CHRONICLES OF ESTRIA
BLOOD AND ASH
BOOK ONE

Also by Stuart Thaman

Praise for Blood and Ash

"Thaman's *Blood and Ash* has it all—vampires (in a good way), epic fantasy, adventure, plenty of betrayal, and best of all, it's gritty. It at once takes what we all expect about the genre and builds it up, honors it, and then breaks down those stereotypes in a very satisfying way. Regardless of your interest in the Chaos Wars game, if you like George RR Martin and Frank Herbert, pick this up."

~ Nick Thacker, best-selling author of the Harvey Bennett thrillers

"After taking a series of body-blows as of late, Stuart Thaman gives the vampire a fresh lease in *Blood and Ash*, a work that challenges many staples of fantasy writing. No convention of the genre is out-of-bounds here, including an anti-hero vampire princess who is so awesome you'll just want to take her home to meet the folks... but should you? Stuart Thaman proves he's the undisputed master of his universe."

~ Ren Garcia, author the *League of Elder* series

"Dressed in the epic trappings of high-powered combat, Thaman's *Blood and Ash* proves entertaining page after page with a wonderful crew of badass characters, viscerally satisfying fight scenes, and a skill at the craft rarely seen by modern novelists. The battles are memorable, the story will keep you guessing, and the gods—they will be nasty."

~ Kell Inkston, author of *Valiance*

"Captivating from the start. Thaman has taken traditional fantasy and turned it on its head: the princess is evil, the orcs are good, the magicians need to bathe. Who doesn't like a good anti-heroine story?"

~ Virlyce, author of *The Blue Mage Raised by Dragons*

"*Blood and Ash* is dark fantasy with a striking anti-heroine. The book is a darker and grittier counterpart to Michael J Sullivan's *Riyria Revelations*. Thaman has breathed life into his strong-willed characters and expertly captured the world of *Chaos Wars* on the page."

~ Louise Stanley, author of *The Flame Owl*

"*Blood and Ash* is out of the ordinary epic fantasy, but with paranormal and horror all thrown together in a very well-written novel!"

~ D. Thomas Jerlo, author of *The Tears of San'Ferath*

CHRONICLES OF ESTRIA
BLOOD AND ASH
BOOK ONE

STUART THAMAN

NEF HOUSE PUBLISHING

Blood and Ash
Chronicles of Estria (Book 1)
Copyright © 2017 Stuart Thaman
www.stuartthamanbooks.com

Ral Partha's Chaos Wars was created by
Bob Charrette, Rich Smethurst, Marc Rubin, and Chuck Crain.

ISBN-13:978-1975814755
ISBN-10:1975814754

Cover design and interior illustrations by J Caleb Clark
www.jcalebdesign.com

Formatting and typesetting by Bodie D Dykstra
www.bdediting.com

Mirrors and daylight are silly lies,
In all those stories you spread about me.
No magic, no covens and terror—
I walk among you as one of you.
~ *Predator,* Vader

Table of Contents

Foreword 1
Map of Estria..10
Prologue..13
Chapter 1 17
Chapter 2 29
Chapter 3 33
Chapter 4 43
Chapter 5 55
Chapter 6 73
Chapter 7 81
Chapter 8 95
Chapter 9 111
Chapter 10 121
Chapter 11 137
Chapter 12 159

Chapter 13 171

Chapter 14.. 181

Chapter 15 193

Chapter 16 207

Chapter 17 221

Chapter 18 239

Chapter 19 245

Chapter 20 255

Chapter 21 263

Chapter 22 275

Chapter 23 291

Chapter 24 321

Chapter 25 329

Chapter 26 343

Chapter 27 359

Chapter 28 371

Chapter 29 383

Chapter 30 395

About the Author 401

Foreword

The World of the Chaos Wars

Generations ago, the known world enjoyed relative stability. Gleaming armies marched off to do battle against one another, vanquishing rivals and conquering enemy lands. The kingdoms of Elves, Dwarves, and Men would squabble amongst one another, but still band together to fend off the assaults of Orcs and Goblins, the Undead, or Chaos Warriors that challenged their borders. There were many threats: the Fae beguiled anyone foolhardy enough to stray into the deeps woods, Beastmen raided caravans, Lizardmen drug captives down into their caves, Demons corrupted the weak-willed, Monsters lurked in the shadows, and Dragons soared amongst the clouds. Life was a struggle, but life was manageable.

In time, the arrogance of Men unearthed an ancient artifact; a chalice imbued with world-shaking power. Unsealed from its mystic confinement, the Chalice's energy lured the mightiest of beings out from the Demonic Realms. The Lord of the Fire Demons sought to claim the chalice and take its power for himself. In the ensuing battle, the Demon clashed with a powerful Grandmaster. The two beings, both brimming with otherworldly power, came into contact with the Chalice, and reality itself began to buckle. As they grappled, the flaming sword of the great Demon pierced the veil, tearing a hole in the very fabric of reality. The Chalice fell deep into the void, and the Demon followed, both instantly transported far away to a distant plane.

With his newfound ability, the Demon rampaged across the lands in an unpredictable pattern, battering away defenses, tearing holes in space and time, and then moving on to the next unsuspecting land to wreak havoc and search for the Chalice. He left a trail of destruction through the kingdoms of Men, Dwarves, and Elves. Into the heavens where the Wind Lords reigned, the Demon flew up and tore portals in the very clouds. The portals brought the Demon deep below the seas where the Atlanteans and Fishmen were locked in battle. Underground, his hellfire lit the way as portals brought him into the caverns where the Lizardmen gathered and into the tunnels where Ratlings scurried. The Demon continued into the forests, cutting a path before him where more Elves, Fae, Gnomes, Tree Creatures, and all forms of Beastmen lurked. Halflings hid in their shelters. Out in the plains, Orcs roared and Goblins hissed at the Demon as he passed overhead. His presence set the jungles ablaze as he raged past Amazonians and Troglodytes. High in the mountains where the Dwarves secluded themselves and Dark Elves hatched plots, the Demon appeared and brought agony with him. All civilizations and lands were subjected to his brief, unyielding presence and the portals he left behind.

The great tears in reality, called different names by different races, proved to be a destabilizing force in every region where they appeared. With no discernable pattern between where portals led, or even if the destination remained fixed, they opened routes to the other lands, other realities, and other times. Though most civilizations were unaware of the Greater Demon's existence, or that it was the cause of these tears in reality, they soon learned of the danger of the portals and the new threats that spilled from them.

Amid the upheaval wrought by the portals left in the Demon's wake, the Black Prince, a High Lord among the forces of Chaos, called his generals to his side and began a reign of terror that shook the known world. In every land, the forces of darkness rose up and struck at the hearts of their enemies. Trade caravans, villages, and monasteries everywhere were attacked. The Forces of Light in turn marshalled their armies and brought low many of the Black Prince's armies. Liches and Vampires were pulled into the sunlight and put to the stake. Witches, Druids, and Heretics were burned. Roving hordes of Goblins were herded into dead-end valleys and gunned down by Dwarf and Elven missile fire. As the years ran on, the atrocities on both sides escalated. None were left unscathed as the Chaos Wars raged on.

During this time, most of the known world's accumulated knowledge was lost to destruction and fire. The great libraries were abandoned as resources shifted to defend more tactically-significant positions. Academies were left open to looting, vandalism, and the scourge of nature. The histories of the great empires have carried on only through the tradition of storytelling, and in many lands myth and suspicion have replaced fact. Few maps survived the great purge of knowledge. Some regional maps can still be found, but these cherished items are closely kept heirlooms, protected at all costs. Many coastal lands have been cut off from the rest of the world. Their interactions with greater civilizations have become limited to raids on other ports and defending themselves from Pirates. Many island nations have been forgotten altogether, and some cities deep in the jungles or atop mountain ranges have fallen into legend. The few remaining maps are highly cherished but of little use, as many were written in now-dead languages, and disasters such as the hellfire storms have remade the topography to the point where former mountain ranges and landmasses are no longer distinguishable.

Now, nearly six hundred years after the beginning of the Chaos Wars, the world is a broken husk of what it had once been. Vibrant fields of wheat and corn have been churned to mud. Poverty and starvation are a way of life. Massive city-fortresses that had withstood magnificent armies are now abandoned monuments to the dead. Ancient Elven towers still gleam brightly in the sunlight, but they now stand alone, surrounded by the crumbled remains of the fallen ramparts and walls that had once protected the villagers below.

All of the most powerful kingdoms have been laid low. The once-great empires have been reduced to nomadic tribes, grappling to hold onto the remnants of their homelands. They live in civilian-armies, constantly on a slow march, fighting for resources and driving off opposing forces. The more powerful Warlords claim the better of the ruins of the great kingdoms in vain attempts to rebuild the mighty structures. Their efforts prove short-lived, and their claims over the castles, fortresses, and citadels of old seldom last more than a generation. The borders between lands have become dynamic and fluid as the battle lines constantly wax and wane. Scarred veterans and war-maddened peasants fight more to survive the day than to claim victory.

Over the centuries of hard-fought existence, the once stoic and disciplined armies have abandoned their reliance on traditional fighting styles and equipment. Even the most noble of armies scavenge the battlefield for every weapon, every scrap of armor and war machine that can be used in the next battle. It is not uncommon to see Elves manning black powder cannon batteries or regiments of wild Dwarves resorting to spear and bow warfare when they find no other recourse. Necromancy has become commonplace among magic-users of all lands, and even Orcs have been witnessed riding atop ornately caparisoned horses after battles against the Kingdoms of Men. Forced by circumstance into seemingly absurd situations, engineers and mages of even the most unrefined races have interwoven science and magic to bring foreign war machines to bear against their enemies. Air Ships, Steam Engines, and Mechanical Giants looted from the Dwarves and Men are a favorite of Goblin and Ratling armies. Some battalions of Elves have reinforced their bowmen with black powder guns and simple rockets found in the conquered armories of Men. Every army steals and rebuilds their enemy's chariots, war wagons, and artillery after each battle. Even the Dwarves and Elves have resorted to capturing monsters and titans, chaining them or mystically bonding them into service.

As territories shift and resources dwindle, old allies treat one another as bitter enemies, fighting over scraps of food, fertile land, and whatever diminishing resources they can unearth. Faced with new challenges and dramatic shifts in power, ancient enemies find themselves fighting alongside each other to protect common interests... if only for the moment.

In this new reality of continuous warfare, the old definitions of 'Good' and 'Evil' no longer hold the meanings they once did. The concept of 'Order' is a notion lost to time. Some scholars and kings do still cling to the concepts of the Forces of Light or Forces of Darkness, but those definitions are from a time and place long lost, and they are mostly a matter of perspective anyway. Dwarves and Elves might see the Ratlings and Beastmen as more of a nuisance than actually evil when compared to legions of the Undead, Chaos Warriors, or Demons. And once the Ratlings and Gnolls came to learn exactly what those Demons and Undead had in mind for the forests, woods, and plains that they called home, those races turned away from their traditional allies for their very survival. They may still be found pillaging Elven colonies, but when full scale war is waged, most Gnolls and Ratlings will be found opposed to the Forces of Darkness, a stark contrast to the ways of old.

There exists now a very fluid concept of what makes for enemies and short-term allies, though classic alliances and grudges still shine through the murky political waters when given a chance.

This is the world of the Chaos Wars, a world where even the most powerful are on the brink of collapse, where certainty and security are the stuff of legends, and instability has become the norm.

The Chronicles of Estria series tells of one such corner of the ravaged world.

By Jacob H. Fathbruckner, Iron Wind Metals, Partner, Chaos Wars Sales and Product Development

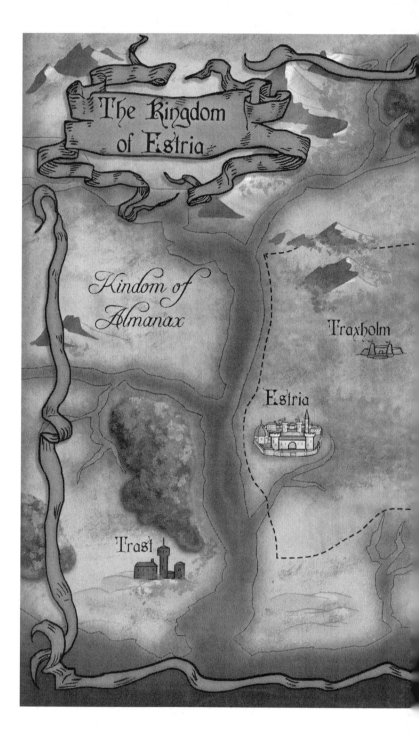

The Kingdom
of Estria

Kindom of
Almanax

Traxholm

Estria

Trast

Prologue

I have been here far too long. My father's kingdom is vast and full of splendor, but it is a kingdom of bondage. When I leave the castle, guards follow me. When I sneak outside these walls to do as I please, my eyes continue to dart over my shoulder in search of my father's men. Sometimes I see them. Sometimes I only think I see them. There can be no peace in this palace of stone, this fortress that has been my prison since the hour of my birth.

I am meant for greater things. I know that now. I'm supposed to be more than a mannequin dressed in fine silk with a silver tiara in my hair. Life has more meaning than appearances, and I intend to fulfill my destiny—though perhaps that is the wrong word. Destiny would have me walk a straight line, a predetermined path whence I cannot stray.

I reject destiny. Fate means nothing to me now. With the proper guidance and a little luck, I'll carve my own name into *the history books. Bards will sing my tales in front of crackling fireplaces in quaint inns across Estria, though I get the profound sense that most of those songs will not be ones of praise or adoration. They will be stories of fear and trembling.*

There are those who will say my path is foolish, who will admonish me for my choices. Those are the men and women who have never truly lived for themselves. Those are the ignorant masses, the blindfolded sheep being herded to their meager ends, the willfully ignorant who will be buried next to their grandfathers—who are buried next to theirs.

When you make a decision to live, you change nothing of the external world. When you make a decision to uproot your entire existence in the name of living along a self-determined path, you change every iota of your internal world. That change must come first.

But the will to live is not something I've seen in more than a handful of people. My father does not possess it, nor my mother. Perhaps they both did at some point in their lives, but that spark has been dead for years. Probably decades.

It took me sixteen years to discover my spark. Some would say it was given to me, but either way, it is mine now. I will not stay shackled in this cold, relentless dungeon of a castle. I will not be buried in the family crypt next to generation after generation of my ancestors. That is not the path I will walk.

The crown in my future means nothing. Its weight, its shimmer: a death sentence.

I will be of my own making.
A horror.

Anathema.

Something to be hunted and killed.

But freedom is my own choice—and it is worth any cost.

~ The final entry in the journal of Princess Lina Arias, discovered in her royal bedchamber two days after her disappearance.

Chapter 1

"Find my daughter, Captain," King Arias growled over a frothy mug of dark stout. The young man in front of him nodded sharply before departing, his armored boots ringing against the stone floor. Behind him, the queen wept over her breakfast. She had not eaten in days, and her face was gaunt with hunger.

"She *must* be in the city," Arias whispered to his wife. He wrapped her in a warm embrace, stifling his own tears as he spoke. "The gates have been closed since she…" he didn't want to say it aloud, but there was no other way to describe what had happened, "was kidnapped," he finished with a heavy sigh.

The queen nodded gently against his chest, but she did not respond.

King Arias led his wife out of the banquet hall to their private chapel on the western side of the keep.

Under normal circumstances, the small octagonal room would be decorated with portraits of all eight gods, but only one remained. A tall tapestry of The Watcher hung on one wall with several offerings placed on a wooden altar beneath. The Watcher was a slender woman with golden hair curling down the sides of her face, beautiful, but not in any striking way—her curves and features were subtle, and they reminded the king of his beloved daughter. He gazed into the tapestry's eyes, searching for some sort of answer he knew he would not find.

His wife moved to the table of sacrifices, tears still flowing down her cheeks. "What if Captain Maxus does not find her?" she asked quietly, her voice shaking with every syllable.

"I still have other options," Arias sighed. "We will never stop searching."

"What happened to our little girl?" the queen sobbed. She looked expectantly to The Watcher, but the delicate tapestry remained motionless.

Maxus, the Captain of Estria's famed King's Shield, practically flew from the keep. He descended a long set of stone steps two at a time, only offering the men at the bottom a curt salute as he ran across the wooden drawbridge toward the barracks a quarter mile away.

The massive headquarters was eerily empty.

Maxus moved through the halls to a chamber near the back where a heavy desk sat with his name carved into its front, a stark reminder of how hard he had worked and how much he stood to lose. As he had expected, a freshly penned report sat on a wooden tray before his high-backed chair. "Nine-tenths of the King's Guard is actively deployed," he read aloud as he paced. "Seven knights have reported illness from spending too much time in the sewers, and another four have still not returned from their last foray into the catacombs." He tossed the report back onto his desk and shook his head.

"Sir?" a stocky man with short, blonde hair said as he poked his head into Maxus' office.

"Come in, Merren, please," Maxus bade him, pointing to an empty chair.

"I'm sorry, sir," Merren began fearfully, "I looked for your steward, but did not find him. I do not mean to barge in. I—"

"It is quite all right," Maxus said, cutting him off. "My steward, along with the rest of the staff, is assisting the search effort currently." He leaned back in his own chair, trying to appear calm and in control, though he knew his face told a different story.

"Yes, sir," Merren replied with a nod. Though he was an officer of the city guard and in charge of controlling Estria's walls, he feared Maxus and the power the King's Shield held. "There might be a new development," he said hesitantly.

"Come out with it!" Maxus yelled, his mind jumping to conclusions faster than he could comprehend. He surged forward in his chair, knocking over an inkwell in his haste.

Merren visibly shrank, his fingernails digging into the arms of his chair. "One of my men saw a stooped figure enter the sewer on the south side of the city near the docks," he blurted out all at once.

"Why was I not informed the moment it occurred?" Maxus chastised coldly, standing and retrieving his sword belt from a peg on the wall.

"You were asleep—"

"Then wake me," Maxus spat with finality. He buckled his sword belt tightly around his waist and lifted a small shield emblazoned with Estria's crest from a wooden rack. "Take me to the *exact* location," he commanded the younger man with a snarl.

Merren practically jumped to his feet to scurry out the door.

The air above the docks reeked of salt and old fish. The smell didn't bother Maxus much, but the relative lack of noise coming from the harbor shook him to his core. It had been two weeks since any boats had entered or departed from Estria's piers. When the princess went missing, King Arias closed the port and all of the city gates, strangling Estria's once booming trade in an instant. Without food coming into the city, Maxus wondered how long the lockdown would last.

With a shake of his head, Maxus threw grim thoughts of inevitable starvation from his mind and followed Merren down a steep set of stairs to the water's edge.

"It was this tunnel, I'm sure of it," Merren said, pointing to a wide opening framed by barnacles a few feet above the lapping brine. "There are lanterns in the harbormaster's office," he was quick to add.

With a stern nod, Maxus commanded him to retrieve a lantern. When the man returned, the two men descended over the rocky bank to the sewer and drew their swords. "Smugglers use these tunnels," Maxus remarked. "Perhaps someone is using them to get the princess out."

Merren nodded in agreement. He opened the front of his lantern fully to allow the meager candlelight to flood through the passageway. "The sewers have been continuously built and expanded for hundreds of years as Estria has grown. They go on for miles."

"Let's hope we find something soon, then," Maxus replied. They walked slowly through the first tunnel, carefully testing their footing in the ankle-deep water, and mindful not to make too much noise. After a hundred or more yards the sewer branched into six different pathways, each one fanning out under a different section of the city.

"This one," Merren said after a moment of

investigation. He pointed his lantern down a narrow tunnel, dimly illuminating the low, slime-covered ceiling.

"How do you know?" Maxus asked. He didn't like the idea of needing to stoop his head to progress farther, but he didn't see much of a choice.

"Look," Merren said, pointing with his sword. "Grooves in the muck. Someone was here recently and left tracks."

"Lead on," Maxus told him. He trusted the man, as everyone in the city did, but Maxus still couldn't shake the feeling that he was being led into an obvious trap. Still, the subtle tracks left in the sewer sludge were enough evidence to at least investigate further.

Merren led his superior through tunnel after tunnel for what felt like hours. The deeper they moved, the worse the stench of the place became. Finally, after Maxus had long since sheathed his sword to cover his mouth with a glove, the two officers rounded a corner and the tracks stopped abruptly. In the side of the tunnel, a small wooden door rested on reflective, silver hinges.

"This is new," Maxus said, running a finger along the door's surface. "It isn't covered in grime."

Merren closed the shutter of his lantern almost entirely, allowing only a small line of light to illuminate their steps. "Should we get the rest of the King's Shield?" he asked, his voice tinted with the slightest hint of fear.

"It would take too long," Maxus answered. The man

placed his palm against the side of the door, gingerly testing it with a fraction of his body weight. Surprisingly, the door was not locked. It swung inward silently, revealing a freshly cut set of wooden stairs descending into darkness.

The two men crept down the staircase as silently as they could. Merren kept the lantern low, only flashing the light ahead every few seconds to confirm his footing. At the bottom, another door presented itself, although it was made of forged iron and looked as old as the city itself. In its center, a rectangular metal flap covered what Merren supposed was a peephole.

Maxus lifted his sword to the iron and pushed, lifting the metal ever so slightly to peer through. The scene on the other side took his breath away. Faster and louder than he intended, he pulled his sword away, letting the metal piece fall back into place.

"Ratlings," he whispered. "An entire den of them."

Merren shook his head. "They must've captured the princess!" he quietly urged.

"Go back," Maxus commanded the guardsman. "Tell the king what we've found. Get the city guard, the King's Shield, everyone you can, and bring them here. Whether they have the princess or not, they must be exterminated."

Merren hesitated, and Maxus—fearing the worst—waited for the man to betray him. If it was a trap, there was little time left to spring it. "What are you going to do?" Merren asked after a brief moment.

"I'll stay watch," Maxus replied, never taking his eyes from Merren's weapon.

Hastily, Merren saluted his superior and ascended the wooden steps behind them. Maxus let a sigh of relief escape his lips, but he still waited several minutes until he turned back to face the door.

More gently than before, he poked his sword through the hole to peer into the ratling den and take stock of his enemies. The humanoids, if they could be called such, were shorter than a grown man by a foot or more, and had ugly, misshapen rodent heads complete with whiskers and long teeth. Maxus counted thirty of the filthy creatures before he gave up.

The den, illuminated by torches on the walls, was no more than sixty feet across in any direction. To the right and left, closed doors lined the underground lair, and Maxus had no way of knowing how many hundreds of ratlings might be beyond each entrance. In the center of the main chamber, the ratlings Maxus could see were mostly sitting at tables. Some of them ate, others gambled with dice or bones, and a score of them attended to weapons and armor stored on wooden racks in one corner.

Why do they have torches? Maxus silently wondered. Ratlings had excellent vision in the dark. *The princess...*

As Maxus watched, one of the doors set against the far wall opened, and a human figure covered by a red lace cape and hood sauntered into the chamber. At once, the room went silent, and most of the ratlings bowed.

Maxus had to stifle a yell when the figure removed her hood. "No!" he couldn't stop himself from gasping. He let the metal flap fall shut and backed away from the door. "Princess Lina…" he muttered. His mind reeled, refusing to accept the reality of what he had just seen.

Was she their leader? A *ratling* leader? Maxus moved back to the door and pushed the flap open once more, but his confusion had made him careless. His sword clanged against the metal, echoing through the silent room and drawing the attention of every single ratling in the den.

Before he could think of a plan, several of the murderous half-rodents came for him, brandishing weapons, and wrenching the door open with their grimy claws. Maxus let his sword fall to the ground as he was dragged by his shoulders into the den. His mind simply would not accept the reality of what he had seen.

"What do we have here?" Lina mocked. She took a few steps forward, and her smile flashed with recognition. "Captain Maxus?" she laughed, her dark hair fluttering around her cheeks. "My father's bodyguard—a most welcome surprise!"

Maxus didn't know what to say. His mouth opened and closed, but no sound came forth. "Rescue…" he finally muttered. One of the ratlings shoved him in the back, forcing him to his knees.

Princess Lina bellowed with laughter. "You came to *rescue* me?" Her cape brushed against Maxus' side as she circled him, one of her fingers toying with a lock of his hair. She leaned over his shoulder to whisper in his ear. "Don't worry," she told him. "I'll let my father keep Estria. I have other plans. Grander plans."

Maxus scoffed. "*Let* him keep the city? You think a few ratlings could topple Estria?" As her captive, he knew he shouldn't provoke her, but she was clearly delusional, and his stupefied mind could think of little else to say. "Come to your senses, Princess," he continued. "Let me take you home."

Lina brushed her cheek against his. A curl of her hair fell in front of Maxus' face. "You have no idea what I've become," she whispered, her voice powerful and dripping with confidence.

Maxus was so dumbfounded and terrified that he didn't notice when her razor-sharp teeth bit into his neck. He collapsed to the ground in her arms, hitting the stone floor with a gentle thud as the woman feasted at his veins.

"I'm not my father's princess any longer," she told him, lines of red running down the sides of her mouth.

Merren stumbled breathlessly into the king's

audience hall, interrupting what appeared to be a rather important meeting between the sovereign and several attendants. The king stood at once, brushing two leather pouches to the side of his desk in the process. There were several members of the King's Shield in the room, and they all had their hands on their weapons.

"News of my daughter?" Arias bellowed. He leaned over his desk with both fists on the wood, presenting a terrifying image that caused Merren to shrink back.

"Maybe, my lord," Merren replied. "We've found a large nest of ratlings beneath the city. Maxus believes they may have the princess held captive. I apologize for interrupting, but I knew you would want to know immediately."

"Ratlings?" the king demanded, though his voice had relaxed. "Did you see my daughter? Was Lina there?"

"Unfortunately not, sir," Merren answered.

"She could still be their hostage," the king concluded quickly. He turned to the handful of attendants waiting respectfully by the side of his desk. "Send word to Ilsander. Whatever price he names, I'll pay it. I want him here as soon as he can be found. Understood?"

One of the attendants bowed deeply. "Certainly, my liege. I will arrange for his escort just as quickly as he can be located." The attendant grabbed the leather pouches from the desk and exited, the others quickly following suit.

"Organize a militia," the king commanded, turning his attention back to Merren. "Pull as many men as you can from the city guard. I want these ratlings dealt with swiftly. But we must be careful—if they fear we are coming, they may harm my daughter before we reach her." The king turned back to the man before him, his mind reeling with possibilities. "And Captain Maxus?" he asked. "Is he currently organizing our strike?"

Merren shook his head. "He stayed in the tunnels, my lord," he explained. "He is watching them for any sign of the princess."

"Good," King Arias said with a curt nod. "Go and gather a force. I will make an offering to The Watcher for your success, and you are to leave as soon as the men are fully prepared. There isn't a moment to waste! Not a single second!"

Chapter 2

"We need to move" Lina told her ratling officers. The beasts had names, but she didn't care to learn their crude pronunciations. The fur-covered humanoids would all be dead within the month anyway.

Lina looked back to Maxus' drained corpse on the floor of her underground lair with a mixture of pity and disgust. She had known the man as a casual acquaintance of her father and had mostly enjoyed his company, but she knew she could not afford to leave any witnesses in Estria. Master Rhaas, the one who had given her the immortal gift of vampirism, had made that clear.

She hadn't seen Rhaas in several months, and she longed for his guidance and mentoring once more. He had since returned to Traxholm, a village quite some distance from the capital, and Lina was out of time.

"Organize the clans," Lina continued. Her voice

STUART THAMAN

of command resonated throughout the ratling horde assembled in the main chamber of her makeshift residence. One of the nearby ratling officers skittered away to one of the doors at the side of the room.

Lina turned toward the short stairwell that separated her ratling force from the several human leaders who had aligned with her cause. Humans and ratlings were never allies, but Lina and Rhaas had spun their lies well, brilliantly manipulating the two disparate groups with promise after promise.

Her human allies were mostly retired or rejected military types, and she also controlled a rather large contingent of convicted men her ratlings had freed from the Estrian prisons. Lina smiled as she remembered how easy it had been to control the weak-minded humans. The threat of a quick death, coupled with the promise of gold and glory, had made them into slaves with barely a moment's hesitation.

"Rally your soldiers," Lina said as she entered the makeshift human barracks. "We leave in several hours."

The men in the musty room were only a small fraction of her human force, and the rest remained in various states of hiding throughout the city. Her men were mostly vagabonds, ex-prisoners, or mercenaries, totaling somewhere between one and three thousand. With her ratling swarm, her combined army reached nearly ten thousand, though their training had been basically nonexistent. In a true war, Lina knew she would never have a chance. But marching to Chancol would be far from a true war—it would be a slaughter, but that bloodshed would give her the souls she needed to crush the city in the palm of her hand.

A few hours before nightfall, Lina gathered with her hodgepodge militia outside one of the larger storm drains on Estria's southern border. She saw the city behind her and felt a pang of longing, a momentary urge to abandon her grand schemes and return to a warm bed in the keep at the center of town, but she had prepared thoroughly for the last moment of homesickness. She took a clear glass vial from a pocket on her traveling belt and held it to her lips. Some of Maxus' blood was contained within the vial, and though it had gone cold, it still energized the vampire greatly.

"I don't want to be seen by any more people than is unavoidable," Lina told the three generals at her side. "If you see anyone about to raise an alarm, kill them and hide the body quickly, but then move on. Otherwise, run quickly. There are bound to be farmers and merchants out on the roads, and there aren't enough trees to fully conceal our escape."

One of the generals was human, standing awkwardly ten or more feet from his ratling counterparts, clearly unnerved by the chittering creatures and their furry bodies. All three of the leaders nodded and turned to their retinues, each eager to spread the word of their flight.

An hour later, Lina was the first to reach their pre-determined rallying point two miles from the nearest Estrian building. Her force had killed over a dozen civilians during their disorganized escape, but the deaths barely registered in Lina's mind. She was in motion, finally taking the first step toward her ultimate goal, and the satisfaction of being free to pursue her goals far outshone any regret that crept into the back of her mind.

Chapter 3

"How long will it take for reinforcements to arrive?" Lina demanded, pacing back and forth in her command tent. She had fifteen hundred ratlings still in Estria awaiting her valiant return, and at the rate they tended to breed, the sewers of her father's city would be teeming with the disgusting humanoids in only a few weeks.

The man, one of her generals whose name she did not care to remember, trembled visibly in front of her. He was a competent man and had the group's trust, but in the grand scheme of a vampire's long life, he was inconsequential. Lina glared at him, waiting for an answer.

"It will take…" he began, nervously casting his eyes everywhere but on his queen.

"Out with it!" Lina barked. "How long?"

"At least two weeks, my liege!" the man said all at once, his words jumbling together in his haste. The general fell to one knee, hoping desperately that Lina's wrath would not mean the end of his life—as it had for his predecessor. It had taken the makeshift army a week and a half to travel from Estria to Chancol, but a force comprised exclusively of ratlings could move much faster than the humans. Two weeks was not the answer Lina wanted to hear.

Surprisingly, Lina did not respond. She continued to pace, but her lips remained frozen in a scowl. In stunned silence, the general knelt and waited for his next order. "Come with me," Lina finally said, brushing a lock of hair from her face. Like an obedient dog, the general scampered after her, making sure not to follow too closely.

Lina's leather boots made little sound on the hard-packed dirt as she marched, and the din of battle soon filled her ears. All around the command tent the fight for Channer's Glen raged, and Lina's small force from Estria was losing badly. Half a mile east of the tent, the high walls of Chancol rose up from the forest like a towering beacon of grey stone.

Lina wanted the city badly. In order to lay siege to Chancol, she first needed to take the glen, but the pesky troglodytes who lived there were proving harder to exterminate than Lina had planned. "How many men have we lost?" she asked the general cowering behind her. "More than half the force, my lady," he yelled back over the sound of a black powder cannon firing nearby. The artillery piece was the only one she had acquired before marching out of Estria, and its thunderous retorts gave her a great deal of pleasure.

"Good," she mused, just loudly enough for the man to hear. She could feel the strength of all those lost souls whirling in the air around her. She called to them gently and they responded, rushing into her fingertips like tiny glimmers of candlelight.

"By the gods!" the general shrieked, slowly realizing what was happening. "No! It can't… It can't be true!"

Lina had planted a number of rumors in her army and the city she had left behind, each one telling a slightly different tale of her magnificent powers, but none of them substantiated. Necromancy, as well as her vampirism, was a crime punishable by death. It would be an ironic punishment, should she ever be apprehended, considering the only person alive who could actual steal that spark from her.

Now was the time. With her army falling all around her, she needed to show them her true power. She needed the troglodytes of the glen and the humans of Chancol to witness her true strength. She needed them to bow.

Turning on the general with fire in her eyes, Lina beckoned him forward. "Are you willing to serve?" she asked the man, grabbing him by the breastplate and holding a jeweled dagger to his throat.

The man swallowed hard. Terror danced across his eyes, but he nodded.

"Good," Lina whispered. "Now we show these wretched beasts the real meaning of obedience. They will know fear."

Lina's dagger slid through the flesh of her general's neck without any resistance. She drank in the man's life, consuming it voraciously until nothing but the hint of blood and a husk of blackened ash remained at the end of her blade.

"Now you will serve!" Lina bellowed into the air. The nearby leaves shook with the might of her voice, and for an instant the battle seemed to cease as time stood still.

From the aether just beyond Lina's dagger, a creature stirred. A wraith, one of the most powerful denizens of the lower planes, answered the princess's call. The creature was small and humanoid in form at first, but Lina fed it all the disembodied souls of her fallen soldiers. The wraith ate and grew, doubling over on itself several times, always rising to stand taller than it had been just an instant before.

When time began to flow once again, the towering wraith existed in the material plane just a few feet in front of Lina's dagger. Fire spewed from the beast's ethereal shoulders and head, though Lina could barely see the creature's torso reaching far above the nearest trees.

It had taken the form of her late general, though only the man's physical shape. None of the general's memories or thoughts were left. The man had been utterly obliterated by the summoning. The wraith knew only one master, and its mind held only raw emotion, completely devoid of logic, reasoning, or even the slightest shreds of disobedience.

Kill these filthy swine, Lina thought, sending her will into the towering menace. It responded with a flurry of emotion the princess could only describe as pure, unlimited rage. She conjured the image of a troglodyte to her mind and sent it as well, imprinting the awkward humanoid's form on the wraith's singular awareness.

At once, the wraith moved forward, crushing trees and humans alike with each thundering step.

The wraith only spoke one word of the human language—one Lina had taught it over the years she had spent earning the being's loyalty.

With a fiery breath that shook the earth and sky, the wraith crashed down on the troglodyte army with cataclysmic force. "KILL!"

Lord Elador, High Magistrate of Chancol, watched the events unfolding in Channer's Glen through a still pool of water one of his mages had turned into a scrying surface. As the chief political officer for the grand city, it was his duty to keep the people safe. Elador was an old man, nearly seventy years of age, and had kept his people safe for decades.

The perils of the world had approached his doorstep once more.

The battle raged in the scrying pool, but the troglodytes seemed to be holding the upper hand. Elador smiled. He had allowed the strange humanoid creatures to settle in the glen outside Chancol for just such a reason. His city was peculiar, of that Elador had no doubt, and with that peculiarity came a host of enemies. Permitting the troglodytes to live so close had created a buffer, another layer of security, and Elador enjoyed watching that buffer in action.

Elador moved his magical vision to the strange commander of the army—a human like himself—and watched her inside her command tent. He could practically feel her trepidation as she paced back and forth under the low cloth ceiling. Another man was with her, but he appeared weak and unfit for command. Unfortunately, the mages of Chancol had not bestowed the power of hearing upon his scrying pool, so Elador had to guess at what the two were saying.

"Sir," someone said from the back of the vaulted chamber, pulling the magistrate's attention away.

"Yes?" Elador responded. He turned to see the newcomer, the only other person he ever permitted in the scrying room.

The man, a tall, strapping figure with sun-touched skin, was Elador's son. As a magistrate, Elador was publicly sworn to celibacy, but even the most honorable of men had their indiscretions.

"The army from Estria has been nearly routed," Saveus replied.

Elador smiled. "I see that," he said. "The troglodytes have bred greatly since they came to the glen. Their numbers alone are enough to crush such a small force."

Saveus nodded, but his face showed anything but mirth. "Our runner has returned from Estria," the man continued, obviously unnerved. "Their king has no knowledge of the force fighting in the glen. King Arias denies responsibility for this attack."

"Oh?" Elador asked.

Saveus produced a parchment scroll from a pocket on his leather vest and unrolled it before his father. "This woman," he began, pointing to the hand-drawn picture, "her name is Lina Arias. She has been missing for some length of time and the king has offered ten thousand pieces of gold for her return, but our men aiding the troglodytes say she is not a ratling captive."

Elador furrowed his brow. He loved the interweaving political plots which ran the city's bureaucracy, but this new development was entirely unexpected. "This woman is King Arias' daughter? She leads their army!"

"There's more," Saveus continued. "The king believes

she is under the control of a necromancer or some other dark magician. She could have brought powerful allies."

The floor of the chamber shook violently, nearly knocking both men from their feet. Elador rushed to the scrying pool and peered into it. His eyes went wide when he saw the colossal beast Lina had just summoned.

Lord Elador's voice trembled when he spoke. "Call the mages," he commanded. He thought he could hear the wraith's distant voice echoing against Chancol's high walls. "Gather the army!"

Chapter 4

Saveus ran from the king's scrying room in the heart of Chancol, sprinting through the dark corridors as quickly as his feet would take him. When he reached the surface streets the bright sunlight stung his eyes, but he didn't have time to stop. Ahead, only several streets away, stood a squat building overgrown with moss and fungus: the legendary Guildhall of the Pestilent, the home of Chancol's most revered wizards and mages.

Saveus was still more than a hundred feet from the Guildhall's entrance when the stench of the place began to overwhelm him. Everything smelled of rot. Long ago, before the mages had uncovered a mystical power source deep beneath the city, there had been businesses and homes surrounding the Guildhall. That had been hundreds of years ago, and nothing had been constructed near the place since.

When Saveus reached the Guildhall's moss-covered door, he could barely breathe. There was a haze of spores hanging in the air, obscuring his vision and making him nauseous. His fist slammed into the rotting wood of the front door, splintering part of it inward. Another burst of spores rose up from his hand, clinging to his flesh like some vile slime meant to consume him.

"Come back later!" a voice called from inside a moment later.

"The city is under attack!" Saveus screamed. He hated opening his mouth and inhaling the strange spores in the air, and he could only hope they were harmless. He heard someone shuffling around on the other side of the door.

With a grunt, he tore away another huge chunk of the door and stuck his head inside. An old man in a tattered brown robe turned to regard him casually. "So impatient," the old man muttered, though he did unlatch the door to welcome the new guest.

"The mages have been summoned," Saveus said hastily. "Gather your order. War is upon us!"

The man seemed unaffected by Saveus' profound assertion. "Korbax is busy," the man replied. "As I said before, you must come back later, perhaps next year, or better yet would be the year after that."

Saveus had to make a conscious effort to resist hitting the man where he stood. "Where is he?" he bellowed, stepping up to tower over the old man.

"If you insist upon your own death," the man smirked, "you may request an audience with Korbax below, though he has not entertained a visitor in many years."

Saveus shouldered past the man toward a decrepit staircase in the back of the hovel. He tested the first step with his foot, unsure if it would hold his weight. When it survived the strain of his body weight, Saveus flew down the staircase. It spiraled several stories underneath the streets of Chancol where it connected to a labyrinth of tunnels which served as the city's sanitation system.

The whole underground compound was easy to navigate, even for someone who had never been there before. A strange mold, something the mages called 'Witherbite,' grew out in a radial pattern along the edges of the stone sewers. To reach the important areas of the compound, all Saveus had to do was follow the fungus. Luckily, the strange Witherbite gave off a slight aura of luminescence which flickered like distant candlelight.

It didn't take long for Saveus to find a wooden door he assumed marked the lair of Korbax. The ancient mage, if he was even human, had been directing the work of the Guildhall of the Pestilent since long before even Lord Elador had been born. As the legends went, Korbax was as eternal as the glowing Witherbite, though other theories claimed that the name was more of a title passed from one generation to the next than an actual person.

Steadying his head against the waves of nausea coming from everywhere around him, Saveus pushed open the vine-covered door before him. He saw Korbax in the next chamber, apparently asleep in a glistening pool of dark sludge. All around him, men and women in earth-colored robes turned in unison to witness the unwelcomed intrusion.

Saveus had seen Korbax a handful of times before when his father had met with the strange mage to discuss various things the leader could influence within Chancol. Living in the literal and metaphorical bowels of the city, Korbax's Order of the Pestilent had a strange arrangement with the city's political officers. Lord Elador had negotiated a deal with the mages long ago where they still paid their royal taxes and were citizens of Chancol, bound by law, and in return, the mages were given unlimited access to Chancol's sewers, something no one else seemed to want.

"You disturb my meditations?" Korbax said slowly, his deep voice resonating throughout the room. The nearby attendants lowered their heads respectfully.

Saveus wasn't sure how the man, or thing, spoke. Korbax was humanoid in shape, though that was where his resemblance to a man ended. Instead of flesh and bone, Korbax was seemingly crafted from some sort of viscous liquid which had been draped over a collection of tree branches. He had no eyes, no mouth, no ears—just sludge continually dripping from his thorny appendages.

"There is an army in Channer's Glen," Saveus said, mimicking the attendants with a bow of his head. "Lord Elador seeks your assistance. You must rally your order at once."

Korbax turned his head, a terrifying ball of black ooze sitting atop his shoulders, to the side. If he was even capable of emotion, it was impossible to tell. "I *must*?" the strange mage replied.

Saveus swallowed hard. He understood the situation he was in. If he angered the mage, he would be killed without hesitation. If he did not secure the mage's help, perhaps he would die anyway. "There is no time," he added, trying to keep the fear from showing in his voice.

"Does Chancol not have an army?" Korbax asked callously.

"Yes," Saveus said, struggling to find an honorific title to add to his answer. When he could not come up with one, he simply remained silent.

"And?" Korbax prodded.

"The force against us is from Estria," Saveus went on. "They have a young woman leading them, a summoner of sorts." He looked up from his bow, hoping to catch some glimpse of an expression from the mage, but he saw nothing.

"The wraith!" Korbax said. His voice moved like a

tendril throughout the room, weaving its way between the humans as a whisper. "I felt it moments ago."

As both an officer of Chancol's military and a high-ranking political figure, Saveus had witnessed many horrors in his life. He had seen the corpses of murdered children, slaves captured and beaten after battles, and more than one person burned alive for the crime of vampirism.

Nothing in his past had prepared him to witness the sight of Korbax unclothed as he rose from his mediation pool.

The mage's body was made of congealed slime. Thick strands of rotting liquid fell off of him as he moved, dropping into the pool with little puffs of spores, filling the room with even more unbearable stench. His bones were small, made of plant matter, and they protruded all over his shifting body at awkward angles. The whole assembly reeked of pestilence.

"Take me to the wraith," Korbax said with terrifying strength.

"Indeed," Saveus replied, happy to turn from such a wretched sight. He made for the door only a few steps behind him.

"Summon the conclave," Korbax commanded his attendants. At once, the robed acolytes scattered throughout the many passages connecting to the central chamber.

Even without looking at the horrific mage, Saveus

knew Korbax was staring at him. He could *feel* the weight of the sludge-visage boring into his back. Cautiously, Saveus turned back. One of the attendants held out a green cloak, the same one Saveus had seen the mage wearing before, but Korbax rejected it. "You've seen much," the mage stated.

"I assure you, I do not understand what I have seen," Saveus replied honestly. He wasn't sure what secrets Korbax was trying to conceal.

For a moment, the chamber was silent. "I should kill you," Korbax said flatly.

"Plea—"

"Though I believe your life still has purpose," the mage continued abruptly. "You shall be my ambassador to your father. Do you agree?"

Saveus didn't know how to respond. The thought of returning regularly to the Guildhall of the Pestilent filled his body with revulsion. On the other hand, the notion of refusing the mage's offer was unacceptable.

"I would be honored," Saveus said. Before Korbax began to speak again, the soldier set himself in motion back the way he had come, eager to be rid of the tunnels and their foul stench.

Saveus and Korbax met Lord Elador atop Chancol's

western wall, some twenty feet above the streets. The fiery wraith was visible just beyond the troglodyte glen, freely crushing combatants with its huge fists. "The army will be assembled in another couple hours," Elador said to the new arrivals.

"Yes," Korbax muttered, though it was clear he wasn't speaking to any human. He leaned over the parapet gazing at the wraith, and his ever-flowing body seemed to accelerate.

"Can you kill it?" Elador asked the mage, completely unfazed by the man's morbid appearance.

Korbax turned again to the two humans on the wall. "Send your soldiers back to their homes," he said forcefully. "Tell everyone in Chancol to take shelter. Tell them to cover their faces. *Tell them not to breathe.*"

Elador shrank back. "W-what," he stammered, lifting his hands up defensively. "What are you going to do?"

Elador wasn't sure if Korbax's face was capable of smiling, but it certainly seemed like it did in that moment. "Estria's pet is cute," the mage whispered. Down below the wall, a contingent of robed mages began filtering out of the city. They turned to face their leader, eagerly awaiting his command.

Saveus coughed down a fresh wave of vomit when Korbax lifted his arms above his head.

"Begin the chant!" the mage bellowed to his supplicants below.

The noise that rose up in response to the command was unlike anything Saveus or his father had ever heard before. Insects began to buzz around the sludge-being atop the wall, and small rodents scurried over the stones, appearing out of nowhere.

"We need to run!" Elador said. He could smell the plague rising from the ground like a heavy fog. The air stung his eyes and burned his lungs.

"The people!" Saveus shouted. "They must be warned!"

Elador shook his head as he ran for the stairs which would take him back toward his keep. "They'll figure it out!" he yelled through a stream of painful coughs.

When Korbax was finally alone atop Chancol's wall, he threw himself fully into his summoning. Civilians would die, of that he had no doubt, but the collateral damage did not weigh much on his mind. He had been experimenting with the strange power source hidden far beneath the city for decades, and it was time to bring it to the surface.

After several minutes of chanting, the rodents and insects were joined by other denizens of the sewers. Snakes, giant stinging creatures, and a host of unnamed reptiles slithered forth from the ground, all drawn to the call of the Pestilent. The soil began to break apart near the acolytes, and hairy, black legs the size of ship masts emerged from the crumbling earth. Korbax pointed to several places, and they all similarly erupted. Huge spiders covered in bristles with bulging, red eyes pulled themselves up into the brilliant daylight.

One by one, Korbax began to drain the energy of his servants. He drank every last drop of life he could without killing them, leaving a ring of unconscious followers below him. When the vital force congealed into a shifting orb of life balancing tenuously between his tree-like fingers, he shot it backward, deep into Chancol—where it exploded on the roof of the Guildhall in a shower of rot and disease.

For the second time that day, the ground began to rumble. Though this time, the rumbling was not subtle, nor did it pass quickly. It built and built, becoming a violent earthquake. Several buildings near the Guildhall collapsed, and Korbax saw many large panes of stained glass on the nearby keep shatter.

"Come to me," Korbax whispered to the power he had harnessed beneath the streets. When he had discovered the beast, it had nearly consumed him, but a century later he had befriended it. And he knew the creature, the *god*, was eager for combat.

"Come, Voktarn," Korbax whispered again. At the mention of its name, the knowledge of which Korbax had spent several decades pursuing, the creature rose up from the ground, utterly destroying the Guildhall in the process. As the creature ascended from the depths where it had lived for millennia, it expelled wave after wave of toxic spores into the air. Wherever the spore clouds touched organic matter they took hold, sprouting into huge tendrils of Witherbite. In the span of a few heartbeats, the city was covered with pulsating, reeking vines.

"Voktarn!" Korbax shouted. "Come!"

The creature continued to rise, growing far taller than the highest spires of Chancol, taller than the walls and taller than the fiery wraith beyond. Eventually, Voktarn emerged. The monster was enormous, shattering even Korbax's lofty expectations. It shuddered, and an avalanche of dust and rot fell from its many heads. The abomination, not previously thought to exist, began advancing at once, crushing buildings and fleeing civilians beneath its four sludge-encased feet. As it breathed, clouds of poison gas emanated from each of its maws.

When Voktarn reached the western wall, it lowered a head down to Korbax, and the mage climbed on top of it. He let his own shifting body sublimate into the hydra, their oozing masses combining to form one terrible creature of rot and disease.

In one of the scrolls Korbax had discovered during his quest to learn more about the magical creature, he had found what the ancient people who worshipped the hydra had called it—and it was a fitting title. With a smile hidden by melting sludge, Korbax yelled into the air, "Voktarn! The Living Plague!"

Chapter 5

Inside his father's keep, Saveus retched onto the stone floor. The stench assaulting his nostrils was beyond putrid, beyond natural. The acrid air wove its way through his sinuses and into his brain, eating away at his sanity one pungent breath at a time.

When he finally managed to pull himself up against a wall in the narrow stairway leading to the audience chamber, he heard a chorus of screams coming from the city around him. Delirious, he pushed himself along the wall until he was standing behind his father's marble throne. A huge, dripping insect with black pincers skittered across the back of the chair. Several of the ornate windows on either side of the room had shattered during the tremors, and more insects flew inside with each passing moment. Most of them resembled the shiny beetle crawling over the throne, but others were much larger, appearing to be massive mosquitoes, cicadas, and other creatures.

The buzz generated from the swarm bordered on deafening. Saveus clamped his hands tightly over his ears, inadvertently swatting away one of the beetles that had landed on his face unnoticed. Several paces in front of the throne, a handful of Lord Elador's personal guards writhed in torment upon the stone, vomit coating their tabards and armor.

"Get below!" Saveus shouted to the men. "Follow me!" He wasn't sure if his plan would work, but his mind could think of nothing other than escaping the horrifying plague of insects befalling the audience chamber. To his left, a red-painted door barred the way to Chancol's vast wine cellar.

Saveus practically crashed his body into the locked door, fumbling for his keys and stifling another bout of vomiting as he moved. Behind him, the contingent of soldiers crawled toward the door, and many of them dropped their arms and armor in order to cover their mouths with the cloth of their tabards.

The red door moved lazily inward, the screech of its hinges muffled by the constant buzzing echoing from the walls. Once the handful of men were gathered on the staircase with the door securely latched behind them, Saveus attempted to gather his wits about him.

"What is it?" a guard asked. A thin arc of blood shone above his brow from where one of the insects had cut him.

"The Pestilent," Saveus said with heavy breaths. "My father has commanded the Guildhall of the Pestilent, and I think they just summoned their god."

"We're doomed," the guard muttered. His eyes were wide with fear.

Under the door, a bristling spider pressed its body into the staircase. Saveus stomped down fiercely on the creature, splattering it beneath his boot heel. "The guild fights for Chancol. Some necromancer of sorts from Estria summoned a wraith, and my father didn't know where else to turn."

"And the city? What will be left?" the man exclaimed.

"I don't know…"

"We should be fighting!" one of the other guards offered.

Saveus shook his head. "This isn't our fight. Though these are our homes and our families behind the walls, we would only get in the way," he said, his nausea replaced by an air of dejection. "We just need to wait it out. If anything is left of Chancol when the fighting ends, we can rebuild."

"You would have us sit here like cowards?" the guard accused.

"Yes," Saveus replied sharply. "You haven't seen the beast outside our walls."

"What is it?" the first guard asked. "What's out there?"

Saveus let out a heavy sigh. The stench of pestilence still clung to his lungs, but his brain was starting to ignore it, or at least it wasn't actively making him retch any longer. "A wraith taller than this keep comes against us," he began slowly, pausing to let his words take effect. "A necromancer summoned it, and the beast that the Guildhall called forth might be our only chance of survival."

"The summoner is from Estria? Necromancy is outlawed there, just like it is here," the man continued.

"We don't know the details," Saveus told him. "I'm sure my father has already dispatched an emissary to Estria in search of answers. Right now, all I know is that if you go out there, if you go *outside*, you're going to die. You will either be burned alive by the wraith, or you will die from whatever hell-plague the guild has conjured. Those are your choices."

The once belligerent guard paled, moving a few steps farther down into the wine cellar. "I'll stay—"

A thunderous boom cut the man off, shaking the whole keep to its foundation. Dust and bits of old mortar fell from the spaces between the stones, and the sound of glass shattering could just barely be heard beneath the cacophony of the swarm in the audience chamber.

"Into the cellar!" Saveus commanded, though his words were wholly unnecessary. The four men scrambled past each other as quickly as they could in the cramped space, spilling out at the bottom of the stairs in a heap of tangled arms and legs.

A second crash sounded from above, louder than the first and long enough to make Saveus' teeth click together in his head. "Stay away from the wine!" he tried to shout to one of the men who had fallen beneath a rack of heavy barrels.

A few seconds later, the entire wooden rack splintered from the force of the keep's vibrations, and the six wine barrels it supported came crashing down upon the unfortunate soldier. Luckily, the man still wore his breastplate, and the polished armor took the brunt of the force, though his head cracked audibly into the stone. The force of the blow silenced the guard at once, and a good bit of the man's blood mingled with the white wine spreading over the ground.

"Pull him up," Saveus ordered the other two guards. "Set him against the wall. We'll get him help when everything is over. We're not leaving this cellar until then."

The two other soldiers offered no protest. They propped their comrade up next to them. Blood ran down the unconscious man's face.

One of the guards drew his sword from its sheath and began cutting his tabard off at the waist. Once the makeshift bandage was more or less secured, the three conscious men finally had a moment of respite. They could hear the insects buzzing up above, but the sound was distant and muffled.

"We will live. We're safe down here," Saveus said,

though his voice lacked all confidence. "We will live…"

Lina Arias stalked beneath the feet of the wraith she had summoned. It was a powerful creature, but the plague elemental brought forth by the mages of Chancol was perhaps something beyond her abilities altogether.

"I need that power," she whispered to herself, a sly grin on her face. The wraith stomped beside her, its fiery foot crashing through a cluster of birch trees as though they were twigs.

Maybe twenty or thirty yards to the right of the beast, a handful of troglodyte warriors lurked with their spears held tenuously before them. One of the small humanoids clutched a heavy shield that looked like it had previously belonged to one of Lina's men. The troglodytes were far from setting an ambush, and the fear emanating from them told Lina they were merely hoping to survive.

The vampire left her tempestuous minion's side, weaving through the fiery air toward the enemy troglodytes. She twirled her jeweled dagger easily in her right hand. The troglodytes wouldn't be much challenge for her, and they would all likely die whether she acted or not, but Lina didn't care. She had her own purpose fuelling her steps.

The troglodytes shrank back from her advance, though they did not break rank to flee. "Your bravery is admirable," the vampire mused, flashing her sharp fangs, "but I'm hungry. Summoning is a tiring task, you know."

She fell upon the group of warriors in a blur of speed, whirling from one soft patch of exposed flesh to the next faster than the troglodytes could perceive. After the span of only a few heartbeats, all but one of the troglodytes had been reduced to a corpse.

"You," Lina whispered, her voice somehow inviting and utterly terrifying at the same time. She beckoned toward the troglodyte holding an Estrian shield, sheathing her dagger and reaching to the creature with an outstretched hand.

It barely took a hint of magic to enthrall the troglodyte's simple mind. Against a human, especially a warrior with a hardened resolve, it would have been too much effort for Lina to bother expending. Enchanted, the stout humanoid wobbled forward and dropped his shield, a befuddled expression lingering on its otherwise blank face.

"Come here," Lina continued quietly. "I won't hurt you. I just… I *need* something from you."

The troglodyte responded softly in its strange, guttural language, and its lips twisted upward in an uneasy smile.

"That's it," Lina cooed, "just a little more. Follow the

sound of my voice. Come to my hand, little one."

With halting steps, the troglodyte fell into Lina's arms, its leathery skin sending a shiver through the woman's spine.

Lina Arias beamed down at the creature. Its eyes swirled with enchantment, and its grey tongue lolled lazily from the side of its mouth.

"Good," Lina said softly. "I'm just so hungry. You understand, right?"

Her fangs sank slowly into the troglodyte's neck, and Lina was reminded of one of the first times she had ever feasted on living blood. She had been young, *terrified*, and the lust for blood she had felt had driven her into a field where she had laid low half a dozen cattle. The troglodyte's flesh tasted almost the same as a cow's, musty and tough, rolling behind her teeth.

Though the troglodyte's hide was tough, the creature's blood flowed freely over Lina's tongue once enough pressure had been applied. It was warm, not hot but pleasingly warm, despite its unrefined flavor. She tasted the earthy notes of the troglodyte's primal lifestyle flowing through the dying being's ragged veins. The troglodyte never resisted the feeding, its muscles limp throughout the minute-long ordeal until it finally died.

Lina tossed the drained corpse down to the dirt with a wicked laugh. She flexed, and her arms surged with new strength. Her pet wraith was nearly upon Chancol's high walls, just seconds from crashing into the plague elemental guarding the city. With unnatural speed gifted to her by vampirism, Lina shot through the smoldering trees, her mission clear in her mind.

She reached the two giants at just the moment they came together, fire mixing in the air with a rain of toxic spores and vile sludge. Thunder boomed as the wraith swung its burning fist into the chest of the elemental, and a second blast threatened to bring down Chancol's walls when the plague god retaliated.

Giant insects and other hideous beasts covered the battlefield in front of the majestic city. Lina looked to the top of the walls for humans to kill, but there were none. The stench she breathed in so near to the plague elemental was foul, but the woman's bloodlust kept her mind razor-focused, steeling her brain against the magical assault.

One of the giant spiders skittering up from the ground appeared only a few feet in front of Lina, and she dove to meet it, her dagger's point leading the way. The beast reared violently at her, lashing its huge, hairy legs in front of it and spitting globs of venom from its mouth. Lina ducked under two of the spider's legs on its right side, spun to her left to avoid the creature's fangs, and sank her jeweled dagger up to the hilt in its abdomen. The beast screeched, shuddered twice, and died, still partially submerged in the dirt where it had arisen.

Lina sheathed her blade as she leapt from the

spider's corpse. Scampering toward the wall, she braced herself for a leap. She was always unnaturally strong after a feeding, but she had never cleared such a height before. With a short running start, she vaulted into the air and planted firmly against the sheer face of the stone wall, only a single body length below the parapet. She grunted with the effort, using all of her extraordinary strength to keep herself from plummeting back to the ground.

A moment later, Lina pulled herself over the ledge of the wall and collapsed onto the narrow stone walkway. A sheen of sweat ran down her brow, and her chest heaved, taking in huge amounts of air. Her muscles burned in her arms and legs, but she felt more than exhaustion. She felt *alive*. She was closer to her goal than she had ever been before.

Lina stood and stretched her legs, relishing in the rush of blood as it filled her veins. She could see all of Chancol from her vantage point, the city spread out in a circular pattern before her as if waiting to be plundered. The very center of the town had been the epicenter of the summoning, and a gaping hole marked the place where several buildings had once stood.

She batted a flying insect from her face and took off for the nearest door, hoping it would lead her down to the street level. Jumping over a series of growing vines coming from the center of the city, she darted from the alley into the complex network of streets that served as

Chancol's arteries.

Windows were shuttered on either side, and Lina saw no one other than a solitary corpse as she sprinted through to the ravaged crater. She reached the gaping hole in the city unscathed, swatting away various insects before they could bite or sting her.

At the edge of the excavation, the stench and putrescence of the plague elemental's home began to break through Lina's otherworldly fortitude. She lifted the cloth of her shirt to cover her mouth and dropped down the ledge to enter the side of a broken tunnel. Her eyes watering from the caustic air, she squinted against the pain as she moved from one passageway to the next.

Lina arrived at her destination after only a minute of frenzied searching. She stood before a large, circular door devoid of any ornamentation or keyhole. She growled and lowered her shoulder, ramming her body into the wooden portal with all of her magical strength. After the third hit, she heard the wood around the latching mechanism on the other side begin to splinter, and the whole door broke inward on her seventh strike. Inside, the Guildhall's vault was massive. The room stretched several stories from floor to ceiling, and its depth was immeasurable at first glance.

She felt the presence of a key in her pocket, a key that had been given to her by Rhaas a long time ago, a key she had kept on her person ever since she had first felt its metal beneath her fingertips.

Quickly, Lina darted from one shelf of relics to the next, giving each row a single glance before moving on to the next. When she found the object of her search, her heart caught in her chest. She sensed the glass vial from two rows away, her vampiric gifts allowing her to smell the blood through almost any barrier. With solemn reverence, Lina pulled back a musty silk cloth to reveal a small box banded with iron.

The vampire plucked her bronze key tied with a lace ribbon from a pocket in her leather pants and slipped it into the box's lock, turning it slowly to ensure she did not damage the antique tumblers. The lock clicked, and Lina felt the tension holding it shut give way, a small puff of dust escaping the fresh gap between the lid and the bottom half of the box.

Again, Lina's excitement threatened to overtake her mind entirely. Years of careful planning spun through her head, the memories becoming a torrent of both pleasure and trepidation.

She lifted the lid and pushed aside a second layer of cloth, eager to finally see her prize with her own eyes. The glass vial was thin, barely holding more than a mouthful of thick, syrupy blood, but it was there and undamaged. Lina smiled. She lifted the vial gingerly from its stand, realizing as she did so that she had not brought a safer vessel to transport such a delicate artifact.

For a moment, she thought about drinking the blood

then and there, and even went as far as to remove the cork stopper and place the glass to her lips. She thought better of her plan, unwilling to risk a debilitating side-effect in the midst of such hostile territory. Lina gathered the two pieces of silk cloth from the shelf and used them to pack the vial tightly in its original box. Once it was locked, she slipped the key back into her pocket, turning quickly for the door, more memories rushing through her head faster than she could make sense of them. The whole plan, Rhaas' plan, had finally come to fruition.

A bit of movement caught her eye from between two nearby shelves, and the woman stopped in her tracks, shaking her head to clear her thoughts. She could just barely hear the sounds of the two colossal beasts locked in battle above her muffled by forty feet of dirt.

"Hello?" Lina asked, directing her voice toward the movement she had seen. She took a few tentative steps forward.

No reply came.

The creature, whatever it was, moved again, and Lina thought she saw a bit of steel flashing in the dim light.

Lina darted forward past another two rows of relics and the figure outpaced her, finally emerging directly in her path. It was a man, a very old man, and he was dressed in a loose-fitting green robe. His face was beyond withered, and his eyes seemed to struggle to hold Lina's gaze. He clutched a silvery rod topped with a clear, jagged crystal in his left hand, and his right did not emerge from the empty sleeve of his robe.

"I have no reservations about killing an elder," Lina said evenly. She drew her jeweled dagger from its sheath. With her other hand, she tightly gripped the box she had stolen. In that moment, she could barely think of anything beyond her escape from the city and the completion of her life's task.

The strange man opened his mouth, but he did not speak. Instead, the crystal on his wand flared with a pinkish light, and then a swarm of oversized wasps and hornets flew from his maw with a torrent of noisy wings. The insects flooded into the archive, surrounding Lina and blocking her vision with their inky bodies.

She slashed once in front of her with her dagger, killing a handful of the creatures, but she knew fighting them would be fruitless. Sheathing her dagger once more, she pushed forward through the swarm with one hand in front of her eyes and her mouth clamped tightly shut.

The winged insects focused their attention on Lina's left arm, stinging her flesh and using their unnatural size to rip bloody wounds all across her flesh. After several steps through the swarm, Lina's body was so wracked with pain that she knew she could not continue.

Searching deep within her magical repertoire, Lina called forth an old spell which she had nearly forgotten. As she whispered the words to the incantation, her face began to glow with unholy fire. She poured herself into the spell, dropping any semblance of a defense she had against the swarming insects and giving herself fully to the power of the magic that had claimed her mortality. When the spell was complete, she arched her back and roared, spitting a thin line of ethereal flames onto the archive's ceiling.

At once, the insects began to move away from the terrifying vampire. They buzzed about her flesh, but refused to land. Lina bellowed again, pushing her magic to its limits, and the stinging creatures retreated, racing for the open door to the archive. Her body heaved with effort and exhaustion, sweat running down her face. The insects vacated the archive in the space of a few heartbeats, and only the old man stood before her once more.

"You would be wise not to anger me," Lina threatened between breaths. Her body was swollen from so many poisonous stings, but her voice still flawlessly conveyed the finality of her statement.

The old man fixed her with his gaze. "You would be wise not to steal, young girl," he chastised.

Before he could blink, Lina lunged upon the man, keeping her dagger low to catch him in the stomach. She expected her adversary to dodge, to roll away with some unnatural show of speed, but instead she felt the man's warm innards spray over her wrist. She twisted her magical blade deeper into the wound, wasting no time. As wave after wave of sticky blood washed out of the man's gut, she stared into his eyes, searching them for some hint of treachery or deceit. All she found was agony.

When the deed was finished, Lina licked the old man's blood from her skin, and the power of her vampirism healed the hundreds of small stings and tears covering her body. Almost as quickly as all the commotion had begun, the archive was quiet once more.

Box in hand, Lina didn't waste a second moment of thought on the man and ran from the complex, vaulting back to the surface streets of Chancol, eager to be away from the strange magic of the Guildhall. Instead of turning back the way she had come, toward the remnants of her army and the fiery wraith she had summoned, Lina ran for the eastern side of the city. When she reached the stone wall, she knew she did not possess enough magic to vault upward and scale the stone, so she searched for a door or gate.

Half a mile to her right she saw a closed portcullis in what appeared to be an abandoned guardhouse. She dashed toward it, making sure every window she passed was shuttered, hoping her retreat would not be seen or reported. At the guardhouse, she found a narrow staircase leading above the iron portcullis, and the room over the entryway was deserted. Several creeping vines wove their way about the heavy chains locking the portal below, and the vines continued to grow as she watched them. They gave off the same foul stench that everything else in Chancol did of late.

On the outward-facing side of the guardhouse, tall arrow slits were aligned every few feet to help ward off attackers. Lina was slight of build, and it did not take much magic for her to blur the edges of her form ever so slightly, making her just barely small enough to pass through one of the gaps in the stone. Once extricated from Chancol, she turned her path northward, running through the wooded foothills toward Traxholm, a small village on the outskirts of Estria's rule.

She pictured her destination clearly in her mind: a small house, a single-story building made of hewn logs with a simple, thatched roof. Inside those four walls was where her master resided. The man who had made her who she was. The man who had given her immortality—and the only one who could take it away.

A man she intended to kill.

Chapter 6

Merren led the Estrian militia into the sewers with a torch in one hand and his sword in the other. It had taken three days to assemble the force, and still no word had been received from Maxus. Behind the soldier, over two thousand armed men and women followed, though they moved slowly—only two or three abreast at the widest parts and single-file the rest of the way.

The force clanked through the wet and smelly tunnels, making a raucous noise Merren feared would alert everyone for miles around. Directly behind the first ranks marched three of King Arias' best personal doctors, though instead of weapons and armor they carried pouches of herbs, a stretcher, and several heavy bags of other medical supplies. Merren hoped they would find the princess, but he didn't think it was likely. The nest he had seen with Maxus had been large and well-stocked, not some ragtag group of ratlings passing through the region on their way elsewhere.

When they finally came to the wooden door Merren and Maxus had encountered earlier, he found it unlocked and partially open. No light came from the other side.

"Not a good sign," he said quietly to the soldier behind him.

Merren pulled the door open fully, wincing as the hinge creaked, and saw that the room beyond was completely empty. Other than a few random pieces of furniture and other miscellaneous items, there was nothing. Merren waited for a moment before entering, scanning every inch of the doorway for a trap. It took a few moments for the bulk of the force to file into the chamber. Standing at the front of the room, Merren broke his charges into smaller contingents to scout the side chambers. He didn't know how many other rooms and passageways there would be, and the idea of separating his soldiers made him uneasy.

"Come with me," Merren told a handful of soldiers nearby who were guarding the medical personnel. The men wore the insignias of town guards, the lowest form of Estrian security, and they looked painfully out of place. He wondered if any of them had ever used the heavy clubs hanging at their sides, or if their entire combat experience had been confined to bar fights and debt collections.

Merren led his band through a doorway and into what he figured would have been the ratling leader's chambers. The room turned out to be completely empty, though it did contain another door, and that one was locked and banded with iron. He placed his ear against the door and held up a hand to silence the others, but heard nothing. "Empty again," he growled, unable to keep his frustration fully in check. "This whole damn complex is empty."

He took a club from one of the men and swung at the lock on the door. With all of his weight behind each blow, the plating holding the iron lock began to pull away from the door itself. "Here," he said, handing the club back to its original owner after twenty or so swings. "Get it the rest of the way." Sweat glistened on his brow in the warm torchlight.

It took four of them alternating turns to bust the strike plate from the door, but they got in nonetheless. The next chamber, what appeared to be one of the complex's termini, had a small bed against the corner and heavy iron hooks dangling from the wall to Merren's right. Two of those hooks held chunks of uncooked meat suspended several feet from the floor.

"What is it?" one of the men said, covering his nose and mouth to avoid the repugnant smell.

"Look, those are the pants he was wearing," Merren said. One of the others brought a torch a bit closer so they could all see it more clearly. "That's the captain.

They killed him."

Shouting erupted from one of the other tunnels, and the group turned back toward the main chamber.

Ratlings swarmed into the largest room of the compound, running and jumping from soldier to soldier. They were fast, but were also unarmored and bore only their claws and their teeth. Merren ran to the center to organize the troops to fight back. Behind him, the doctors cowered in fear.

"Form a line!" Merren commanded loudly. Some of the more veteran soldiers found each other in the chaos and made some semblance of a formation. The ratlings flooded in faster than the human militia could rally, and they were quickly becoming overwhelmed.

Merren dove into the fray, slicing back and forth in front of him as one of the ratlings charged for his gut. His blade caught the creature in the shoulder and bit deeply, but the ratling kept coming. It stretched out its long claws, and when Merren tried to jump backward he hit one of his men. All three fell to the ground, the ratling on top of the two humans screeching furiously.

Pain flooded Merren's mind. He felt the other soldier's weapon digging into his back through his heavy brigandine. Blood poured from the wound down the blade's fuller, sapping Merren's strength with every heartbeat. The man tried to push the ratling from his chest, to throw the beast to his side, but he couldn't get any leverage.

Long whiskers brushed against Merren's face as he struggled. The ratling's angular snout dripped hot liquid onto Merren's forehead. The beast dug its claws into the man's chest, tearing through armor and flesh with relative ease. Grunting with pain, Merren squirmed backward on top of the other soldier and managed to get his legs free to the side of the menacing ratling. He kicked with all his remaining strength, creating just enough space to get his sword between himself and his attacker.

When the ratling dug in again, Merren was able to wrench his sword up toward his own chin, severing the claws that were scraping away his flesh. Merren smiled weakly when the ratling howled and scampered away, leaving the man bleeding profusely from both the front of his torso and the back. Underneath him, the other soldier rolled away, clearly dazed.

Merren struggled to his feet. He saw the medics still bunched together in the corner, but a swarm of ratlings cut off his path. To his right, a handful of his soldiers had formed a small circle of blades and shields, and they looked to be prevailing against the horde. He didn't know how many ratlings there were, and all he could do was hope that he had brought enough soldiers of his own. His vision blurring, Merren pulled himself a few feet closer to the circular formation of fighters just before he lost consciousness.

He couldn't tell how long it had been before he awoke again. Thankfully alive, the only thing Merren could feel was pain. He opened his eyes and saw the same room where he had gone down, but the battle had thankfully ended. There were voices in the room with him, but only a handful. When he tried to turn and see what was happening, the pain in his back was so intense he had to stop.

"You're with us," a voice Merren immediately recognized said from somewhere nearby.

"My king," he whispered past the pain. "Did we find her?"

King Arias let out a heavy sigh full of emotion. "No," he said, not trying to hide his sadness in the least.

Merren managed to prop himself up on his elbows and look around. The room was full of soldiers, most of them lying on the ground tending to their wounds, and the king sat nearby on a low stool, his personal retinue of guards within easy reach.

"Maxus," Merren said, remembering the half-eaten corpse hanging from a hook in one of the other rooms.

"He'll get a proper burial tomorrow," the king replied. "You did good work here. The ratling nest was fully exterminated."

Merren could barely believe what he heard. "Fully

exterminated?" he asked. "How many did we lose, my lord?"

"Over a hundred," King Arias answered. "But the threat has passed. Your soldiers killed them all."

"Did we find *anything*?" Merren wondered aloud. Losing a hundred men to clear the sewers of ratlings felt like a needless waste, and the thought of a hundred corpses being the only result made him shiver. There *had* to be some other gain.

"Lina was there," the king confirmed quietly. "They clearly left in a hurry, and we found some of her things."

Merren felt his heart sink in his chest. He hated the thought of the king's daughter being dragged from city to city by such wretched creatures as ratlings—and he hated to think what they were doing with her while she was their prisoner.

"Where did they take her?" he asked.

"I don't know, Merren," the king said solemnly. "But we will find her. We will find Lina and bring her home."

Chapter 7

A singular goal imprinted on her mind, Lina traveled toward Traxholm through the forests of Estria for a week and a half, stopping whenever she fancied to run down a wild beast in order to feed. She didn't particularly like eating deer and wolves, but their blood sustained her—and that was the only thing she needed. On the second day of her strenuous run, she noticed a black spot of corruption beginning to form on the tips of her fingers on her right hand. She had tried to wash away the pox in a stream, but it had not budged. Day after day, the spot had spread through her flesh.

By the time Lina arrived in the blustery north, still a day from Traxholm, the black sickness crawling through her flesh had made it nearly to the elbow. It wasn't even, but splotchy and spindly, like a thick spider's web lacing itself around her arm. She had wrapped the corruption in a bit of untanned hide from a deer, and she shuddered whenever her mind wandered to the black, unknown patches of affliction.

She thought of the man she had killed in the Guildhall's archive, cursing her recklessness. The man's blood had coated her hand, and she knew it must have been the source of her contamination. Everything in that Guildhall had been doused in some aspect of plague, and the man had been no different.

Still tucked away in a box secured to the side of her belt was the vial of blood she had stolen, the object she had risked her life to acquire. The blood in the glass had once run through the veins of a powerful lich, a necromancer who could raise the dead with a mere thought. Consuming such powerful blood would certainly bring about profound and potentially catastrophic side-effects, but Lina was confident that she could steal the lich's magical strength, and that was a prize worth any price, though a flicker of doubt formed in her mind whenever she eyed the blackness spreading through her skin.

She saw the outskirts of Traxholm early in the morning, a few hours before the sun's light arrived to melt some of the frost from the dormant fields. A few farm houses stood on the edge of the village, their chimneys spewing thin lines of smoke into the air. Lina could hear the soft sounds of animals in their stables coming from a nearby farm as she passed. The hardy folk of Traxholm would be awake soon, and she knew being seen could seriously interfere with her plan. Her father would have the entire kingdom looking for her, of that she was sure, and every report of her whereabouts would bring them one step closer to interfering—though anyone the king sent to arrest her would surely end up dead at Lina's feet.

The princess ran into Traxholm's center coming to a stop near a large, stone fountain carved into the shape of a long-forgotten local mayor the people exalted for some unknown reason. The village square was calm and peaceful. A beggar slept under a heap of blankets next to an empty trader's stall, and the man was the only other living creature to be seen. Lina considered draining the beggar's blood while he slept to send a message, but she knew the idea came from her unrestrained bloodlust, not her logic. Going for longer than a week without human blood to sate her vampirism was something Lina was accustomed to, though it was not a pleasant experience by any means.

Slowly, Lina crept to a storefront on the northern edge of the square and climbed to the building's roof. In the week she had spent traveling she had gotten all of her water from streams and ponds, and her palate longed for something stronger. She bent low to listen inside the building for any movements, and when she heard nothing she dropped down to the back where a lock protected the store's cellar. It took her several seconds, but her vampiric strength crushed the lock in her palm. She threw the pieces of the mechanism far away and slipped silently into the cellar.

The wine arbors of Traxholm were nothing even close to well-known, but the vintner did make a distilled spirit whose reputation exceeded the borders of the small village. She found a small cask of the clear, potato-based spirit aging on a low shelf in the back of the cellar. Lina plucked the stopper from the barrel and breathed in the earthy aroma, eager to feel its burn in her throat. The locals called the drink Liquid Silk, but Lina thought it tasted more like fire than anything else. Despite its wicked burn, merchants all over the world paid exuberant amounts for barrels of the stuff.

She tipped the container up to her lips and swallowed a mouthful of the Liquid Silk, smiling as it seared her insides and fogged her mind. The batch was relatively fresh and unrefined, still lacking the woody notes that made it such a delicacy, but it was a far cry from cold stream water or hot animal blood, and that alone was enough to satisfy Lina's desires. She drank another mouthful and replaced the stopper, promising herself that she would return later when the Liquid Silk had had more time to properly age.

Up above, she heard the telltale creak of footsteps on the store's floorboards as the vintner began opening the shop for the day's business. Lina darted silently back to the stairs leading to the outside and left the store behind before she could be discovered. The sun's rays were just appearing over the horizon, dawn only a few minutes away.

The house Lina sought was situated on the northeastern corner of Traxholm, slightly removed from the village center, but still close enough to put her in view of the common folk milling about the square. About a third of a mile south of her master's dwelling, a dirt path led to Traxholm's mayor's house, a quaint cabin sporting only minimal ornamentation.

Lina pressed herself flat into a muddy depression in the land roughly equidistant from the mayor's cabin and her master's house, her eyes glued to the northern building, her heart racing in her chest. She hadn't seen her master in several years, and she had to hope that he hadn't moved away without telling her. If he *was* still there, he had probably smelled Lina the moment she had gotten within a mile of the village. She hoped the alcohol in her blood would help mask her scent. She shook her head at the notion, stifling a laugh. Nothing would keep her hidden for long if her master wanted to find her. Lina's only true concealment relied upon not being sought.

Several hours later, she finally caught a glimpse of her master moving within his austere hovel. She recognized his silhouette behind a small, frosted window. He was stretching, waking up late in the morning as usual, and he stoked his fire a moment later. Lina watched him prepare a meager breakfast for himself, thankful that it seemed her master was still living alone.

At her side, she couldn't help but fiddle with the box hooked onto her belt. She knew she should drink the vial then and there to gain every possible advantage before confronting the powerful vampire before her, but the corruption crawling up her right arm gave her pause. It had been a week, and she had not felt any adverse effects from the growing darkness, but it still worried her nonetheless.

What terrified her most was that the only person she trusted to properly diagnose her magical ailment was the very man she stalked—the man she intended to slaughter.

With a sigh, Lina dug out a small patch of dirt from under her body. When she had enough of a hole to bury her box, she unlatched it from her belt and lowered it carefully down. Once it was buried, she drew her dagger and held its point to her left wrist. Pricking herself would immediately give away her scent to her master, but it would also cover the smell of the vial beneath the ground, hopefully hiding it from Rhaas' keen nose.

Lina spent close to an hour contemplating her next move, all the while holding the sharp point of her dagger against her flesh. Finally deciding that diagnosing the corruption on her arm was more valuable than murder, Lina sliced a thin line down her wrist and let her blood drip onto the ground.

Almost at once, the man inside the house turned

toward the window. There was no use hiding any longer, so Lina stood, making sure to allow her wound to bleed freely over her buried treasure.

She walked toward the small structure with purpose, only making minimal efforts to keep her marred skin from view. The man inside took a massively large sword from a set of hooks above his door and came out to meet her.

"Lina Arias," he said evenly, dragging the huge sword alongside him. The weapon was so unwieldy it bordered on comical. It was one and a half times the man's own height, the hilt alone longer than most ordinary blades.

"Master Rhaas," Lina replied. Her voice shaking slightly as she spoke.

"I did not expect your return," Rhaas continued. "What brings you all the way to Traxholm? I trust you have not come to secure your immortality." He held his colossal weapon easily in front of him.

"No, Master Rhaas, I have not come to kill you," Lina said, and the words tasted like a lie on her tongue. "It is just the opposite." She held her corrupted arm out before her as she drew near to him. "I have need of your expertise, if you would be so kind."

Rhaas relaxed at the sight, moving his sword back to his side and beckoning Lina forward with his other hand. "Come into my home," he said casually, though he never took his eyes from the woman's dagger.

Lina entered the small dwelling before Rhaas. She moved to sit on one of only two chairs present at a roughly hewn wooden table in the corner. To her right, Rhaas' bed was covered in a haphazard assortment of blankets. On the small counter that served as a kitchen area, the vampire had a modest collection of glass jars filled with blood. Their scent was pungent, and Lina recognized each of them as coming from animals, not humans.

Rhaas hefted his mighty sword back to the pegs above his door and turned, a curious expression on his face. "There are no healers in Estria who could analyze your ailment?" he asked.

"Not exactly," Lina said with a half-hearted laugh. "Estria doesn't know what I am, and I'm fairly certain they don't know where I am, either."

"You never told your father," Rhaas concluded after a silent moment had passed between them.

Lina smiled. "I imagine news is slow in traveling to Traxholm, but you're bound to hear it sooner or later," she went on. "I recruited an army of humans and rat-lings, the dregs of Estria, and I sacked Chancol."

Rhaas' eyes went wide with surprise. "And what, pray tell, was the goal of such a reckless plan?" he asked coldly.

"You know what Chancol has in that smelly Guild-hall of theirs," Lina answered with a devilish grin.

"Lich blood," Rhaas said, sniffing the air.

"I was unsuccessful," Lina added quickly. She watched Rhaas' eyes for any sign of recognition, any sign that her ruse might have come undone.

The male vampire nodded slightly. "Chancol has powerful allies," he stated. "It would take much more than a makeshift army to topple those mighty walls. You'd need professional soldiers, siege equipment, months of supplies, and much more."

"Yes, Master Rhaas," Lina said with a dutiful nod of her head.

Rhaas let out a heavy sigh of disappointment. He pointed to Lina's blackened arm. "I trust you earned that scar fighting the Guildhall of the Pestilent?" he said, a bit of judgment lacing his voice.

"Yes, Master Rhaas," she said again.

"How? Some sort of incantation?"

Lina shook her head. "One of their mages. It was his blood," she clarified. "I stabbed him in the chest, and his blood stained my hand. It has been spreading as well."

Rhaas turned her arm over in his hands. He pushed at the black tendrils of corruption with his fingertips, gently at first, then more forcefully. He watched Lina's expression for any signs of pain, but she gave none. "How far has it reached?" he asked when he finished his physical examination.

Lina pulled up the sleeve on her shirt to show her shoulder. "Only one line has made it onto my back, but it's there," she said. "Do you know what it is?"

"I've seen it once before, I believe," Rhaas stated. "You must have killed a very powerful member of the Guildhall. The type of enchantment protecting him, and now afflicting you, is typically reserved only for their highest-ranking members."

"What's it called?" Lina asked. She could feel her heart rate accelerating in her chest. One of the many disadvantages that came with immortality was disease. No illness or poison could claim her life, but they could destroy her organs or cripple her body nonetheless. Such a fate was worse than death, confining her to an eternity of misery that she would never be able to escape.

"I don't know the name," Rhaas said. He stood and went to his kitchen area for a jar of blood. "Do you fancy a drink?" he asked. "Though I'm afraid I don't have any alcohol in the house."

"Can you cure it?" Lina demanded to know, ignoring the man's question altogether.

"Would you prefer wild boar or groundhog? I'm afraid those are the only palatable critters I've found this week, though I do have a few pounds of boar's meat left if you're hungry." Rhaas fetched two jars from a shelf and returned to the table, presenting them for Lina to choose.

"I don't want your blood," she growled. "Tell me how to cure my sickness!"

Rhaas set both of the jars down on the center of the small table. "I'm not sure you can be cured," he said. "Or at least not fully."

"What do you mean?" Lina begged.

"I would venture that the darkness covering your body is irreversible," he answered.

"And the sickness? What of it?"

Rhaas took the lid from one of the jars and held it to his lips, savoring the scent a moment before drinking a mouthful. "It will spread. When the black reaches your chest, when it gets to your heart, your body will begin to die."

"Is there a cure?" Lina demanded. "Tell me!"

Despite the gravity of the situation, Rhaas smiled. "I know a way you may live, but I do not know any method that will remove the stains of the corruption from your flesh," he said slowly, drawing out his words.

"And?"

"As I told you before, I don't know what they call it. What I do know is how they make it, and that might lead you to a cure. The enchantment is derived from a rare plant, a vine with green petals and yellow root and trunk. It grows somewhere to the west, though I'm not sure where. In the past, the guild members would make an annual pilgrimage to gather more of the crop, but I'm fairly certain they discontinued the practice several years ago."

Lina shook her head. "They must harvest an antidote. Where can I find it?" she asked.

"You don't know much about the Guildhall of the

Pestilent, do you, Lina?" Rhaas mused. "The strange acolytes of Chancol do not concern themselves much with antidotes. It is their belief that a guild member who contracts the affliction is purposefully doomed by their god and therefore unworthy of saving. You won't find your cure residing in their vault, I'm afraid."

Lina hoped her sour expression conveyed all the anger and frustration she felt.

After a moment, Rhaas continued. "The corruption from which you suffer is a slow and insidious disease," he said, "and I know of a place where disgraced members of the Guildhall of the Pestilent go in search of relief from such a poison. *That* is where you will find your cure, if one exists."

"What do you mean?" Lina asked. Sitting in such a confined space, she was keenly aware of her racing heartbeat thrumming in her ears.

"I'm not convinced that such a cure exists," Rhaas stated. "I keep a more watchful eye than most on the operations of all the various magical groups throughout Estria, and I have never heard of a disgraced Guildhall member with the affliction returning to the fold. You might have better luck than most, or you might not."

"Where can I find them?" Lina asked, standing to leave as she spoke.

Rhaas went to a small cupboard and rooted through a stack of parchments until he found one with a crudely drawn map on it. "Here," he said, his finger over a completely blank section. "I believe it is a very small encampment, probably horribly pungent, and likely well-hidden. I'd expect to meet resistance, but nothing you cannot handle. If a cure exists, you will find it there."

Lina studied the map and committed it to memory as best and as quickly as she could. "South of Tiaman City, west of the Roaring Fjord. Are there any other landmarks?" she asked.

Rhaas rolled the scroll back up and returned it to its place in his cupboard. "You'll find a waterfall there, though to be honest my knowledge of the area is limited at best."

"And why should I trust you?" Lina asked. She narrowed her eyes at her master, eager to be off but determined to be thorough.

Rhaas laughed. He held his hands out wide as if to reveal any clandestine motivations he might harbor. "Lina, my dear," he said. "What choice do you have?"

Lina laughed and pushed open the door, stepping into the brilliant light of the day. She thought of recovering her stolen box from the ground, but there was no opportunity for her to dig up the vial without being seen. Instead, she turned her course toward the east, shielding her eyes from the sun. Tiaman City was far away, likely farther than any distance she had traveled before, but the crawling black plague on her arm was better motivation than she needed.

Chapter 8

Much to Lina's dismay, there was no straight route from Traxholm to Tiaman City. Rugged mountains and biting cold bordered her path to the north, and the direct line leading to the city was blocked by Azanthium, a large trading port which belonged to her father. As Estria's third largest city, Azanthium was a vital economic and military outpost. A garrison of several thousand Estrian soldiers made it their home, each one under the pay and supervision of King Arias.

Covering as much land as possible, Lina used her immense strength to sprint through the forests and fields, avoiding the villages along her path, but always staying close enough to eat a farm animal when her vampiric hunger took hold.

She reached a small trading town on the side of a quiet lake a week after leaving her master behind. The village didn't offer much to be seen, but the towering spires of Azanthium rose up against the horizon, glittering as they reflected the sea against their bronze statues. The city was a day's walk from the trading post, and the road was crowded with merchants and peasants alike.

Lina unwrapped a bit of stolen cloth from her right arm to inspect the corruption. The flesh of her hands and fingers was completely black, and most of her forearm had darkened as well. The narrowest of slivers had crept up just beneath her earlobe, and she wasn't completely confident that she could hide it if anyone gave more than a passing glance.

When she had her disguise in place once more, she slipped herself into the steady stream of people walking on the main road, her eyes darting from one pedestrian to the next, waiting to see a flash of recognition that would expose her identity to the masses. Ahead of her, the town square was alive with merchants. The most common wares being traded appeared to be various food items, and Lina used a few pilfered coins to get herself a piece of dried meat to better blend in with the locals. She hated the taste of such a desiccated hunk of beef, but it was always her food of choice when she needed to present a mortal, inconspicuous facade. Dried meat was common, and no one questioned her if she took several minutes chewing each revolting piece.

A few taverns and inns flanked the busy central square on either side. Lina selected one which looked like it had the fewest Estrian soldiers within and ducked inside. The common room was warm, bordering on musty, and a pot of stew bubbled over a smoldering fire in one corner. There were a dozen or so patrons, and Lina ignored them all as she approached the barkeep.

"I need a room, just one night," she stated quietly. She held the cloth wrapped around her right arm as tightly as she could, and she made sure the hilt of her jeweled dagger didn't show at her waist.

"Four silver," the old barkeeper replied. He was a short, gruff man with a patchy beard and no hair left atop his head.

"Silver?" Lina asked. "For a single night?"

"Aye," the man responded. He didn't look up from the tankard he was working in his hands.

"I'll give you one," the woman responded.

The barkeep let out a sigh and set his tankard down on a shelf behind him. He looked Lina over with disinterested eyes. "I'll take three, but that doesn't include a meal," he stated flatly.

"Why?" Lina challenged. She kept her voice down as quietly as she could while still sounding normal, and only one other patron had taken an interest in her conversation.

"The price is the price," the man said. "Besides, I only have two rooms left, and I don't like you. You look sinister, a woman traveling by yourself and all. It isn't right."

Lina raised a brow in surprise. "Two pieces of silver, and it will be like I was never here," she said with a disarming smile.

"Fine," the man replied after a moment of consideration. "Two silver, but you'll eat none of my food, and you'll cause no trouble. I want you gone by dawn."

Lina nodded and set two coins down on the man's bar. "I want the better of the two rooms you have left," she told him.

The man nodded. He fetched a key from a drawer beneath the bar and set it next to the coins. "Top floor, take a left. The window has a draft and it gets cold at night, but the door locks and the floors don't creak, so it's the better room," he explained.

"Thank you," Lina replied, sweeping the key from the bar and moving toward the staircase in the same motion.

The room was exactly as the barkeep had described it. It was cold, and the window facing the market square didn't fit exactly right into the wall so it whistled when the wind blew over it. Lina stood at the window for a long moment, watching the people beneath her move about through the square. A few of her father's soldiers roamed through the market with spears in their hands and armor gleaming in the sunlight. She didn't fear their physical prowess in the least, but she wanted to remain unseen by the kingdom's spies. An open war against Estria's army would slow her down, and that would allow the corruption to spread.

What she needed was to move through Azanthium as quickly as possible, and she wanted information as well. According to Rhaas, Azanthium was only a few miles north of the conclave she sought, and the people were bound to know more than she did about the strange, rotting fanatics.

When night fell, Lina was in her room sitting in the center of a wax circle preparing to commune with the fiery wraith she had summoned to sack Chancol. She could feel her magical connection to the beast, but it was weak. Once she had finished readying her spell, Lina spoke the words to the incantation which transformed her circle into a scrying surface.

The wraith stood tall in the ethereal plane, though it was far diminished compared to the towering inferno of rage she had produced two weeks before. The souls of her soldiers swirled angrily through the wraith's body, trapped in their hellish prison for all eternity.

"You survived," Lina said quietly. Her voice was a whisper in her third-story room, but it boomed throughout the wraith's homeland.

"Burn the plague!" a chorus of souls chanted in unison within the wraith. "Burn the plague! Burn!"

Lina smiled. "How much did you burn?" she asked.

"The plague is dead!" the souls hissed at once. "The plague is dead!"

"Good," Lina cooed.

"Burn!" the wraith continued to chant. "Burn! Burn!"

"Soon enough, my darling," Lina replied. "I'll call you soon, but now you must rest. I require more souls to pull you forth from the abyss—"

"More souls! Burn with more souls!" the wraith bellowed. The unfortunate spirits trapped within the wraith were in a perpetual state of torment, but they were bound to the creature's will, so they chanted their forced response together without protest.

Lina waved her hand and the scrying surface vanished, leaving behind only a circle of melted wax on the wooden floorboards of the room. She waited for the wax to cool before cleaning it up, setting the solidified pieces next to the many lit candles on the room's dresser. The scrying exhausted both her mind and body, and she succumbed to sleep on the scratchy mattress a few moments later.

When morning broke, Lina was already on the move. The room showed no signs of use as she closed the door behind her, the cloth covering her arm fluttering in the air. She had her dagger sheathed at the small of her back, perfectly concealed beneath her shirt. The barkeep was awake as she left, and shot her a glare when she passed, but remained silent nonetheless.

In the center of the market, a few traders had their stalls opened and ready for business. Lina stopped at one of them to purchase a skin of syrupy-sweet wine. She hadn't fed on blood in several days, and the wine fortified her mind at least temporarily against the debilitating effects of her vampiric bloodlust.

Lina went first to the nearest stable. She found a pair of horses in Estrian barding with a single stable boy tending to their needs. "You there," she called, putting on an innocent look.

The boy turned to regard her and stretched his back with a grunt. "What do you want?" he asked. He had the voice of a lifelong stable hand, a born peasant destined to serve and do nothing else.

"These horses," Lina began. "Are the soldiers who are riding them en route to Traxholm?"

The boy screwed up his face in confusion. "Traxholm? Never heard of it. What are you doing here?"

Lina moved closer, hoping some of her feminine charm would help loosen the young boy's lips. "You haven't heard?" she said, feigning shock. "Traxholm was attacked by smelly men in green robes commanding frightful magic!"

"You're thinking of Chancol," the boy countered. "Big battle fought there, or so the soldiers say."

"A battle? I hadn't heard," Lina lied. "And what became of said battle?"

"Some upstart rebel army got routed," the boy

replied casually. He took a shovel from one of the walls and began cleaning a stall.

"Chancol isn't terribly far from here," Lina went on, finally directing her manipulation toward a more relevant path of questioning. "Is there an army coming for Azanthium? Are we in danger?" She held her hand over her chest, mimicking the noblewomen of her father's court when they pretended to be frightened.

"An army?" the boy scoffed. "Not here. Just the king sending troops to hunt for his daughter—nothing out of the ordinary."

Mention of her manhunt made Lina smile, but she concealed her enjoyment beneath a fake cough. "And the green-robed men?" she pried. "Have you seen them? Are they here now?"

"You mean sludge-ones?" he clarified.

"Yes," Lina answered, though she hated the term. It made her shudder to think of the implications, and she wrapped the cloth tighter about her corrupted arm. "But why do you call them such a name?" she asked.

The stable boy laughed as he shoveled a fresh pile of horse droppings into an old bucket. "They come through here all black and twisted and turning to sludge, maybe one every couple weeks or so," he said. "You've never seen one?"

"Where do they go after Azanthium?" Lina pressed, ignoring the question.

"Why would I know?" the boy retorted, waving her

off. "You ask a lot of questions."

Before the stable boy had a chance to look back on Lina again, the woman darted silently from the building, satisfied with the answers she had gotten, but still looking for more.

Back in the sunlight of the town square, Lina wondered where she might be able to garner an earful of more reliable information. She turned first toward the local magistrate's office, a squat stone building flying her father's banner at the apex, but a hand-drawn poster made her stop in her tracks. The proclamation was for her capture and return, offering a reward written just beneath a startlingly accurate representation of her face.

Her father had announced the sum of twenty thousand pieces of gold along with a modest fiefdom of three hundred acres for her safe return. She thought of the two silver coins she had exchanged for her room in the inn, stifling a laugh when she considered how many entire taverns she could buy with the reward for her own return. Scrawled in thick ink to the side of the reward was another mention of gold to be collected, though it offered only five thousand pieces of gold for her corpse, should she be discovered in that condition.

Lina quickly turned away when a soldier exited the building, and she stooped low as if lacing her leather boot. Luckily, the soldier passed by without a word, hurriedly walking toward wherever he needed to be. Lina kept her face to the ground as she retreated from the poster, deciding not to take it down for fear of raising any undue suspicion.

"I need a cloak," she said softly to herself. Her hair, raven-black and curled in tight, silky tresses that ran down to the nape of her neck, was her most recognizable feature. Her father had sandy-blonde hair and pale skin with light eyes to match, but her mother had darker, more angular features, like a fearsome warrior queen.

She didn't see any cloak merchants setting up to peddle their wares in the town square. There were two silk sellers on the western side of the market, and Lina purchased a small swatch of black silk with the intention of fashioning herself something more secure to hide her disfigurement.

Lina left the trading post around midday, walking inconspicuously behind a line of three oxcarts carrying barrels of beer toward Azanthium. None of the other travelers said anything to her, and no one questioned the dark silk sleeve she had attached to her shirt. She kept her eyes peeled for any of the so-called 'sludge-ones' the stable hand had mentioned, but she saw no travelers who could have fit the description.

The merchant caravan reached Azanthium a few hours past nightfall, turning toward the port town's seedier waterfront district. Lina split away from them to the north, moving as far away from the garrisons of soldiers dotting the city as she could. Azanthium was too large to warrant walls to protect it, so the men stationed there were concentrated mostly in circular barracks rising up between the roofs every few streets.

Azanthium's northern sector was dominated by one of the most unique trades in Estria, an open market for body modifications both magical and mundane. Tall brick buildings loomed over a circular marketplace larger than the entire village of Traxholm. At every stall, merchants called out their services, and eager customers created long lines for the more prominent sellers. Most of the officers stationed in Azanthium avoided the northern district, looking at body modification as something gritty and wholly beneath their station—and Lina figured the lower-ranking men she might run into would be too distracted to pay her any attention.

Though she had never been to the city before, she had heard stories of the Azanthian enchanters and the achievements they touted. Lina sought out one merchant in particular: a man in front of a marble building wearing a large, feathered hat. There was a short line of noblemen waiting to enter his business, and Lina stood behind them with her coin purse in hand.

Lina had to wait a little more than an hour for her chance in front of the merchant. Only a handful of people had looked her way during her time in the line, and none of them had shown any sort of recognition. A few stray screams of pain drifted out from the building as the customers inside received their augmentations. "What'll it be?" the man in the plumed hat asked. His voice was soft and melodious, fitting his dapper appearance quite well.

"I need to find someone, and I think you might be able to help," Lina answered. She made sure her coins jingled just enough to let the man know she was serious.

"Aye, I can help," the man replied with a charming smile. He held out his hand expectantly, and Lina dropped a single gold coin onto his soft leather glove. She knew she was overpaying, but she wanted the best, and added discretion always came at a higher rate. "You want Timmit, he's upstairs. You'll know him when you see him."

"Thank you," Lina said. She walked quickly up the flight of stairs that took her into the building, a tinge of blood making its way to her nostrils. The scent was enticing, and she had to actively focus her mind to keep her feet moving in the correct direction. Despite her concentration, she found herself hesitating a moment as she passed by an open door. Inside, a tall elf strapped down to a metal table grimaced as a group of three dwarves moved about his back with wicked-looking tools in their hands. The elf's shoulder blades had been split open, and one of the dwarves was positioning a leather wing over the creature's back. Another dwarf held a heavy spike with a thick leather thread attached to one end.

Lina shuddered as she walked past the grisly scene.

Once at the top of the stairs, it didn't take Lina long to determine which room she needed to enter. Gears and lenses hung in row after row on the walls, and a short halfling sat behind a desk with a collection of magnifiers protruding from a leather strap around his head.

"Timmit?" Lina asked.

The halfling lifted his gaze for a moment before returning to his work. "You need help seeing?" he asked, obviously preoccupied. "There are other vendors who can fashion you a monocle for far less than what I will charge."

Lina shut the door behind her. A blood-stained leather chair sat in the center of the room beneath a mirrored candelabra. "I need to be able to see magic," she said, not quite sure how to phrase her request.

"Tracking someone?" Timmit asked without missing a beat.

"You're a perceptive one," Lina mused.

Timmit tapped a finger against one of his many lenses. "I see much more than you can imagine," he said plainly. "Included that bit of plague wandering up your arm."

"I suppose there's no use hiding it," Lina said, trying to cover her surprise. She pulled back her silk sleeve and held her arm in front of her. "Can you heal it?" she asked.

The halfling shook his head. "I can see many things I cannot fix," he stated. "Though I suppose the person you want to find is not a specific person, but rather a *type* of person, yes?"

"I need to find the place where the Guildhall of the Pestilent sends their disgraced members," she answered.

"Ah," Timmit sighed. "There's your purpose. You did well hiding it before, but I saw *almost* everything."

For a moment, Lina wondered if the strange creature could see her vampirism. She could control the presence of her fangs at will, but she had little reign over her bloodlust, and the halfling had already seen so much. "Can you help me track the path of the sludge-ones?" she asked.

"Yes," Timmit was quick to reply. "How much gold have you brought?"

"I have twenty-one pieces of gold," Lina said honestly. It was a massive sum by a commoner's standard, but she had no way of knowing what Timmit considered a fair price.

The halfling thought for a moment before speaking again. "I can do it quickly for ten pieces, but you will not enjoy the process. For all twenty-one pieces, I'll make it painless and unnoticeable."

Lina took her dagger from her belt and held it forward, making sure the jewels in the hilt reflected the light in the room. "What would you do for ten pieces of gold and my dagger?" she asked.

Timmit rose from his desk to inspect the weapon, eyeing the item, but not touching it. "Marvelous craftsmanship," he whispered. "Where did—"

"And your silence," Lina quickly added. Timmit stole

several glances at her under the guise of inspecting the dagger, and an uneasy feeling grew in Lina's stomach.

"Agreed," the halfling said after a minute. "Come back tomorrow and I'll have something for you."

"Thank you," Lina responded with a nod. "Your discretion is something I value above all else."

Timmit smiled. "Certainly, my lady."

Chapter 9

Lina arrived at Timmit's workshop the next day an hour or so after dawn. She had fed on a pig the previous night and felt her bloodlust was fully under her control. She walked through the door to Timmit's workshop with more than a little trepidation, and the halfling was ready for her. He wore a heavy leather apron, a pair of glass lenses set in goggles over his eyes, and held a small drill with a thin bit in his left hand.

"Before we begin, I'll need your payment, my lady," Timmit said. He ushered Lina to the chair in the center of the room, and Lina offered him her dagger and the promised gold.

Lina closed her eyes and relaxed her breathing. "What are you going to do?" she asked, though she wasn't sure she wanted to know the answer.

Timmit tapped the back of her head with the end of

his drill. "The rear of the brain is where we perceive our sight," he explained. "And emeralds have been found to be more attuned to magic than anything else of similar size. With a little magic, I will combine the two, allowing you to perceive magic with your mind's eye."

Lina felt queasy. Her stomach turned, threatening to expel the blood she had consumed several hours before. "I'll be able to find the ones I need to follow?" she asked one last time.

"Yes, my lady," Timmit replied. "It will take some getting used to, but you'll be able to see the disease that afflicts them as clearly as you now see your own."

"And how many times have you done this before?" she questioned.

"Someone always has to be the first," the halfling answered. Before Lina could protest, Timmit placed a wet rag over her mouth and nose, filling her head with a pungent scent she could not identify. A few heartbeats later, the halfling removed the rag, though Lina did not slump forward as he expected. Instead, her head wobbled back and forth in a lazy, distracted manner.

"What…" Lina murmured. "What… is that?"

Timmit placed a hand to the woman's neck and waited, counting her heartbeats silently to himself.

"It seems my usual anesthetic does not affect you," he mused after a moment. "Tell me, is there any enchantment protecting you? Anything I should know about?"

Lina let out a weak laugh. Then she tilted her head

back and bared her fangs, her eyes wildly delirious.

"That… complicates things," Timmit said quietly. "I'll give you the ether as often as I can, but too much will be worse than not enough." He fixed a leather strap around the top of Lina's head and another around her neck. "This is going to hurt," he whispered as he brushed her hair aside.

Roughly three hours later, Timmit finished sewing the skin back together over the rear of Lina's skull. The woman had felt almost everything, but she had thankfully been able to resist the urge to scream, though her fortitude had proved so colossal it had actually frightened the halfling. "That's it," Timmit said with a sigh. There was a little bit of blood left on the back of his hands, and he wiped them off on a piece of cloth at his desk.

Still groggy, Lina reached back and fumbled with the leather straps immobilizing her head.

"Perhaps you should rest a bit," Timmit told her.

Lina undid her straps and attempted to stand, but she fell back into the chair almost immediately. "How…" she tried to speak, "how do I see magic?" She drooled as she spoke, though it was apparent the effects of the ether were quickly fading.

After only a few minutes, Lina was nearly fully co-gent once more, but the pain in the back of her skull bordered on intolerable. "How does the gemstone work?" she asked once she was confident her mouth could formulate the words correctly.

"You'll feel it," Timmit said. "Or at least you should. Like I said before, you're my first. I've put enchanted emeralds in lenses and other items plenty of times, and those things always end up with obvious activation methods. I think your brain should be no different. You'll know how it works when you know."

"Do you have anything to drink?" Lina asked. Every time she moved her head the pain would flare up again, incessant and throbbing, though she knew it would not last as her vampiric abilities quickly knit her body back together.

Timmit fetched a waterskin from a drawer in his desk, smelled the contents once, and passed it to her. Lina drank the entire skin quickly, though her vision blurred slightly when she tilted her head backward.

"Your..." Timmit hesitated. "Your ability to resist the ether," he said, fumbling for words that didn't involve admitting the woman was a vampire. "That secret is safe with me as well."

Lina smiled. "Good." When the pain in her head began to subside several minutes later, she stood once more—still wobbling, but keeping her balance nonetheless. She looked to Timmit, and an unusual feeling pervaded the back of her mind all at once. She couldn't place the sensation, but she knew it was there, right beneath the pain, waiting to be discovered. "You have some magic about you," she wondered aloud.

"Of course, my lady," Timmit answered. "See if you can find out where."

Lina focused her thoughts on the unusual feeling, and her eyes drifted down to Timmit's old, worn boots. There was magic also coming from the lenses now sitting on Timmit's desk, but the stronger presence emanated from his feet. "You keep a blade in your boot," she said when she thought she had it figured out.

"That's very good," the halfling said with raised eyebrows. "It seems the emerald is doing its job well."

"Perhaps it is not a blade, but something else," Lina said, honing her new skill in on the exact place where she felt the presence of magic.

Timmit loosened one of his laces and pulled a small shell fragment from his boot, holding it aloft for Lina to see. "Not a blade at all, just something to keep my hands steady," he said.

Lina realized that she had no way of knowing if the halfling was telling the truth or not, and she immediately became suspicious. The emerald in her brain only told her *where* magic was coming from, not *what* the magic could do.

Footsteps in the hallway stole Lina's attention from the enchanted shell, pulling her eyes toward the door.

Almost at once, she felt a strong magical presence accompanying the footsteps. Images of guards coming to arrest her flashed through her head. "You've betrayed me?" Lina demanded as quietly and as harshly as she could.

Timmit backed away toward the wall with his hands raised before him. "Never, my lady. Why would I perform the augmentation just to have you hauled away?" he countered.

"I don't know," Lina admitted, her head swimming. She tried to put everything together in her mind, but her thoughts kept returning to the source of magic approaching the halfling's door. A moment later, a sharp knock issued from the other side.

Lina slipped past Timmit's desk and lowered herself into a crouch, the pain in her head slowing her steps. Her dagger was sitting only a few feet away next to the pouch of gold coins she had also traded. Quietly, she reached for her dagger's hilt and plucked it from the table just as Timmit opened the door.

"Yes?" the halfling asked. He blocked the doorway with his small body, not letting those on the other side enter at will, though they could easily see over his head.

"Have you seen this woman?" a male voice asked. It was clear from the way he spoke that he was confident and commanded a great deal of authority.

Lina's heart sank.

"I don't believe so," Timmit answered the newcomers.

"She was seen entering this establishment by one of my men."

"I'm sorry, I don't recall," Timmit stated. "And I'm quite busy, so if you don't mind, I—"

Timmit gave a surprised yelp of pain. At once, Lina smelled the scent of his blood filling the room, and her lips turned up into a nefarious smile she could barely control.

She heard the sounds of three men entering the room as they stepped over the halfling's corpse. "She's here," one of them said. "No one has seen her leave."

Lina stood from her position behind Timmit's desk, her sharp fangs showing clearly over her bottom lip. "I liked that little halfling," she said with a hint of a laugh. "You didn't have to kill him."

"Bring her down!" the leader shouted, a snarl on his face and a bloody sword in his hand.

The three men leapt into action without another word. Lina jumped over the desk, meeting their charge head on, her dagger flashing side to side. She parried the first two strikes without much effort. Luckily, the room was too small for the third soldier to get to her without shoving his comrades out of the way. Ducking under a horizontal slash, Lina pushed forward and knocked one of her assailants backward. The man stumbled into the wall, and a shelf of various surgical implements crashed down on his head.

Lina turned back to her left. The second attacker

was more poised and cautious than the first. All three were her father's men, guards sent from Estria to bring her back. Lina didn't want them to die, but she had no choice. They were there to arrest her, and whether they knew she was a quasi-immortal vampire or not, they had come prepared for a fight. She rushed in at the second man, catching his short sword on the crosspiece of her dagger and turning it wide. She punched hard with her left arm and made the man double over, but the third soldier was upon her before she could react.

The sword smashed down on her back, and Lina's vampiric fortitude was the only thing that saved her from a swift death. Blood rushed out over her spine and down her legs, the skin knitting itself together as quickly as it could, though her mind was scrambled by pain. Delirious, Lina slashed to her right, shredding the third soldier's shoulder down to the bone. The man screamed and fell.

Lina scampered backward to give herself a moment of respite. She felt the power of her unnatural gift surging through her skin and keeping her standing, but it sapped her strength at the same time. She parried another blow in front of her, and she barely managed to knock the blade slightly wide. She needed to feed, or she'd be cut limb from limb, left as a crippled husk to be dragged back—still breathing—to her father's city where she would be burned at the stake.

With a flash of her fangs, Lina leapt forward with

her arms wide, taking a slash to the right side of her ribcage in the process. Her ploy worked, and she landed on top of the soldier's neck as the man's sword clanged to the ground.

She ripped a chunk of the man's flesh away in her teeth.

The second soldier stopped in his tracks. "Vampire!" he screamed at the top of his lungs.

Fresh adrenaline surged through Lina's body. Suddenly emboldened, she threw her victim to the ground and stalked toward the last enemy, blood running freely from her mouth.

"Vampire!" the man gasped again, his face pale. He backed away with his hands in front of him like a man condemned to die before the gallows.

"Say another word and I'll make it slow," Lina growled. The skin of her back had fully healed, and she stood upright with a smile. She placed her bloody dagger down gently on Timmit's desk.

"Wo—"

Lina lifted the man off the ground by his throat with a single hand. She stared into his eyes as he squirmed. "If my father is going to send his dogs to arrest me, he might as well get someone competent. Run home, cur." She spat a bit of blood onto the man's face. "Tell him to find someone worth my time."

Lina tightened her grip, crushing the man's windpipe just enough to prevent him from screaming. With a sinister grin, she used her free hand to claw through the soldier's stomach. She sank her fingers into the man's organs, but didn't rip them free. She poked and prodded, then retreated from his innards and let him fall to the ground. "You'll live for a few days," she told him casually. "Perhaps my father's surgeons can save your life. But you don't have much time. You need to run *now*," she said, kicking him toward the door with her boot.

When the man was gone, Lina wasted no time collecting her dagger and as much gold as she could find before exiting building through a second-floor window. The sun was high overhead, and she was covered in gore, so she hurried toward the edge of Azanthium as innocuously as she could.

Chapter 10

The northern side of Azanthium had a few houses alongside a well-planned grid of streets, though most of the area was still being developed. Lina passed a handful of pedestrians as she ran, and one of them shrieked when she saw the amount of blood covering Lina's clothes.

After the vampire was a substantial distance from the nearest house at the edge of town, she stripped off her shirt and licked the blood from her arms. It tasted stale, but there was no stream nearby to wash the stains from her skin. She looked back toward the city streets, and her enhanced vision showed her several locations of magic, one of them moving toward her at a slow and easy pace.

She crouched behind a few low bushes to watch the magic approach. No sounds of guardsman's footsteps or the telltale clink of metal armor came toward her. When the magic was nearly within reach, Lina pulled her shirt back over her chest and stood, her hand at the hilt of her dagger. The person approaching turned out to be a child. The boy was perhaps ten years old, and the magic on his person emanated from a small necklace under his roughspun shirt.

"Hello," Lina said quickly, somewhat startled by the boy's presence.

"Umm," the boy responded. He eyes went wide when he saw the amount of blood coating Lina's clothes.

She could see the boy starting to inch away, and she grabbed him firmly by the wrist. "I need your shirt," she demanded, though it didn't look large enough to fit her well in any kind of convincing manner.

The boy yelled, struggling against her unsuccessfully.

"Just give me your shirt," she said again. She pulled him closer and ripped the garment from his chest before pushing the boy back the way he had come.

With plenty of time left before her planned departure, Lina circled wide around the northern edge of Azanthium until she saw a tailor's shop which appeared to only sell items cut for women. She took off her own shirt again once the boy was out of sight, put on her stolen garment as best she could, and walked into the shop with her head held high, putting on the air of a noble.

"Can you believe it?" she scoffed when the tailor

came around a corner to greet her. She pointed to the flecks of blood still staining her pants. "A goat, slaughtered right in front of me!"

The tailor didn't look completely convinced, but he didn't cry for help either.

Lina decided to press her ruse further. "And the butcher gave me his shirt as his only means of recompense! The audacity, I tell you. It is absurd what this city is becoming," she pompously declared with a wave of her hands.

"And what exactly does my lady desire?" the tailor asked after a moment of contemplation. He was an older man, likely around Lina's father's age, and was impeccably dressed in a crimson waistcoat with matching leather gloves.

"Well I can't go to Lord Barrington's estate looking like a butcher's assistant, now can I?" Lina scolded. She did her best to put on an aristocratic air, and it seemed to have its desired effect.

"Lord Barrington?" the tailor questioned cheerfully. "I hadn't heard he was in town. But yes, you must be more finely equipped for such a momentous occasion. Here, come follow me."

Lina breathed a subtle sigh of relief when the tailor turned his back to lead her deeper into the shop. She had fabricated the loftiest sounding name she could think of, and the fact that it had turned out to be a real person amused her greatly. Passing a few racks of petticoats and bustiers, the tailor showed her to a section of the store filled with dresses of every imaginable color and fit.

"If anything is to your pleasing, my lady, you may try them on. I'll have one of my assistants help you," the man said.

"Oh, that won't be necessary," Lina replied quickly. "I was wondering, do you have something more suitable for riding? I believe there might be a fox hunt tonight, and I would like to attend."

The tailor nodded, a bit of interest sparking in his eye. "Right this way," he said, ushering Lina to the second floor of the store. All manner of utilitarian clothing items hung on neatly organized racks at the top of the stairs.

She browsed through a collection of leather equestrian pants until she found a pair that looked to be roughly her size. Above the pants, the tailor showed her a shelf with a few stacks of blouses designed to be cinched at the waist. Lina selected a darkly colored one with a bit of embroidery around the neck. It wasn't perfectly pragmatic, but it would work.

"And if it gets cold, do you have a cloak?" Lina asked.

The tailor smiled and extended a hand toward a small alcove overhanging the street. Inside, a few dozen heavy cloaks hung from wooden pegs.

"Thank you," Lina said, running her fingers over a garment made from wolf hide stitched to a linen interior. "This will do just fine."

"Would you like to try them on, my lady?" the man asked. He pointed her in the direction of a closed wooden door.

"Certainly," Lina answered. "And if it is not too much trouble, I would very much like to never be seen in these rags again. Would you be so kind as to dispose of them for me?"

"With all due haste," the tailor said politely. Lina dropped several coins into the man's palm before entering the changing room. When she emerged, she felt refreshed and capable. She had kept her belt, though moved it higher on her torso to properly secure the blouse she had purchased, and her dagger still hung from her back, hidden well under her heavy cloak. She wore the hood of the cloak tucked down against the back of her neck to hide her fresh surgery scar, turning the garment into more of a cape than anything else.

When she had properly thanked the tailor, she made a point of casually inspecting a few other items before leaving to ensure the man's suspicions remained low. Thankfully, he did not question her peculiar story nor her behavior, satisfied as he was with his sale.

Once more on the streets of Azanthium, Lina walked toward the eastern quarter of the city, to the governmental buildings and the barracks. Moving among so many officials made her nervous, but it was the quickest way to get out of the city, and Lina welcomed the challenge of traveling so near to her potential captors. With every glance thrown her direction, a fresh wave of exhilaration flooded her mind. The slaughter she had wrought in Timmit's office had filled her with adrenaline, and some part of her never wanted that rush to end. She wondered how much of her enjoyment from killing had come from her vampiric bloodlust and how much had simply blossomed in her as she aged. For a moment, she considered the possibility that she had become *evil*, that her vampirism was not as controlled as she believed it to be, but then she remembered what her 'normal' life had felt like. With a disinterested scoff, she pushed the notions far from her mind.

Lina reached the eastern end of Azanthium around nightfall. She had searched for some sign of a sludge-ridden acolyte of the Guildhall of the Pestilent to follow to their hidden enclave, but she didn't know exactly what to look for. The corruption on her skin had made it nearly to the top of her shoulder, and a few wisps of the darkness stretched to either side of her collarbone. The looming threat of the plague quickened her steps with every passing minute.

Several low barracks stood on Azanthium's eastern end, and where there were soldiers, there were always seedy gambling halls and dingy brothels. In every city in Estria, the worst parts of life clung to the military like the sickness clinging to Lina's right arm.

After a cursory examination of several noisy bars, Lina decided to enter the one with the least amount of magic emanating from within, a sailing-themed tavern called The Slippery Deck. Inside, most of the patrons had the burly build of dockhands, and one of them wore a fine coat with a matching hat. Lina figured he was a captain from one of the ships moored nearby, but he spoke with a unique accent none of his drinking mates shared.

Lina spotted an open chair not far from the staircase heading up to the rooms, and she took it nonchalantly. Living under her father's ever-watchful eye, she had never grown accustomed to taverns and raucous drinking. Fortunately, Master Rhaas had taught her much in the ways of the world, including a great deal of charisma she had not had before her transformation. She was confident she could work her way through conversation until she got what she was after.

One other patron sat at the table Lina had chosen, and he was a haggard old man who smelled like the sea. Much to Lina's approval, the man barely acknowledged her presence when she sat down across from him.

A young serving girl came to offer Lina a drink and some food a few moments later. She accepted the frothy mug of beer in exchange for a coin, but turned down the sad-looking beef with a wave of her hand. "Is it always this loud?" Lina casually asked the man at her table.

"What?" he said, barely paying any attention to her. Instead, his glassy eyes were fixed on some nondescript section of the wall across the room.

"The bar," Lina said. "Is it always this loud?"

The man nodded.

"Seen anything interesting?" she asked. She wasn't sure how to naturally work the sludge-ones into such a brief conversation.

"Bah," the man said. He took a drink from a cup half-full of a pungent liquid that smelled like the alcohol made in Traxholm. "Nothing beyond the usual," the man added after swallowing his sip.

"Any sludge-ones come through recently?" Lina posited. She kept her gaze cool and noncommittal, moving from one sailor or dockworker to the next as though the answer to her question was of little consequence.

"The last one was killed just a week ago," the man grumbled. "Didn't you see it?"

"Ah, now I remember," Lina said with a smile. The heat of the tavern was starting to make her skin perspire under her heavy cloak. She elected to finish her drink quickly, letting the conversation fade into oblivion before leaving.

Once more outside, Lina made for the nearby government buildings. Executions in Estria were only carried out with the express permission of her father, and the dungeons were all owned by the crown. Azanthium's gallows was bound to be near some gaudy bureaucratic center.

When dawn broke the next day, Lina was soundly asleep within her cloak in a narrow alley near Azanthium's public gallows, dagger in hand. She rubbed the fatigue from her eyes and sheathed her weapon on her back, eager to take up the hunt once more. A homeless woman had slept in the alley perhaps twenty-five feet from Lina, but she hadn't been a bother.

Lina could smell the stench of old blood coming from the scaffold when she was still a good distance away. In the center of the cobblestone square stood a tall gallows, three stocks, and a messy chopping block where the vilest of criminals met their swift ends. One man was bent over in the stocks, and his bare back was severely sunburned. She approached him cautiously, though she was more concerned about dirtying her new clothes than any threat the man in the stocks could possibly present.

"The sludge-one who was killed here," Lina said quickly when she was sure no one was within earshot. "Where was he found?"

The prisoner spat at her feet.

Lina snapped her dagger from its sheath in an instant and held it behind one of the man's burned ears. "Just tell me, scum, and I won't disfigure you beyond what has already been done."

The prisoner laughed, though it was a weak noise strangled by his unforgiving posture. "Why do you care?" he wheezed, stretching his neck to look at Lina's shoes.

She pushed her dagger down slightly, drawing a few drops of blood from the flesh between the man's ear and his skull. "Where was he found?" she demanded again.

"In the sewers!" the man cackled. "Where they're always found, you halfwit!"

Lina growled and pushed her dagger down farther. The man's incredulity was frustrating, and she felt the corruption growing up her arm adding fire to her veins. Under normal circumstances, Lina typically prided herself on keeping her emotions reined in, but the way the prisoner spoke incited her passions. The sign near him said he was an adulterer, a member of one of the lowest levels of filth Lina could imagine. She sank her blade another inch, cleanly severing the ear from its head.

The prisoner screamed, and someone walking nearby took notice. Lina concealed her dagger and turned, shaking her head as she stomped away.

Lina was no stranger to the sewers. Though it was her first time in Azanthium, the sewers of Estria had been her temporary home, and she felt safe there. The darkness concealed her vampiric gifts. Other creatures made the sewers of the major cities their home, but they were inconsequential to her. Just as she had done in her father's capital, the ratlings of the underworld would submit to her power when they saw the might she wielded. Ratlings were easy to mold to her will—easy to control.

She dropped into a nearly lightless tunnel a few streets south of the stocks. The place reeked, though the smell was nothing compared to the stench she had experienced in the Guildhall of the Pestilent.

Her augmented sight saw the lingering signs of magic everywhere in Azanthium's sewers. Several people had been in the tunnels recently, and more than one of them had carried a magical object with them. Lina followed the trail, certain that it belonged to the sludge-one the city had just executed.

After a few turns that brought her deeper under the center of the city, a familiar smell found its way to her nose. She thought of the old man she had killed in the archive beneath Chancol, and she knew she was on the right trail. Another minute or two later she caught the scent of blood mixing with the putrid rot she followed. She bent down to investigate the area and saw several splatters of old, stale blood staining the sewer wall around chest height. "This is where he was apprehended," Lina concluded.

She followed the smell of blood in a new direction, hopefully tracing it backward to find where the sludge-ones congregated in the darkness. She found what she sought a few minutes later when the smell brought her to a loose hatch on the bottom of the sewer floor. Some of the sewer's liquid fell through the portal around the uneven edges, and she heard several voices mixed with the sounds of splashing water.

Lina removed the metal lid and saw the opening beneath was barely large enough for her slender frame to squeeze through. She wrapped her new cloak tightly about her shoulders to keep it from getting ruined and dropped through. The lower tunnel was small and cramped, forcing Lina to bend at the waist to move. The tunnel opened up after the first turn, revealing a larger area connected to a rough cavern and illuminated by a single sputtering torch that filled the air with a heavy smoke that had nowhere to go.

On the cavern floor, two humanoid figures were motionless beneath a pile of dirty blankets.

"You're alive?" Lina asked loudly when she finally stood to her full height in the cavern. One of the blanket piles rustled in response. The rustling heap radiated with magic similar to Lina's arm, and she knew she had found a disgraced acolyte of the Guildhall of the Pestilent.

"Stand up, sludge-ones," she said. "We're leaving this place."

A young man pulled the blankets from his head to look at her, his eyes bloodshot. He was no more than twenty, and the corruption eating his body was nearly complete. Black tendrils of rot crept up his face, ending just beneath his eyes, and he appeared only moments from death.

"Get moving," Lina commanded. She took her hand away from her dagger and let her silk sleeve fall from her right arm. When the man saw her corruption, he appeared more interested, though only slightly.

"Why are you here?" he asked weakly.

"You're going to take me to the enclave to be healed," Lina responded flatly. She flashed her fangs. "If you do not, I will kill you."

"I'm already dying," the man laughed. "I'm doomed. I'll never make it to the enclave."

"You want to end up like that one?" Lina asked, pointing to the other pile of blankets that had not yet moved.

The man rubbed some of the sleep from his eyes. His wild hair was matted with all manner of filth and it clung to the skin of his head. "I don't have a choice," the man said after a moment. "She died two days ago. I'll be dead in a week."

Lina stepped closer to him. "I can keep you alive for longer than you'd have without my help," she said. "I can make you what I am, though you won't like it. But vampirism slows the corruption's spreading. If you show me the way to the enclave, I'll get us both there."

The man considered her offer for a long time before speaking again. "I would become an anathema," he said.

"You already are," Lina shot back. "But you would be a living anathema, not a dead one."

"Fine," the man said, meeting her gaze. He pushed himself up from his filthy blankets and stood. He was a little shorter than Lina, perhaps only a hair over five feet tall, and his body was so emaciated his ribs showed beneath his corrupted skin.

"When it reaches your heart, you'll die," Lina told him.

"I know," he answered. "I tried to join the Guildhall of the Pestilent back in Chancol, but apparently my devotion was not strong enough."

"How long ago was it?" Lina asked.

"Maybe a month," he replied. "Maybe a little longer. People were rejected by the guild every week, but I never thought it would happen to me..."

"The enclave isn't far from here, or so I've been led to believe. I can keep you alive until then, but we need to move quickly," Lina said. She reached a hand out and pulled the man up from the ground.

"Can I bury her?" he asked, sadness overwhelming his voice when he looked at his dead companion.

"There's no time," Lina told him sharply. "Will this cavern take us out of the city?"

The man nodded. "My name is Ayrik," he added. "What's yours?"

Lina considered lying to Ayrik to conceal her identity, but it didn't matter. She already knew she would kill him once she had been cured. "Lina Arias," she said with a bit of pride. "Daughter of King Arias, sovereign lord of Estria, and heir to the realm."

Ayrik's eyes went wide with disbelief. "You—"

"Let's get moving," Lina said, cutting him off. "The

sooner we leave Azanthium, the sooner I can turn you and save your life."

"I'll have to... eat people, won't I?" the man asked, fear filling his voice.

"Only if you want to," Lina told him honestly. "But you will have to drink. Normal food will taste like ash and mold in your mouth, but blood will sustain you unlike anything you've ever felt."

Ayrik nodded. "I don't want to kill people," he said. He began walking, presumably leading Lina from the sewers, though his pace was painfully slow.

"You can feed on animals, but most of them taste like dirt," Lina said. She pushed the man in the back, urging him forward.

Chapter II

King Arias sat in a small chamber off to the side of his grand audience hall. There were bags under his eyes that had been there for a week or better, though his stress had been mounting for months. In front of him, one of his regally attired advisors stood nervously at a wooden door.

"Well, I don't have much choice, do I?" the king said.

The advisor licked his lips nervously. "I think it would be wise to see the man, my lord," he said. "I have thirty guards stationed behind you, out of sight, but ready to intervene. If the man makes any sort of threatening movement, he will be killed. Though it might be wise to relocate this meeting to somewhere more open, if it pleases you, my lord."

King Arias shook his head. "Calling an orc a 'man' might be a stretch," he laughed. "And I want to know I can trust this hunter with my life. If I never let him get close enough to kill me, I'll never know he *wouldn't* kill me if given the chance."

"As you command, my king, though I have been told he is a half-orc, my lord, not a full-blooded orc," the advisor dutifully replied, doing nothing to hide his own trepidation. His hand shook as he reached for the door behind him. When he had it opened, he told the guard on the other side to bring the half-orc forward, and then they both waited.

Half a minute or so later, a burly, green-skinned humanoid stepped into the private chamber. He wore a leather vest over his muscled chest, and his tusks were adorned with metal rings and small, gleaming barbs. Two swords dangled in leather sheaths at his sides. Each one was thin with an intricate, silver handguard on the pommel. The king knew they must have cost a fortune, and he assumed they were magically enchanted as well.

The half-orc sniffed the air, a look of disappointment on his green face.

"Thank you for coming, Ilsander," Arias said. The fear in his voice was palpable.

Ilsander shifted his weight from one foot to the other. He was massive, and the king wondered if the non-orcish part of his heritage came from a giant or some other colossal being. "My payment?" the hunter said. His orcish voice was gruff, like a bull speaking the human language, and his heavy tongue added weight to his words that was further reinforced by his menacing tusks.

King Arias nodded to the advisor in the chamber, and the man handed Ilsander a single bar of hammered gold. While the human advisor had required both hands and a considerable amount of energy to lift the gold from the table, the half-orc handled the piece of metal easily. Ilsander tested the weight in his hand, tossing it up from his palm and catching it again as though it weighed little more than a few ounces. When he was satisfied, he dropped the bar into a sturdy leather pouch hanging from his belt. The belt itself was attached to his vest, preventing the heavy gold from dragging the leather band down to his knees.

"What makes you think she's a vampire?" the half-orc wasted no time in asking.

Arias let out a heavy sigh. "I have eyes and ears in every city in Estria, and a few in cities not yet under my rule as well. The town of Traxholm is also subject to my purview. I received word yesterday from Traxholm's mayor that some of their livestock had been killed by a vampire. Furthermore, my daughter knew a man from Traxholm by the name of Rhaas, and some of my attendants suspected him of being a vampire himself, though I foolishly never listened." The king looked down to the ground, defeated, only moments from letting his grief get the best of him.

"Circumstantial evidence at best," Ilsander replied.

"There's more," the king added quietly. "I trust you've heard of the attack that happened at Chancol?"

Ilsander nodded.

"We received a message from the city just two days ago. They more or less repelled the assault, but they said a woman had led it. She summoned a wraith, a colossal one, and used it in her attempt to sack the city. She had humans in Estrian colors under her command, along with a significant host of ratlings," the king explained.

"Summoning a wraith is not indicative of a vampire," Ilsander reminded the king. "Has she been witnessed feeding?"

Arias shook his head. "The messenger from Chancol did see her personally, though only for a moment. He had watched her jump from the ground to the top of the city walls."

"*That* is certainly indicative of a vampire," Ilsander stated. He smiled between his tusks, an awkward expression that looked more menacing than anything else. "Do you know where she is now?" he asked.

"I do not," the king said. A tear slipped from his eye and slid down his cheek. "After the attack on Chancol, we know she went to Traxholm—likely to meet with Rhaas—but she was never actually seen there. Perhaps she is heading east for the coast. If she boards a ship at Azanthium, I fear I may lose her forever."

Ilsander flexed his imposing muscles as he stood. "If she sails for another kingdom, I can pursue her, though I will expect payments to be made every month," he said.

"Do whatever it takes," King Arias commanded, finally meeting the half-orc's gaze for the first time. "Bring my daughter back alive. Do *whatever* it takes."

"And if your overzealous soldiers get in my way?" Ilsander asked.

The king nodded toward his advisor, and the man handed a medallion to the half-orc. The coin was etched with the king's seal on one side, a rolled scroll emblazoned on the other.

"You have my writ of passage," the king said. "Only three others in Estria bear such a token. Simply put, it gives you freedom to do anything within the boundaries of the realm without consequence."

Ilsander turned the coin over in his hand before slipping it into a small pocket on his vest. "And if I must kill?" he asked.

"Keep the bloodshed to a minimum," the king responded sadly. "But as I said before, do *whatever* it takes. If you must level a city to rescue my daughter, find a way to send me a message first so I don't accidentally go to war, but do it. I want my daughter home."

"Certainly," Ilsander said with a strange grin. "I'll need horses. Will your writ allow me to requisition new steeds from your garrisons?"

"It will indeed," the king answered. He looked to his advisor. "Give Ilsander my own mount. Remove the barding so no one thinks he stole it, and get him a different saddle. I want him fully outfitted with everything he needs, is that clear?"

"Yes, your majesty," the man said at once. He turned to leave in the direction of the stables.

"Anything you need, just let my assistant know," Arias said.

The half-orc bowed, his green skin reflecting the light coming through the windows above them.

"Bring Lina back alive, understood?" the king said one final time.

"If she is a vampire, only the one who turned her can take her life," the half-orc replied. "Hunting vampires is my specialty." He patted the pommel on his right hip. "I cannot kill them, but I can certainly subdue them and bring them home."

"Thank you," the king added. He stood and raised a hand toward the door the half-orc had come through. "Again, if there is anything you need, do not hesitate to ask. I will offer a sacrifice tonight to The Watcher for your safe travels."

The half-orc studied Arias for a moment without saying anything. "I do not bow to your human gods," he said after a moment. "If you must feel as though you have a hand in this, the mighty Kraxblade is the spiritual leader of my clan in the north."

Arias leaned forward in his chair. "What does your god demand?" he asked.

"Have you ever witnessed an orcish religious

ceremony?" Ilsander questioned.

Arias shook his head.

"Because we don't have them," Ilsander went on. "Kraxblade demands skill in battle and conquest on the open plains, not worthless pieces of silver left on a tray."

Ilsander exited the room before the king had time to formulate a response, his swords making muted clinking sounds as he walked.

"Do you really think you can find her?" Arias' attendant asked hesitantly as he helped Ilsander mount the king's own horse. The beast had been bred for hunting, and it was one of the fastest creatures the man had ever seen.

"The boat theory makes sense to me. I'll likely find her in Azanthium with her master, if what your king said is true," Ilsander said. He didn't bother looking at the human when he spoke.

"And you can bring her back alive?" the man asked. He handed the reins up to the vampire hunter with a bit of awe in his eyes.

"Moonsilver," Ilsander said. "I've captured dozens of vampires in the last twenty years. None of them were able to summon wraiths, but I have other things for such problems."

The man nodded and walked the horse out of the stable. Once they were in the open, Ilsander wasted no time urging the beast into a full gallop. The half-orc was heavier than any other rider the king's horse had carried, but the vampire hunter looked at ease in the saddle, perhaps even more comfortable than the king himself.

Lina and Ayrik returned to the surface sometime around noon, emerging from a different sewer tunnel than the one either of them had first used to get beneath Azanthium. They stood in an alley next to one of the shipping warehouses near the docks, and Lina was thankful that the smell of brine covered up most of the sewer's stench clinging to her cloak.

Sadly, Ayrik had little in the way of concealment. He kept one of his wretched blankets wrapped tightly around his shoulders, but he could not hide the two lines of black that had twisted themselves beneath his eyes. He looked like a beggar, and his appearance contrasted sharply with Lina's finer attire, making them an odd pair to be seen. A pair that could possibly draw attention.

"We need to move quickly," Lina said under her breath, her corruption ever-present in her mind. Ayrik's own contamination had sapped his strength, and the once youthful man struggled to keep up with her.

Nearby, a few dock workers busied themselves with a huge wooden crate that was nailed shut. They struggled to lift the cargo, making a great deal of noise with each step.

"Come," Lina whispered. "Go now."

The two darted from the alley where they had emerged to a nearby customs office, hiding behind a tall stack of empty barrels next to the door. A few seconds later, Lina ran for the next obstacle, ending in a crouch behind a counter full of herrings with Ayrik close behind her.

"Hey—" a fisherman began to say, but the words dried up in his mouth when he saw Ayrik's skin. Lina shot him a glowering look as she considered eviscerating him where he stood, but another opportunity presented itself farther down the docks and she took it, hoping to be done with the entire city as quickly as possible.

The two ran for the better part of twenty yards as a lounging group of sailors all turned their backs at once to welcome a new ship sailing into port. They made it to the back of the harbormaster's officer where only one other person stood, and the man there appeared to be thoroughly intoxicated from the night before.

"Only a few more streets to cross," Lina said. She pointed to the nearest gatehouse, though they didn't need to exit through it, as Azanthium had no walls.

"I'm too slow," Ayrik said breathlessly. He had barely

been able to keep up thus far, and the final stretch was longer than the rest they had done.

"If I turn you now, you'll be stronger. But you'll need to feed right away," Lina told him. "It isn't worth the risk."

Ayrik's eyes wandered to the drunk at the other end of the alley.

"You can't feed on him," she said sternly. "Not unless you want to be stumbling around as well, and that isn't going to help us right now. Besides, you're going to scream when it happens."

Ayrik nodded, though he kept staring at the man with a crazed look in his eyes.

"Focus," Lina demanded. She grabbed him by the shoulder and shook him to bring his awareness back to the task at hand. Inside the harbormaster's building, she heard footsteps coming near and a door opening. "We have to go now," Lina urged.

She pulled Ayrik roughly by his matted blanket to the edge of the alley. Peering around the corner, she saw a group of sailors going into the harbormaster's office, and two of them stopped at the door to chat. Lina looked back down the alley for a different escape, but the path let out near a barracks that teemed with soldiers.

"Now!" Lina said, bolting across the wharf as quickly as she could. She didn't wait for Ayrik to follow, but trusted that he wasn't stupid enough to stay behind.

Lina reached the edge of Azanthium quickly, and, as

far as she could tell, hadn't raised any suspicion. If the sailors had seen her, they hadn't cared.

Ayrik's journey across the wooden decking was a far different adventure altogether. He tried to run, but his tired and decrepit legs could barely keep him upright. Lina watched with a grimace as the sludge-one collided into a sailor, stumbled past the doorway to the harbormaster's office, and nearly collapsed into the sea. One of the sailors attempted to help the man back to his feet, but when he saw Ayrik's facial disfigurement, he called out in distress.

Lina cursed her luck.

She darted back toward Ayrik and looped her arm hastily under his shoulder, wrenching him back to uneasy footing. One of the sailors coming from the building nearby tried to brush her away, but her grip was like iron, and she pushed through him with ease.

"Hey!" a voice called from inside the office. Fortunately, the sailors were only confused, and none of them had raised any sort of alarm. When Ayrik fell to the ground and ripped Lina's silk sleeve off in the process, their demeanor changed drastically.

"Sludge! Another one!" yelled a pompously dressed man Lina assumed was the harbormaster. A handful of sailors ran off in the other direction shouting for the guards.

The harbormaster stepped in front of Lina's path and held his hands out to stop her. "Just put him down, miss," the bureaucrat said in his most official-sounding voice.

Lina repositioned her weary cargo on her shoulder and reached behind her back to procure her dagger. "Back off," she growled.

The harbormaster stood his ground.

"Let me pass!" Lina yelled in his face. She stepped forward and stuck the point of her blade beneath the portly man's heavy chin. Somehow, he still didn't get the message.

"Now just—"

Lina rammed her dagger through the man's skull. He fell to the deck at once, his considerable weight tearing Lina's weapon from her hand.

"Stop her!" a voice shouted from a dozen or so yards behind the two. Lina charged forward, hefting Ayrik fully onto her back in the process, and ran for the edge of the city. She reached the last line of buildings before any of the soldiers caught up to her and wasted no time sprinting for the wild parts of the forest farthest from the traveled roads.

With her vampiric speed pumping blood furiously through her veins and engorging her muscles beyond what any human could ever hope to achieve, Lina easily outran her pursuers. She only slowed her brutal pace when she was several miles from the city. By then, the bloodlust living within her chest had mounted to a nearly ferocious level. The exertion had drained her reserves, and she needed to feed.

Looking around the tall pine trees and crunching leaves of the woodland, the only blood Lina could find was making its way through Ayrik's body, just beneath his tainted flesh.

"Are there villages nearby?" Lina asked. "Trading posts?"

Ayrik shook his head.

"You're going to die if I don't turn you soon, and we will both need to feed," she said. "I could get a squirrel or maybe a rabbit, but it isn't the same. We need a person."

"Back to the road… travelers…" Ayrik murmured.

"You might be right," Lina said. "But we've already given ourselves away. My father is searching for me. Ambushing anyone but a lone traveler on the road might prove too risky. I don't want to leave a trail of bodies that leads directly to my feet."

"I think you already have," Ayrik said weakly. He groaned on the ground and pulled up his shirt, running a hand over the tendrils of darkness twisting all around his body.

Lina knew he was right. "A few more bodies probably won't make a difference," she conceded.

Leaving Ayrik behind to wallow in pain on the forest floor, Lina ran back toward one of the dirt roads that stretched from the city's eastern border to the next town. Azanthium was near the edge of the Estrian kingdom, so the roads were sparse, and Lina knew it might be several days before she saw a group small enough for her to easily ambush.

The sun had fallen by the time Lina heard anyone coming down the road to Azanthium. She saw a sliver of torchlight meandering through the trees, and a pair of voices accompanied it a moment later. The empty sheath on her back gave her pause, but the insatiable hunger within her chest urged her onward. She needed blood, and she needed it soon. Even stronger than the pounding bloodlust resonating throughout her body was the corruption, the darkness tainting her skin and threatening to overcome her.

Lina finally saw the small group up close a minute or so later. There were three humans, and one of them rode a horse. Metal clinked within the saddlebags on the horse's sides, and one of the men walking carried a banner. "A knight," Lina guessed. She thought back to her own bounty with a smile. "Perhaps he searches for me," she said under her breath. She smiled, though her heart pounded more ferociously behind her ribs with every passing moment.

The man in the saddle—the knight—looked tired. The horse moved slowly, and only one of the squires carried a torch. All three of them wore swords on their hips, though Lina assumed the knight to be the only one proficient with his weapon.

When the small retinue had passed, Lina emerged from her hiding place flat on her stomach by the side of the road. She stalked behind the group quietly, focusing her attention on the squire to the knight's left, the man farthest back. Utilizing her magical speed, Lina darted forward and wrapped a hand over the squire's mouth. She twisted, and the familiar sound of breaking bones accompanied her violent motion.

The knight and his second squire did not notice the loss of their companion.

Then Lina's bloodlust overcame her, and she immediately dug her teeth into the man's neck. Like a cat toying with a mouse, a deep growl resonated from Lina's chest which she could not control.

"Ordrick?" the knight called, turning in his saddle. The remaining squire shrieked when he saw his comrade being drained.

Lina let the body fall limp from her arms.

The knight drew his sword, and the hammered steel rang against his scabbard. "Monster!" he yelled valiantly. He turned his horse to charge, wild fury flashing in his eyes.

Lina rolled to her side as the knight galloped past, his weapon sweeping harmlessly overhead. She came up quickly, energized by her feeding, and leapt onto the back of the horse. She tore at the knight's back with her hands, and it took her only the space of a few heartbeats to knock him from his saddle.

The man grunted as his hit the ground, and then the tip of his sword poked up through his back. He slumped to his side with a solitary groan, dead on his own blade.

Lina turned the powerful warhorse back toward the final squire. The man was either smarter than the others or a coward, for he had dropped all of his belongings and was sprinting away at full speed.

The horse's hooves pounded into the ground, closing the gap in the blink of an eye. As a princess of Estria, Lina had grown up around horses. Her father had loved to ride and hunt, and he had ensured that his daughter became an expert in the saddle. Lina lowered her body off the right side of the horse as she neared the squire. She slammed the palm of her hand into the back of the man's head just an inch above the top of his neck, rendering him unconscious in a single strike.

She jumped fluidly from the horse, holding its reins in her right hand. When she had the living squire loaded on the beast's back, she went to collect the knight's sword and scabbard from his corpse.

"A little unbalanced," Lina said to herself as she turned the bloodied weapon over in her hands. The scabbard was well-detailed and had likely been expensive, but the blade itself left quite a lot to be desired. She tested its weight with a few slow strokes, then cleaned the blood from its edge on the side of the knight's shirt.

"You're back," Ayrik whispered from his position seated against a moss-covered tree. His eyes were sunken and dull, barely capable of holding Lina's gaze for more than a second at a time.

"Get up," the woman commanded sternly. She jumped from her horse and landed with a thud next to the sludge-one.

Ayrik struggled to his feet. He was weak, but he was also determined to live. He panted when he stood and would have surely fallen back to the ground had the tree not been there to support his weight.

"How..." he breathed. "How does it work?"

Lina pulled the unconscious squire from the horse's back and let him tumble unceremoniously to the ground. "I'm going to bite you," she began evenly. "When I bite a human I have the choice to turn them, kill them, or take what I need and let them live. It will be incredibly painful, and there is still a chance that you will not survive the transformation."

Ayrik's eyes showed an uncanny mixture of trepidation and resolve. "What are my odds?" he asked.

"I've never turned anyone before," Lina laughed. "And the only time I saw it happen was when my master turned me. It was a horrible experience I wouldn't wish on anyone—but I need you to live."

"The... vampirism," Ayrik stammered, "will stave off the corruption?"

Lina shook her head. "I think it moves slower in me than in you, but vampires cannot die like other mortals. If I am disemboweled on the end of some soldier's spear, I will not succumb to the wounds, but I will require months and months to heal—though my regeneration would certainly leave me disfigured and impaired. If the corruption reaches my heart, I do not think I would die, but it will eat away at my body, reducing me to a helpless beggar despite my strength. Only the one who turns a mortal into a vampire can truly kill the creation, though the student is also capable of ending the master."

Ayrik only sighed in response.

"So," Lina continued, "this is going to hurt."

She sank her fangs into the side of Ayrik's neck, holding back her tongue and resisting the almost insurmountable urge to drink. Pulse after pulse of life-altering magic poured into the man. He convulsed wildly in her arms, and his feet kicked sharply beneath him.

He didn't scream as Lina had when she had been turned, but Ayrik was simply too weak to make any noise at all. Lina held him in her arms when the deed was done, waiting to see any indication that the process had been successful.

Finally, several minutes after he had been bitten,

Ayrik's eyes started to flutter open. His pupils were huge, and his pulse was so fast Lina feared his heart might give out before he would have the chance to partake in his first feeding.

"I don't feel—"

"Wait," Lina cut him off. When she had first awoken after being bitten by Master Rhaas, she had experienced the same whirl of emotion. She had felt nothing at first, then every change had flooded her brain all at once.

Ayrik's eyes went wide in horror. He fell screaming from Lina's grasp to his knees, crawling through the underbrush as though the answer to his unimaginable torment was hidden away beneath the leaves and sticks. His body spasmed violently, cracking his ribs and limbs, then quickly began to reassemble itself into whatever internal configuration was required for one to be a true vampire.

Master Rhaas had told Lina of some of the internal changes, but she had never seen another vampire splayed out on a doctor's table for her to examine, and so she wasn't quite sure exactly what the transformation entailed.

Vomit spilled from Ayrik's mouth onto the ground. He gasped through the retching, his body in a constantly fluctuating state of contortion, and then he collapsed in the filth he had spewed.

"The vision," Lina said grimly. Whenever a vampire was turned, they received a vision at the end of their physical transformation. The body's changes were certainly profound, and the bloodlust had altered Lina's mind in ways she barely understood, but the vision that had accompanied her vampiric gift had affected her the most.

She shuddered as she watched Ayrik's still form, knowing full well the sheer horror he was experiencing.

When the man finally regained his senses some twenty minutes later, he was exhausted. His body was covered in a rank combination of sweat, vomit, and petulant corruption. "I lived," he said to no one in particular. His voice was unchanged, though ragged from screaming.

"What I saw..."

"I'll explain it later," Lina said. She had the squire propped against the nearby tree Ayrik had used for support, and the man sported a fresh bruise on the side of his head. "For now, you need to feed. The transformation isn't fully complete until you feed."

"What do I do?" he asked.

Lina showed him the pale underside of the squire's wrist. She bit into it gently, just enough to tear open the flesh, and handed it to Ayrik.

"You don't have fangs yet," Lina told him. "You'll need a dagger or razor of some kind to make it easier."

"When will I get fangs?" Ayrik asked. His eyes were stuck on the blood flowing from the unconscious man's wrist. The bloodlust was slowly enveloping his mind, forcing him closer and closer to the feeding with every heartbeat.

"Do it. Drink as much as you need," Lina answered. "Your fangs will come in after a few weeks. For now, you just need strength to fight the Guildhall's infection."

Ayrik's last shred of resolve broke, and he dove into the squire's arm like a vicious animal tearing the throat from its prey. He came up for breath only once as he drained the knight's unfortunate attendant.

"Good," Lina said when there was no blood left to drink. "You should be able to move soon. We can't start again right now, but soon." She got to her feet and turned eastward, eager to take up her journey once more.

"How often will I need to feed?" Ayrik asked, his voice emboldened by the warm blood flowing down his gullet.

"You'll know," Lina said. "Just don't get carried away. The blood makes you stronger, but bloodlust begets bloodlust. If you don't control yourself, you'll never be satisfied. Roving from one village to the next and leaving behind a wake of exsanguinated bodies is not how you want to live."

"Right," Ayrik said, some of his confidence stolen away. "But first we must find the enclave."

"Exactly."

Chapter 12

Lord Elador surveyed the wreckage of his city. He stood on what was left of the western wall with a handful of Chancol's construction specialists next to him. A little ways down the stone parapet, Saveus and a few other soldiers looked out in the opposite direction. Behind him, the battle had left gaping holes in the city's infrastructure. The charred wreckage of an entire neighborhood the wraith had crushed served as a sorrowful reminder of what the rest of the city could have become. Luckily, the damage had been limited to the western section of Chancol, and most of the remaining bits of plague had been scraped from the streets.

"Most of the population has recovered, sir," one of Chancol's other magistrates said when he reached the top of the wall to join the meeting.

"That is good news indeed," Elador responded. "For

a moment I feared we would all succumb to the plague."

"The death toll stands as it was yesterday, my lord," the man added.

Elador let out a sigh. "Chancol mourns for them all. I'd like a monument constructed to memorialize those lost to the plague. How do you think such a vote would fare among the other magistrates?" he asked.

"Quite likely to pass," came the answer, soliciting smiles from both magistrates.

"Then let us get on to the matter at hand, gentleman," Elador said. He unrolled a large scroll and held it down on the nearest rise of the parapet. "With the center of the city essentially gutted, we have ample room to improve Chancol at its core, to make it a beacon among cities that invites people from all corners of the realm to settle here."

While the magistrates and their builders debated the specifics of Chancol's reconstruction, Saveus and two of his officers surveyed the battlements in Channer's Glen. Everything was destroyed. The quaint, forested land where several thousand troglodytes used to live had been reduced to a charred wasteland of death. Where flowering trees and rolling hills used to rank Chancol's countryside as some of the most beautiful, the battle had reduced it all to ash. The few trees that still remained were blackened husks. Even the stream that had wound through the troglodyte land had ceased to flow, its spring destroyed by the plague elemental's death throes.

Beneath the three soldiers, a ten-foot swath of the wall had been shattered by a black powder cannon blast. Cannons were incredibly rare in Estria, and even more rare in Chancol, and the one brought against the city had been the only such black powder weapon Saveus had ever seen. That cannon was currently being taken to the city's largest barracks on the northern end of town to hopefully be reverse engineered.

"Do you think a second attack is likely?" Chancol's only commissioned general asked. He had become severely ill after the summoning of the plague elemental and had only just recovered enough to return to his duties.

"As far as our intelligence suggests, the attack was a rogue maneuver not sanctioned by Estria's king, though some of the soldiers wore their standard," Saveus answered.

"We have a few of them in custody," the general added "Almost no one survived the attack. They're deserters from the regular army, probably hired as mercenaries."

"Good," Saveus said. "I'll need to interrogate those men. Have they said anything useful on their own?"

"Their leader's name was Lina, but that's the only thing they have all agreed upon since they were separated," the general responded.

"The king's daughter's name is Lina," Saveus wondered aloud. "But it doesn't add up. There must be someone else behind it. Did any of our men get a good look at their commander?"

"Unfortunately not," the general said.

Saveus clenched his fist on top of the stone parapet. "Why would they attack us? We've been trading partners for years, decades!" he raged.

"Sir," one of the officers said, pointing toward a distant location on the field below. "Someone is riding for us. An emissary from Estria, perhaps?"

Saveus watched for a moment before commanding the others to follow him down to the ground level. They waited for the mounted rider in front of the western gate. A few armed guards patrolled in front, and the heavy portcullis had been taken down for repair after a cannon ball had torn a hole clean through it.

When the rider approached, Saveus' confusion only continued to mount. A burly half-orc sat in the saddle, and he had one of the finest horses the men of Chancol had ever seen. Orcs and half-orcs were rare, and many cities had outlawed the race of green-skinned humanoids without question. In Chancol, Saveus had known of orc traders moving through on their way to larger towns, but he had never laid eyes on one himself.

The half-orc sharply reined in his horse a few paces from the military cadre. Above them, the magistrates on the parapet also fell silent to watch the curious exchange.

"I have the Estrian king's writ of passage," the half-orc said without any semblance of introduction. He produced a metal coin from one of his pockets and held it in the palm of his hand.

"Chancol isn't under Estrian rule," Saveus answered uneasily.

The half-orc turned his head back and forth to take in the wreckage. "All of this was done by a woman, yes?" he asked.

Saveus nodded. "What do you know of her?" he asked.

Ilsander slid easily from his saddle and strode forward to meet the group. He stood a full head and a half taller than Saveus. The half-orc rose near to seven feet tall, and his tusks looked razor sharp. "Her name was Lina Arias," Ilsander explained quickly. "She is the king's daughter, and I have been hired to hunt her down."

"So it was her," Saveus said. "But how?" He pointed to the destruction all along the wall. "She had soldiers under her command—humans and ratlings—and a cannon. The troglodytes living in Channer's Glen fought her force and nearly had them defeated, but then she summoned a wraith unlike anything you've ever seen."

If the half-orc was surprised, he didn't show it in his dark, fearsome eyes. "It seems you won," he stated gruffly. "Was Lina's body among the dead?"

"No," Saveus answered. "But most of the casualties were burned by the wraith. It is hard to tell them apart."

"Were there any witnesses who saw her?"

"We have several of her soldiers in custody," Saveus replied with a proud smile. "Perhaps you would like to meet them alongside our inquisitor?"

Ilsander extended his green hand for the man to shake. "I'll see them now, if they're available," he said. His voice was a bit softer than when he had first ridden up, but the force behind it still filled the human retinue with an uneasy feeling.

Saveus told one of his men to summon the inquisitor, then led Ilsander and the others to Chancol's small dungeon after taking the horse to a private stable near the keep. The few cells had been constructed on the second story of a barracks that housed members of the city guard.

"We captured six of the bastards," Saveus said when they reached the first cell. "We put the ratlings to the sword and saved these four wretches, though that one in the corner might not live much longer." He pointed to a prisoner who had been badly burned. The man cowered in the corner of his cell like a beaten dog, and his breath came in ragged gasps that shook his entire frame.

One of the other humans was coughing badly. He spat a huge glob of blood onto the stone floor and wiped his mouth across the back of his hand, smearing his face with more blood in the process.

"You have a unique dungeon," Ilsander remarked casually. Iron bars were set into the walls as windows, allowing ample sunlight and fresh air to be enjoyed by all those within.

"Indeed," Saveus replied. "There isn't much crime in Chancol, so we never found a need for harsher measures of deterrence."

Ilsander nodded. Behind him, the man he assumed was Chancol's inquisitor appeared at the top of the staircase. He was old, probably close to dying himself, and he wore a grim expression that matched his torn black clothes.

"Where do you want to begin?" the inquisitor croaked, his voice raspy with age.

Ilsander looked the man up and down. "You sure you're up to the task?" he asked.

The inquisitor smiled. "I've been prying secrets from vagrants for sixty years," he said somewhat jovially. "I'm not going to let some big green wretch tell me when it's time to stop."

"I could break you in half with one hand, old man," Ilsander shot back, though there wasn't any venom in his words.

"Oh, I'm certain you could," the inquisitor said plainly. "Now, where would you like to begin?"

Ilsander inspected each of the prisoners in turn before selecting the one he thought looked the healthiest. They took the man down to the room below to isolate him from the others, and two of Saveus' soldiers tied the man to a simple wooden chair.

The inquisitor pulled a thin silver rod from the side

of his old boot and set it on the table in front of the prisoner.

"I've told you everything," the man said quietly. "I don't know who she was."

"Her name was Lina Arias, yes?" Ilsander asked.

The prisoner nodded.

"Why was she here?"

"We were going to sack the city," the prisoner said. "We could have taken it for ourselves and set up a new kingdom."

"Why?" Ilsander demanded.

"I'm a deserter," the man said. "I needed somewhere to live, someone to protect me."

"Lina offered you sanctuary," Ilsander concluded. "Was she a vampire?"

The man hesitated, but spoke quickly when the inquisitor's hand brushed against the metal rod on the table. "Yes, and a necromancer as well," he explained.

"And where has she gone?" Ilsander asked.

The man shook his head. "I've told you before, I don't know. If she survived the battle, perhaps she returned to Estria. I don't know!"

Silver rod in hand, the inquisitor walked behind the prisoner and tilted the man's head back. He aligned the tool with the inner edge of the prisoner's eye. "Where is she?" the old man demanded.

"I don't know!"

The rod shifted downward in the inquisitor's grip,

sliding painfully into the narrow gap between the man's eye and his nose. "Don't move," the inquisitor told him. "You certainly don't want to move."

"One more chance," Ilsander said.

"I told you!" the man said evenly, trying his hardest to remain as still as possible. "I don't know! I was just a soldier, not one of the leaders. They didn't tell me anything!"

Ilsander turned back to Saveus and the others. "If none of these men were officers, they'll probably all be useless," he said. He moved past them and walked back into the city, eager to be away from the torture that would gain him nothing. Time was critical, and he hated wasting even a moment.

From a leather pouch attached to his belt, Ilsander produced a bag of coarse orange powder that he took outside the western wall. He sprinkled some of the powder on the ground, and it flared to life with a bright yellow pulse.

"What is it?" Saveus asked from the gatehouse.

"I was wondering when you would say something," Ilsander told him, not at all perturbed that the man had followed him. He waved Saveus over to see the powder for himself. "It shows where magic has been. If the vampire was here, it will track her."

"I don't think it will work," Saveus said. "The hole in the center of the city was made by a plague elemental our guild of mages summoned. The thing was comprised entirely of magic."

Ilsander sighed and scooped most of the powder back into his pouch. "I'll try in a few other places," he said, "though you're likely right. A vampire's magical trail is powerful enough to follow, but a wraith and a plague elemental will make her tracks difficult to find."

The half-orc moved closer to the wall where a wagon-sized crater held the corpse of a giant spider. "How did this creature die? It barely got free from the ground," he said.

"I'm afraid the plague elemental had driven me underground by the point any of this had happened," Saveus answered. It was clear to see the man was disappointed by his own lack of action, but Ilsander didn't think less of him for it.

The vampire hunter spread his orange powder out across the ground in a wide arc, distributing almost the entire bag in a circular pattern. A set of footsteps appeared in the dust.

"I think we have her," Ilsander said. He scooped some of the dust up in a hand and threw it against the stone wall, but none of it stuck. He tried again and aimed higher, and there the orange powder showed Lina's boots clearly marked on the sheer rock face.

"I didn't know vampires could jump so high," Saveus said. He looked up at the glowing mark in wonder.

Ilsander didn't share any of the man's awe. "She could still be in the city," he growled. "Alert your guards.

If she's still here, we need to flush her out."

Saveus instinctively fumbled with the sword at his side. "And if we find her?" he sputtered.

"Hide."

Chapter 13

A yrik required almost a full day to become strong enough to move again. The vampirism added power to his muscles that would have been impossible to achieve naturally, but the corruption eating his body had nearly been complete when he had turned. He teetered somewhere just between being stronger than the average man his age and being only a moment from death at the same time.

Standing in the center of a small grove of trees, Lina held one of her hands into a shaft of sunlight that filtered through the pine needles. Her father had told her stories of vampires, dragons, and other monsters when she was a little girl, and she smirked when she thought of how little the average Estrian must know of her state. The legends described vampires as decrepit old men unable to enter the sunlight for fear of burning. Other

STUART THAMAN

than an occasional sunburn, she had never experienced anything of the sort. Lina pulled her hand back from the dawn to the hilt of her stolen sword. "My father knows nothing," she mused. Some part of her still missed the man, but she shed not a single tear for the life she had left behind.

"What?" Ayrik's voice came from behind, breaking her trance. He rubbed the sleep from his eyes with the palms of his hands. "I'm hungry," he said once he stood.

"For blood?" Lina asked.

Ayrik thought for a moment as he stretched his legs. "I think so." His nervousness was clear on his face.

"You'll probably need to feed tonight," Lina explained. "The hunger is strongest right when you turn. You can learn to manage it over time."

"What do you do? How do you control the urge?" Ayrik asked. The newfound strength in his voice was a stark contrast to his crippling weakness of the day before.

"Ratlings," Lina answered. "They taste like shit, but there are always plenty of them."

"Ratlings?" Ayrik questioned.

"They live in the sewers in Estria, though I'm not sure my father knows of their presence," Lina went on.

Ayrik gave a sullen look to the corpse he had drained the previous day. "Does the king know you're a vampire?" he asked.

Lina laughed. "He would probably have me killed!"

she said. "I'm an abomination." She thought of revealing her necromantic abilities to the man as well, but decided to keep at least one secret from the companion she fully intended to kill.

"*We're* abominations," the man corrected. "We would probably both be put to death if we're found."

"My political station cannot grant me immunity from my crimes," Lina affirmed.

Ayrik gave the body one final glance before he began walking toward the rising sun. "The enclave should be this direction," he said, though his voice betrayed his lack of confidence.

Lina untied the dead knight's horse from a nearby tree and followed him. "How do you know where it is?" she asked. She fell into step beside him, eager to be rid of her affliction as soon as possible. "And why did you choose to join that wretched Guildhall in the first place?"

Climbing over a fallen tree trunk, Ayrik could feel the strength returning to his legs with every pump of his heart. "I was always an outcast, and the Guildhall of the Pestilent offered me somewhere to go," he said. "They really aren't that bad, you know. Most of what they do is really research and experimentation. Chancol was built on top of a long-forgotten god. The priests and acolytes were trying to harness that energy."

"And the affliction?"

"The Blood of Voktarn," Ayrik said. His own

corruption had spread to most of his face, streaking his otherwise fair skin with jagged lines of black. "It is the ultimate gift. When you join the Guildhall of the Pestilent, the priests cast an enchantment on you that melds your blood with the ancient god's own lifeforce. I guess my mind wasn't ready for the enchantment, otherwise I would still be in Chancol."

Lina remembered the old man she had killed in the archive and wondered how much of the battle Ayrik had heard of, if anything at all. "I killed a priest of the Guildhall, and his blood got all over my arm," she said casually. "I'd like to get rid of this infection before it scars my entire body."

Ayrik began to recite in a sing-song voice:

East by east by down, a poisoned jewel in a fetid crown.

Forever forsaken, forever entombed, submerged, but not yet drowned.

"That's supposed to lead us to the enclave?" Lina asked. She recited the rhyme in her head a few times to commit it fully to her memory, though it didn't quite make sense.

Ayrik laughed as he moved through the underbrush. "I think 'by down' means 'south,' and perhaps the rest of it will grow clearer when we get close," he offered.

Lina frowned. "Your confidence is astounding," she replied dryly. "If the enclave is hidden behind a riddle, we may need more time. We'll move faster if we get back on the road."

The two made it back to the dirt path in good time, and Lina took the horse's reins in her hands as she mounted the beast. Luckily, the knight's horse was strong, and it didn't seem to mind the extra weight of a second rider as Ayrik got on behind her.

They rode hard toward the east, and Lina kept her eyes moving back and forth across the landscape, scanning for any clues that might lead them to the enclave. They passed a handful of other travelers, though none of them warranted a second look from the pair of vampires.

The trees and other foliage began to thin after several hours, and Lina stopped their mount when the terrain started to become more rocky and jagged, indicating that they had nearly made it to the mountain range that once marked the eastern border of Estria before Chancol and several other principalities had won their independence.

There was an inn to their north with a small trading post which Lina assumed served as some halfway point between Azanthium and whatever city was nestled in the foothills of the mountains a day's ride away. Without any other obvious route presenting itself, the two turned left up the narrow path toward the small collection of buildings to glean what information they could.

Smoke curled from the chimney of the large inn at the center of the square, and only a handful of other buildings stood on either side of the dirt road. Behind

the inn, a middle-aged man was busy tending to a meager assortment of chickens and rabbits.

"What village is this?" Lina called to the farmer
when she was within earshot.

The man held a hand to his brow to block out the
sun as he replied. "Just a farm and my wife's tavern, not
a village!" he shouted back. He had a distinct accent,
one Lina had heard several times from travelers visiting
her father's court, though her recognition alone was less
than helpful.

"And the nearest city?" she asked.

The man pointed north along the road. "Raagstadt is
a day or so that way," he told her.

When they were close enough to be clearly seen,
Lina let some of her silken sleeve fall aside to reveal her
corruption. "We're looking for a specific place," she told
him, waiting to judge his reaction.

The farmer took a hesitant step backward, though he
did not cry out as Lina had expected.

"You have seen my kind before?" she asked. Lina
dropped from the horse's back and walked up to the low
fence that kept the animals secure.

"Once or twice," the farmer said. His grip on his
rake visibly tightened.

Lina gave him a disarming smile. "Then you know
what I seek," she continued. "Which direction is it?"

The man pointed back to the south, toward the area
from which Lina and Ayrik had traveled. "That way," he

said quickly. "I don't think it is far."

"Thank you," Lina said. "Now, my companion and I are hungry. How much for two of your rabbits?" She pulled a few copper coins from her pouch and held them out to the man.

The farmer looked skeptical, and when he moved to take the money he did so quickly, as though Lina would snatch her hand away at the last moment. "My wife has food in the tavern. I'll take you there and you can eat, then you'll have to leave," he said nervously.

One of the rabbits hopped close to the fence to nibble on a blade of grass near Lina's feet. "I'll take this one," the woman said. She bent down and lifted the creature by the scruff of its neck.

"M-My wife," the man stammered. "She cooks. You can both take a meal at the tavern."

Lina pointed to one of the other rabbit as well. "I paid for two rabbits, not just one," she reminded him. The animal in her arms squirmed as though it suddenly realized what would soon befall it. Lina snapped its neck.

"Fine," the farmer replied quietly. "Take it if you must."

Lina stepped over the low fence and scooped the other rabbit from the ground. She killed it in similar fashion to the first before returning to her horse. "Thank you, sir," she told the farmer. Handing one of the carcasses up to Ayrik, she pulled herself back onto the mount.

"At least wait until we're out of sight," she whispered when Ayrik began to lift the rabbit to his mouth.

Startled, Ayrik lowered the creature back down to his lap. "I..." he muttered. "I didn't even realize what I was doing."

"I know," Lina said. "You have to learn to control it."

When they were once more outside the vision of the small outpost, Ayrik wasted no time devouring the rabbit held in his clutches.

"So what are we looking for?" Lina asked when they had both consumed their bloody meals. "What is a poisoned jewel in a fetid crown?"

"Perhaps a rock formation that looks like a crown will mark the entrance of the enclave?" Ayrik posited.

Lina looked around in every direction and determined that traveling farther eastward would lead them toward a rockier landscape than any other path. "Does 'poisoned jewel' mean anything specific to the Guildhall of the Pestilent?" she asked.

"I didn't get to officially join," Ayrik lamented. "It might mean something, but I never heard it outside the context of the riddle."

"So we just wander through the wilderness until we see something that looks like a crown or a jewel?" Lina scoffed. "There has to be more to the riddle, some piece you don't remember."

Ayrik's brow was furrowed in thought. "That's all there is," he said.

The two corrupted vampires continued through the countryside at a much slower pace for the rest of the day. When night fell, they hadn't come any closer to finding the first clue.

Chapter 14

Ilsander followed Lina's magical signature to the center of Chancol. He had to wrap a cloth around his mouth to keep the stench of the Guildhall from making him vomit, but he descended into the archive nonetheless. At the top edge of the crater, Saveus and the rest of the military retinue stood and watched.

The inside of the archive was covered in several inches of dead insects, and Ilsander's boots crunched through them as he followed Lina's footsteps in the magical orange powder. The powder took him to one shelf in particular near the middle of the archive, and it was apparent that the bed of dead insects on the ground had been recently disturbed. Ilsander saw a large blood-stain spread out across the floor, and it looked like a corpse had been dragged from the room out a rear door.

Tossing a small pinch of powder on the shelves

where the footprints ended, Ilsander saw a dusty outline of the object Lina had stolen. He tried to save as much of the magical powder as he could, but it was impossible to collect every particle and his bag was starting to run low. After a few moments of investigation, Ilsander climbed back to the surface to rejoin Saveus and the others.

"She stole something from the archive," he told them. "I'd like to know what it was."

Saveus shook his head. "Not many members of the Guildhall survived the attack, and the ones who did aren't saying much," he said.

"I have ways of making people talk that your inquisitor could never fathom," Ilsander said with a curt laugh, his right hand resting easily on the pommel of one of his swords. "Where is the entrance to their complex?"

"Well," Saveus said, looking around the crater, "the house they used to mark tunnels with was destroyed. I guess you could just look for them down in the rubble, but be warned: the priests of the Guildhall don't take kindly to strangers."

Ilsander looked back to the crater for the area that had been damaged the least. Across the hole from the archive, several tunnels abruptly ended, though they looked structurally sound enough to still be traversable. The big orc dropped into the nearest one of them with a heavy thud. He was too tall to stand fully upright in the passage, but it didn't bother him much.

The hallway ended after only a short distance, and Ilsander ducked through a wooden doorframe into a larger room with cages of animals lining one wall. The creatures were swarming with insects, and large cysts bubbled up on their flesh. All but one of them appeared to be dead.

Ilsander walked to one of the cages in the center of the line. A grotesque forest critter he could not name scurried back and forth, and weeping sores oozed insect larva onto the bottom of the cage. The half-orc slid one of his fine swords through the bars of the cage, ending the beast's miserable existence quickly and quietly.

He kept his sword in his hand as he exited the room. The next chamber in the complex was some sort of ritual hall that reminded Ilsander of his upbringing. He had been born far north of the Estrian kingdom in the orcish tribal lands and had witnessed several sacrificial rituals before leaving his homeland half a century ago.

The center of the Guildhall's ritual room was dominated by a stone table stained by decades of use. Creeping vines climbed up the sides of the altar like curling fingers rising from the ground itself. There were two extinguished torches behind the structure, and the room's only light came from two holes that had been blasted in the ceiling from up above.

A door opened to Ilsander's right, and a man covered in a green robe entered. He was looking down at something in his hands, and the half-orc was able to sidestep past the man unnoticed. When he was behind the robed figure, Ilsander purposely clanged his sword against the stone wall.

"Wh—"

"I need to meet with your leader," Ilsander said evenly.

The man set the book he was holding on the stone altar and turned. "You intrude upon the Guildhall of the Pestilent!" he accused.

Ilsander relaxed his grip on his sword. He tried to look as unthreatening as possible, but he stood two feet taller than the priest and sported a pair of menacing tusks. "A vampire stole something from your vault," Ilsander stated. "I need to know what it was."

The priest let out a deep sigh. "You are not permitted here, beast," he said.

"I don't want to hurt you, but I need to see your leader."

The priest looked Ilsander up and down. "A vampire stole from the archive?" he asked after a tense moment of silence.

"Yes," Ilsander answered. "I've been tracking her. She came here during or right after the battle and took something, a box. I need to know what was inside that box and why she wanted it."

"Come with me," the priest acquiesced, leaving his book where it sat. He led the vampire hunter down a series of long corridors, each one sloping deeper under the city. There was barely any light at all in the tunnels, yet the priest navigated them without any problems.

Finally, the two reached the largest of the Guild-hall's rooms, a central chamber carved directly into the bedrock. Ilsander kept his sword at the ready and his second weapon on his hip, though he got the sneaking suspicion that some sort of trap would spring at the last possible moment.

"Korbax has been sleeping since the battle," the priest said. "He won't take kindly to being awoken."

Ilsander pushed through the door without wasting any more time. The smell of rot assaulted him the moment he entered the room. He pulled the band of cloth from around his neck back to his face, but it did nothing to save his throat and nose from the acrid burning attacking him with every breath.

A pool of black, tar-like liquid bubbled and oozed in the center of the room, and several robed figures moved about the pool completely oblivious to Ilsander's presence among them.

"Korbax?" Ilsander said, pronouncing the strange name poorly. The orcish language he had grown up speaking was rough and loud, and the guild leader's name didn't sit well on his tongue.

The black pool of sludge stirred. Someone was there beneath the surface, and whenever it moved it released more putrid spores into the air.

"You disturb a god, half-orc," Korbax said as he rose.

His body was covered in sticks and moss, and the shifting ooze obscured most of his features.

"A vampire stole something from you," Ilsander stated. One of the acolytes near Korbax moved to the side to lift a pitcher from a stone table. He poured the pitcher's contents into the pool at Korbax's feet where it steamed and released a cloud of spores into the air.

The strange being just roiled in response.

"She took a box. I need to know what was inside that box," Ilsander said. He lowered his sword, unsure it would even be able to harm such a strange and foul being.

The tar-covered Korbax shifted forward slightly in his pool. "A vampire would only be here in search of one thing. The lich blood," he hissed, his voice so unnatural it made Ilsander pause.

Ilsander felt his pulse quicken. "If she gained the power of a lich…"

"Voktarn's Guildhall houses many priceless artifacts," Korbax hissed. "The lich's blood is one of many such relics." He shifted his countenance to one of the attendants in the room. "Go and confirm this half-orc's tale. If he lies, I will enjoy sublimating his flesh into Voktarn's hide. It will be a curious spectacle to behold."

Ilsander waited patiently for the acolyte's return. The room was silent once the servant was gone, and the half-orc moved nervously from foot to foot. He thought he should sheath the sword in his right hand, but the thought of breaking the uneasy silence made him nervous.

When the robed acolyte finally returned, Ilsander breathed a sigh of relief. "The box is missing, my lord," the man said. He bowed and moved to the corner of the room where he had stood before.

"You are hunting this vampire woman?" Korbax asked.

Ilsander nodded. "I am."

"Good," the plague lord said. "Bring her here so I may extract her blood and add it to the collection. You will be rewarded handsomely for the woman's return. If you fail, Voktarn will find you. If you fail, Voktarn will kill you."

Ilsander bowed out of formality. "Certainly," he answered. He turned on his heel to leave the putrid room as quickly as he could, eager to take up the hunt once more. Knowing that Lina had stolen lich's blood made him uneasy, but he had handled other extreme tasks in the past and survived, though he had to admit that a vampire imbued with a lich's abilities would easily top his impressive list of achievements.

When he finally emerged on the surface once more, Ilsander knew what he had to do. He scattered a small pinch of magical dust on the ground where knew Lina had escaped the Guildhall, and followed her footsteps to the edge of the city. Saveus followed behind him as he worked, always watching with a mixture of curiosity and apprehension.

"I'll bring your horse," Saveus said when Ilsander had concluded his search within the city.

Once more outside the walls, Lina's tracks led northeast, though Ilsander didn't have enough dust left in his pouch to keep following her step for step.

"Thank you," Ilsander replied, taking his reins.

"Where are you headed?" the soldier asked.

"The king believes his daughter might have gone to Traxholm," Ilsander explained. "Apparently she had an acquaintance from there, and the village is not far from Chancol."

Ilsander reached the small village of Traxholm three days later. He had ridden his horse nearly to its breaking point, and the beast could barely carry him any farther. Patting his mount gently on the side of the neck, Ilsander almost immediately smelled something in the air he recognized.

No chimneys spewed smoke into the air, and no voices could be heard from any of the farmsteads. Ilsander rode past the largest building in the village, which he suspected was where the local leadership resided, and everything was eerily quiet. No matter where he turned, the stench of death filled his lungs.

When he was almost in view of the town square, Ilsander dismounted and tied his horse loosely in front of a water trough that had barely any liquid left. The sun was high overhead, and only a few thin clouds drifted by. If he had been there under different circumstances, the half-orc would have enjoyed the clear weather and the crisp, cool breeze blowing in from the north.

He moved carefully beside the buildings near the town center, and soon he heard the sound of someone working, though it was the only voice in the entire village. Peeking quickly around the side of an empty business, Ilsander saw a man moving in front of a freshly dug mass grave. There were several tables set up around the grave, each one holding various collections of books, alembics, and other industrial elements the half-orc could not easily identify.

The entire population of Traxholm was motionless in the mass grave, save for the single shirtless man working around the corpse pile. On the man's back, a circular rune glowed with vibrant blue light. He wore loose-fitting black pants tied around his waist that fluttered in the strong breeze.

Transfixed, Ilsander crouched behind the corner of a building and watched for a long while as the man moved about his strange work. He moved his alchemical implements with his hands mostly, but Ilsander saw him once beckon to a glass beaker with a word, and the beaker floated through the air across the table.

"Well… I found the lich," Ilsander said under his breath.

Sometime after midday, the lich issued a string of words that made the symbol on his back flare to life. A bluish haze rose up from the mass grave behind the man, and it meandered through the air to the magical symbol. When the glowing mist entered the lich's flesh, he issued a satisfied groan as though he had just taken a sip of fine wine.

As the man in the square consumed more souls from his charnel pit, any doubt Ilsander had harbored concerning the lich blood evaporated. Liches required souls and the power of death to fuel their arcane arts, and the entire village had paid the price.

Unfortunately, the magical presence surrounding the lich was bound to be so powerful it would make Ilsander's dust useless. Anywhere he dropped the magical powder it was sure to come alive if the lich had been anywhere near a hundred yards of the location. He needed to move away from the village, back to the road, and simply hope he would get lucky and find Lina's tracks once more.

Then he considered the possibility that Lina's corpse was at the bottom of the mass grave, her soul along with dozens of others fueling the lich's power. If she was there, Ilsander needed to know. The lich only had one weapon visible nearby, a greatsword probably a foot or so longer than Ilsander's seven feet. The huge weapon rested on one of the wooden tables within the man's reach. The hilt alone extended over the table's edge by more than a foot, easily as long or longer than the blades on Ilsander's hips. The half-orc was an accomplished swordsman, stronger than any human and faster than most as well, but he knew a single parry against the lich's monstrous blade would shatter his steel.

He waited until the lich appeared completely occupied in his work and then crept forward slowly in a low crouch. He kept his sword sheathed and clamped a hand over one of the pouches on his belt to keep the contents within from clinking together. Ilsander had made it nearly to the edge of the freshly-dug grave before the lich sensed his presence.

The man's body went rigid, and Ilsander could see him sniffing the air to either side. The lich turned before Ilsander had a chance to retreat.

"I—"

A blast of frigid, necrotic energy released from the lich's chest, rocketing directly for the half-orc. Ilsander rolled to his side in the blink of an eye, coming up with his swords in his hands. "I don't want a fight!" he yelled quickly.

The lich glared at him with black eyes set against his pale, dead skin. The rune on the man's back glowed so vividly it gave the man a strong blue background no matter where he stood or faced. "You dare to attack me?" the lich said, his voice surprisingly human and unchanged.

"No!" Ilsander shouted. "It doesn't have to be this way."

"I can kill you with a thought," the lich answered.

Ilsander took a step closer to the pit, searching the bodies as best he could from his poor vantage point. "I'm looking for someone," he said. "Then I'll be gone."

The lich sneered. "I cannot let you leave."

"I know..." Ilsander muttered.

Chapter 15

Despite his newfound vampiric strength, Ayrik was nearly dead by the time Lina spotted anything resembling a crown in the wilderness. They had scoured the countryside for several days, finding nothing. Lina hadn't eaten in quite some time, opting to devote every minute of her time to searching for the enclave rather than hunting animals or civilians to devour.

And there it was.

A circle of tall trees dominated an otherwise barren landscape, arranged in a semicircle similar to the formal tiaras King Arias had made Lina wear to official government events when she was younger.

"Hey," she said, nudging Ayrik with her elbow. The man slept against her back on the horse, and every now and then he would nearly fall and then startle awake. "I think we found it."

Ayrik lifted his head to look around the strange stand of trees, but he was barely strong enough to maintain his posture for even a minute. Vampirism had saved his life and made him more or less immortal, but it could not stave off the effects of the corruption. He was drained, and he knew it.

"East by east by down," Lina repeated for what felt like the hundredth time in the past couple days. She left Ayrik on the back of their horse and walked to the center of the trees. They were redwoods by Lina's estimation, though she didn't think it mattered. Farther east, she could see mountains rising up in the distance several miles away. There wasn't anything to see to the north and south, and the landscape was bleak, with the circle of trees one of the only interesting features breaking up the monotony. Back toward the west, she could see the darkness of the woodland they had left behind.

Lina circled each of the trees, expecting to find ancient words or symbols carved into their bark, or perhaps even another riddle, but she had no such luck. The redwoods appeared normal in every regard except location. "It has to be the crown," Lina said when she had investigated the final tree. She looked up to the tops of each plant, searching for any type of sign, but again, there was nothing.

"Ayrik!" she called back to the horse. The man was leaning over against the horse's mane, a line of drool falling from his open mouth. He startled slightly when he heard his name, but he was barely able to open his eyes to see what was happening.

"Ayrik," Lina shouted again. "There has to be something more. There's nothing to the south at all!" She paced from one tree to the next, unable to accept the possibility that she had not yet found the crown from the riddle.

"Down," the man replied weakly. "Maybe it's literal." The horse lowered its head to nibble on a scraggly patch of grass, and Ayrik fell from its back to the dirt.

"Down…" Lina repeated. "East by east by down…"

She pounded her boot on the soil in the center of the grove. It made a dull sound like dirt normally does, revealing nothing about what might be underneath. Lina kicked a clod of soil away toward the trees. "We don't have a shovel," she remarked.

Ayrik was silent on the ground next to the horse.

"Fine," she said. "There's no other way." She pulled her cloak behind her back and sank to her knees, digging through the soil with her hands. She shoveled it away handful after handful, hoping beyond reason that the dirt contained some epic secret hidden just below the surface.

She continued to dig for hours. Ayrik didn't wake up, and his breathing was far from strong. Lina tried once to rouse him by shaking his shoulders, but it was no use. The corruption had covered most of his face, and the black tendrils had wrapped fully around his chest.

His vampirism kept his heart slowly beating and brain partially functioning, and that was it. Only by the strictest interpretation of the word could Lina consider the man 'alive.'

When sunset came, her hands were covered in bloody bruises, and sweat had soaked most of her clothing. She had a decent-sized cavity dug out from the center of the copse by midnight, and still she had found nothing out of the ordinary.

"A poisoned jewel in a fetid crown," she said to herself as she worked. "I hate riddles."

Sweat poured from her body, and she had removed her cloak long ago to keep the heat from being trapped against her skin. She considered removing the sole of her boot to use it as some kind of makeshift trowel, but she had no replacement. Swinging her stolen sword against a particularly tough patch of dirt a foot or so beneath the surface, she knew she had ruined the blade. Without a proper whetstone to repair the edge, the weapon was no better than a primitive club.

Swing after swing and handful after handful, Lina excavated the center of the clearing until the light of dawn found her resting on the edge of the hole she had made. "What is the poisoned jewel?" she asked the blood and the dirt on her hands. "Nothing about the trees is fetid… And it merely *looks* like a crown."

Frustrated, Lina walked back to the horse and her meager supplies. "If I had an axe, I'd chop one of those trees down," she muttered. "Perhaps there is a poisoned jewel buried in the roots. But disgraced acolytes seek the enclave often. If there was something underground, the soil would be disturbed from the last attempt. There *must* be an answer."

Ilsander backed away from the pit of corpses with his swords held loosely by his sides. "Just let me leave," he growled, though he felt anything but threatening.

The lich smiled. His eyes flashed with arcane magic the same shade of brilliant blue as his back, and he unleashed a swarm of glowing missiles from his fingertips. In all his years of hunting, Ilsander had defeated three powerful wizards, one of which had been a necromancer. He knew their attacks and what could make them suffer, and he knew the magical assault from the lich was only the smallest demonstration of his power.

Ilsander vaulted backward, and the missiles crashed into the ground a foot or two in front of his feet. They froze the ground solid, creating a black sheen of ice over the village's flagstones. A second wave of missiles followed the first in rapid succession, chasing Ilsander away from the pit of death. All the while the lich laughed, toying arrogantly with the powerful half-orc.

When Ilsander was thirty feet away, he felt a sinking

cascade of gloom erupt in his chest. The ground beneath his feet turned a sickly shade of green, and even the air became tinted with palpable sorrow. He leapt into the air to a nearby merchant's booth on the side of the road. The feeling of hopelessness receded from his thoughts the moment his feet left the tainted ground, but another wave of missiles already headed straight for him.

The half-orc waited as long as he could to give him the most time to steady his mind. The cursed ground was everywhere, rapidly spreading out through the village. Ilsander jumped from the merchant's empty cart and rolled, steeling his mind against a fresh onslaught of despair, and came up on the other side of the street with his weapons sheathed. His back to a wall, he had nowhere to run that would take him from the harrowing landscape.

"I'm not here for you!" Ilsander shouted.

The lich laughed, his overt enjoyment a stark contrast to the wasting depression marring all the land.

Images of slavish servitude flashed through the half-orc's mind. *Submission is the only way...* echoed through his mind. He couldn't tell if the thought had been his own delusion born from the sorrow wrapping its cold hands around Traxholm, or if the words had come directly from the lich's mind. He dropped down to one knee, his eyes averted from the power he had witnessed.

"No!" he growled, gritting his teeth and forcing himself to stand.

A blast of icy death thundered into his chest, knocking him backward with more force than he had ever felt before. Ilsander crashed into the wall behind him, and his green head left a smear of blood on the stones.

He fought his way back to his feet using the wall for support, and his thoughts swam with a confusing mixture of melancholy and pain. Everywhere he looked, all Ilsander saw was more gloom. The village was dead, and the lich had poisoned the very ground to infect the minds of the living with morale-breaking desperation. Ilsander knew the withered earth was having its desired effect on his mind. No matter where he turned his thoughts, they always found their way back to the hopelessness of his situation.

Ilsander knew he could not escape. A layer of frost covered his chest and arms from the lich's powerful missiles, and he knew that was only the barest fraction of the man's capabilities. Still, the proud half-orc would not fall without a fight.

He drew his swords once more and focused his mind on victory, pushing all the swarming notions of desolation as far from his mind as he could. The frost covering his muscles crunched and flaked away as he flexed, swinging his honed steel in easy circles around his wrists. His two-blade fighting style was considered unorthodox by both the full-blooded orcs of his tribe and the other half-orcs like himself, and it was a technique that had taken him decades to master, but Ilsander knew his capabilities well. He had dueled human swordsmen from Estria and dwarven masters from across the sea, and still he stood. A smirk took hold on the half-orc's face when he realized how few scars he bore from his conquests.

"It doesn't have to be this way," he growled again toward the lich. "I won't die like those helpless villagers. I will fight." His words helped sharpen his resolve, creating a nearly impenetrable mental barrier against the sorrow pervading Traxholm.

"You would stand against me?" the lich called across the pit.

Ilsander stood his ground.

"Come, my pet, teach this fool humility," the lich beckoned, and a creature emerged from the pit of corpses. It crawled from the hole toward Ilsander, emanating an aura of frigid ice over the ground as it moved.

The being that rose up from the pit was something Ilsander had only heard mention of once: an elemental of death—the purest form of unlife incarnate, a creature made of dessicated, unholy flesh and encased in chilled steel wrought somewhere in the hellish forges of the underworld. The creature carried a scythe with a handle made of bone, and a wicked edge of gleaming ice that could cut through stone. It sported wings stitched from unholy bits of tattered flesh, a hideous amalgamation that shook Ilsander to his very core.

He wasted no time. He charged forward with his

sword held before him, his left hand ready to parry the creature's scythe and his right poised to impale the elemental where it stood. Laughs echoed up from the lich when Ilsander stumbled through the space where the elemental had been. The creature had taken flight at the last possible moment, leaving Ilsander to stumble head-first into the wretched pit of slain villagers. His swords ripped through the flesh at the bottom with ease, but it was a position he did not want to remain in for long.

Ilsander whirled back toward the death elemental, ripping his twin weapons free of the death pile and hap-hazardly throwing gore around the pit in the process. The death elemental peered down at him from the edge of the pit. It hovered over the half-orc, then descended on its morbid wings to land in the pile with Ilsander. Its face hidden by a steel helmet, the thing screeched, and then the two clashed in the center of the pit.

Bodies crunched beneath Ilsander's feet as he swung. He kept his left sword vertical to protect that side of his body, and he hacked downward with his right hand, only hoping to test the strength of the death elemen-tal's guard. That strength became apparent in less than a heartbeat. The steel of Ilsander's sword crashed into the elemental's scythe, and an enveloping chill spread up Ilsander's arms faster than he could react. When he finally pulled his weapon away a few seconds later there was frost clinging to his arms and neck. The ice had spread to the bodies beneath the elemental as well, turning the gore pile into a slick mess of frozen blood, skin, and bones.

The elemental pulled its scythe in quickly, dropping the weapon's head low to put it in line with Ilsander's neck. He ducked down to avoid the swing and struck out with his right-hand sword again, stabbing directly for the creature's legs. He hit armor, but the elemental's frost response bordered on overwhelming. The ice shot up Ilsander's body and made his teeth chatter together.

Rolling away, the half-orc scrambled to be free from the pit. He needed some other advantage if he was going to destroy the elemental, and his swords felt useless in his hands. The lich's laughs still filled his ears, a painful reminder of what would be left to face if he could somehow find a way to prevail against the elemental. Ilsander's mental defenses faltered, and images of his own body lying dead in the pile flooded his thoughts once more.

He ran to one of the closest businesses and shouldered through the door with a crash of wooden splinters. The inside was stocked with wine bottles and casks of other spirits, and Ilsander got an idea. He rammed both of his swords through an oak barrel on the nearest shelf, and it spewed a clear, pungent liquid all over his blades. Grimacing at the thought of what it would do to the workmanship of his weapons, he clanged them against the stone wall over and over, hoping desperately to get a spark.

The elemental swooped through the splintered doorway, a blast of cold air preceding it. Ilsander struck his swords harder against the stone and, finally, his plan worked. Both weapons came alive in his hands, the strong alcohol burning all along their lengths. He knew the fire would not last long, but it was the only path that presented itself.

Ilsander barely got his swords in line quickly enough to block the creature's frozen scythe swinging in at his head. The resulting crash knocked him backward into another shelf, and the burly half-orc's weight easily pushed all the bottles onto the ground where they shattered. He turned in to his right, away from the scythe but closer to the elemental's steel-clad body, and swept his flaming blades across in a vicious horizontal arc that would have instantly killed any weaker opponent.

The flaming alcohol splattered from the swords onto the elemental's armor, and the thing shrieked. For a moment, Ilsander thought he might have found the creature's weakness. It writhed and bellowed, but the flames sticking to its body went dormant only a moment after they had begun. Ilsander backpedaled over the crashed wine and liquor, encouraging the mindless elemental to follow him. In the single-story building, the creature had no route to easily fly away. When the elemental was directly over the pool of flammable liquid on the ground, Ilsander drove his swords down into the floor, sparking them off the stone and setting most of the building immediately ablaze.

Ilsander smiled as the creature burned, its frozen scythe falling to pieces in its hand. The thing flapped its wings and took flight, ramming its head into the ceiling with a resounding clang. Disoriented, it turned twice in the air in search of the exit, but the flames had consumed most of its corporeal form by the time it was able to locate the door frame. Ilsander choked on the thick smoke and used his arm to shield his eyes from the particulate floating through the air. He flicked the rest of the liquid from his blades and returned them to their sheaths, then backed into the corner farthest from the fire.

The elemental twisted in fiery torment directly between Ilsander and the only exit. Overhead, part of the roof began to cave in, showering them both with flaming splinters of wood and thatch. When Ilsander could tolerate the heat no longer, he began slamming his body into the wall behind him. Weakened by the fire, the structure buckled beneath his strong blows, and he burst free from the building before much of his flesh was burned. His horse whinnied not far from where he had emerged, and Ilsander sprinted for the beast without looking back.

He could still hear the lich's shrill voice laughing above the sounds of fire as he made his escape. Ilsander's left shoulder and part of his neck and back had been badly burned, but he was alive. He stole a single glance over his shoulder to ensure he was not being pursued, and didn't stop galloping until he had put Traxholm several miles behind him.

Chapter 16

"Perhaps a poisoned jewel refers to a piece of your corrupted skin," Lina said sometime around dawn on the second full day of her excavation. She was tired and her body ached, and still she had not come any closer to finding the enclave that potentially held her cure. Her sword was significantly blunted by the all the work it had done serving as her shovel, and the cut it made on Ayrik's arm was jagged and gruesome. Lina sawed back and forth with the dented blade until she held a layer of tainted, blackened skin in her fingers.

"Is this your poisoned jewel?" she shouted at the copse of trees. She threw the bloody piece of meat at one of the trees and waited. The man, clinging to life, groaned beneath her.

Nothing happened.

Lina paced back and forth through the copse, her

frustration transforming into fury. She screamed at the trees, and when they did not respond, she stalked back to the barely-conscious Ayrik and grabbed him viciously by his throat. "You led me here to die!" she yelled in his face.

She shook him violently, and his eyes opened ever so slightly, revealing nothing but black ichor staining his sclera. "Is this your poisoned gem?" she demanded. Her blunted sword rested in the dirt nearby, just in the corner of her vision. She snatched the weapon from the ground and held Ayrik's eyelid open, revealing his jet-black eye underneath. The corruption had tainted his entire face, and Lina could see the unsated bloodlust of his vampirism doing its work on him as well.

The rough blade made garish work of Ayrik's face. Lina hunched over the man's head as she pried and cut, and the black eye was in the palm of her bloody hand before long. "Is this your poisoned jewel?" she screamed at the crown of trees. She hurled the gooey morsel into the pit she had dug and stomped her foot. "Take it!" she yelled over and over.

The ground beneath her feet shifted, silencing Lina at once. She felt the rumble slowly at first, then building to get stronger and stronger. Some of the dirt she had piled on the edge of the hole shook violently enough to fall back into her pit.

A staircase down into the earth presented itself before long, much to Lina's disbelief. The woman stood at the precipice, gawking at the spectacle. Creeping vines wove their way over the stairs and grew up to Lina's feet as if inviting her into their midst, coaxing her down into some ancient tomb known only in legends, folklore, and a single riddle.

Before she descended the stairs, Lina returned to Ayrik and her horse with a grim task on her mind. It had been several days since she had eaten, and she could keep the bloodlust at bay for a while longer, but not forever. She was famished and far from full strength.

Lina went first for Ayrik with her sword in her hand. She was the only one who could kill him—who could truly end his life—and there was no use keeping him in such a ravaged state of uselessness any longer. She pulled the man's shirt up from his torso and saw the utter corruption of his body. The black tendrils were so complete that almost no untainted flesh was visible. Lina aligned her sword with the man's heart and stood above it, using her weight to drive the point through his flesh. It didn't take long, and Ayrik breathed his last.

She turned then to the horse, her final remaining companion. It whinnied, weakly stomping at the ground with its hooves, far too dazed from dehydration and strain to do anything else. Lina knew the beast would not survive long, and she felt a twinge of pity deep in her chest. With a hand gently on its muzzle, she whispered softly to the uneasy creature, calming it as much as she could before taking its life. Her fangs sank into the beast's hide where she drank deeply, giving the horse its final rest and filling her own veins with a fresh burst of strength.

Lina continued to feed until she could drink no more. When she had collected two waterskins full of the horse's thick, warm blood, she dragged Ayrik's corpse beside the horse's. There was no food to take with her and no other supplies of value, so she spent a few minutes stretching and twisting her sore back, and that was all the preparation she needed. Pitted blade in hand, Lina began down the staircase in the darkness.

The path smelled like the earth, but in a good way, far from the pungent pestilence of the Guildhall back in Chancol. For a moment, the environment was so pleasant that Lina almost forget exactly where she was. The sun was high in the sky and the stairs did not turn, giving her a meager amount of light by which to navigate. On every step, more of the creeping vines padded her footfalls.

Lina could sense the magic in the vines. It was everywhere around her, and Timmit's augmentation made her keenly aware of it. She touched one of the leaves of the vine next to her and rubbed it between her fingers, hoping to glean some sort of information as to the plant's magical properties, but she learned nothing. It smelled faintly sweet, though she did not have the courage to taste it, knowing that the Guildhall of the Pestilent's chosen method of both attack and defense was poison.

After thirty or so stairs, Lina came to a square landing no larger than the smallest of rooms at the poorest of roadside inns. The floor beneath her feet was worked stone, and the air was noticeably cooler than at the surface. She wrapped her heavy cloak around her shoulders and looked ahead to the only door, a stone portal covered in vines just like everything else in the underground complex.

She waited at the door for a long time, listening and hoping to hear something on the other side that would prepare her for what was to come. When she was fairly confident that anything behind the door was either dead or silent, Lina pushed against the heavy stone tablet with one hand still on her sword. The door moved inward noisily, making her cringe with every squeak and squeal. Anything inside would surely know she had arrived.

The next room reminded her somewhat of the Guildhall of the Pestilent, from what little she had seen of that underground complex in Chancol. The chamber after the staircase was clearly a temple, with towering statues along each wall and a huge, monolithic spiral of stone at the front. Everywhere she looked, the creeping vines were there. They moved slightly when she paid attention to them, but Lina's focus was too drawn by the grandeur of the temple to worry about something so seemingly innocuous. There was light streaming in from somewhere overhead, but she couldn't figure out exactly where it came from—as though it was simply there and required no physical origin.

Above her, the ceiling was high and vaulted. Lina paused to wonder how much more she would have had to dig before hitting the stone roof from the other side. The ceiling was so far above her it didn't look like there was much room left before the surface. Returning her gaze to the temple, Lina moved toward the obelisk, trying to step on as few of the vines as she could, though avoiding it altogether was impossible.

As Lina walked, the temple felt oppressively silent. "Hello?" she called somewhat quietly, and her voice refused to echo through the tall room as she knew it should have done. No sound, not even her own, answered her call.

When she reached the spiraling black stone at the front of the temple, Lina searched for any signs that other beings inhabited the place. She found nothing. Other than the vines and the statues, the temple was empty. She placed her corrupted hand tentatively against the monolith, and it was cold to the touch like the marble pillars of her father's keep.

"Hello?" she asked again.

Still, no response came back.

She walked a slow circle around the strange pillar, looking for anything that might be relevant to finding her cure. She pushed aside some of the vines curling around the structure. The surface was smooth everywhere, unmarred by any sort of carvings or other manmade marks.

In that moment, Lina was painfully aware of the spreading corruption working its way up her neck. The inky darkness of her curse had climbed past her shoulder and collarbone the day before, and it was getting dangerously close to her heart. She cringed to think of the possibility that it would cripple her in the temple, rendering her helpless and unable to die for an eternity until the next afflicted person happened to find her.

"East by east by down," she recited, trying to keep her mind calm despite her hopelessness. "A poisoned jewel in a fetid crown. Forever forsaken, forever entombed, submerged, but not yet drowned."

She hoped for some sort of rumbling indication that she had just spoken the words to a magical spell, but she heard nothing in reply. Lina repeated the short poem with more emotion, aiming the words directly at the stone pillar. Still, the temple was unnervingly quiet.

Pacing back and forth from statue to statue, Lina pondered the words in her head. "Water," she concluded after a moment. "There must be water to feed the vines. There has to be something submerged." She knelt down to the nearest group of vines and traced them away from the center of the room, following them to the edges of the wall where each tendril of the plant disappeared into a fired clay tube. She grabbed one and yanked, and the part that slid out was wet.

She pulled and pulled, wrenching the vine free from the small channel as quickly as she could. When it was completely free, she knelt down to look through the hole to the other side. She saw water, but not much else. Whatever was beyond the clay pipes was too dark to be clearly identifiable.

Quickly, Lina moved to the next tube a few feet farther down the wall. She pulled that vine free as well, and a trickle of water began streaming through into the temple. She ripped more and more vines from their places, and the flow of water into the chamber increased substantially. Before long, Lina had half of one wall clear of the vines, and water flowed rapidly from the pipes.

She moved back to the black pillar to watch the chamber flood, curious as to what would happen next. Being a vampire meant drowning would not kill her, but it could damage her brain if she was not careful. The temple was huge and Lina was rather impatient, so she ripped more vines from the walls until the water was fully covering the ones that were left, making them difficult to dislodge. She figured it would take quite some time to fill the room, so she took off her heavy cloak and placed her sword at the top of the staircase in anticipation of swimming.

Once, only a month or so after Rhaas had first turned her, Lina had tested the limits of her immortality under water. She had gone into one of the rivers just west of Estria and used stones to sink herself to the bottom.

Part of her had wanted to die that day, ashamed of what she had become, but of course it had not happened. She had stayed at the bottom of the river for what felt like an eternity, though it had been less than half an hour. Her lungs had burned with incredible pain, and she couldn't see a thing in the bleak depths of the murky river. In those agonizing minutes, all she had known was terror and despair.

Luckily, the water filling the temple was far clearer than the river near her father's keep. Lina lowered herself a foot to submerge her head in the rising waters, and she found that she could still see almost the entire structure. Everything was blurry and shifted in the dappled light, but she could see.

When she came back to the surface, her feet no longer touched the stone ground. Lina floated gently on her back as the water rose, breathing in deeply to try and prepare her lungs for the trial she knew was ahead. No matter how much she told herself she would survive, she couldn't keep her mind free of panic as she reached the temple's stone ceiling. The final moments of her ascent felt painstakingly slow. Her last breath came as her face touched the stone that had once been several stories above her head.

Lina turned and pushed off the ceiling with her feet, propelling herself downward. Her ears rang from the pressure, and she struggled to equalize them as she descended. Once back by the pillar's base at the head of the temple, Lina ran through the riddle again in her head. *Forever forsaken, forever entombed*, she silently repeated.

She searched for any sign of change in the room, and the only thing she found was that her sole exit from the temple was blocked, the stone door once more in place. Using the vines to pull herself along the bottom, she moved to the nearest empty pipes to peer through. There was something on the other side, and it cast a faint shadow as it moved through the opposite room, though the clay tubes were far too small to ever pass through.

Her stored breath ran out with a pang of fire in her chest. She opened her mouth to let the water flood her lungs, and the pain of drowning began to build. Lina pulled the sleeve from her right arm and reached as far through the clay tube as she could, hoping that by revealing her affliction she would catch the interest of whatever it was on the other side of the wall. Her plan didn't work. The creature on the other side did not come any closer, content in its seemingly endless journey back and forth.

Reeling with pain, Lina swam away from the tube with only one idea left. *Submerged, but not yet drowned*, she told herself. She clenched her fists to calm her nerves, and then let go of her fighting spirit.

Lina breathed in the water and exhaled it again, closing her eyes as she floated in the center of the room. The water crushed her lungs and chest with brutal force. *Not yet drowned*, she told herself, hoping that exact moment would come very quickly.

She knew it wouldn't.

Drifting listlessly in the sunken temple, Lina felt her mind slipping away. She had been submerged for over two minutes, and the pain was reaching a level no lesser human would be able to withstand.

Another three minutes of sheer agony passed, and still Lina hung limp, suspended in the temple like an insect caught in amber.

Seven more minutes crept painfully by.

Lina fought the urge to scream with every second, and her thoughts blurred in a dizzying sensation of near-death oblivion.

An inky, black tentacle prodded through one of the clay tubes on the eastern side of the temple. A second and third tentacle appeared to either side of the first, and then the rest of the being from the other room pulled itself through. A jet of dark liquid followed behind it, churning the water violently in the creature's wake.

Lina watched the scene with barely any awareness at all, only fractionally cogent of her own existence as she drifted. The creature below resembled a slender squid, but it quickly transformed into the humanoid shape of a little girl when it had fully extricated itself from the second chamber.

"What?" Lina tried to say, temporarily forgetting her submerged state in the midst of her delirium.

The little girl wore a simple green robe similar to the

one Lina had seen on the caretaker of the Guildhall's archive. Somewhere in her befuddled mind, Lina was thankful the girl had emerged, though she had not ruled out the possibility that what she saw was nothing more than a fleeting hallucination brought on by the oxygen deprivation wreaking havoc on her brain.

The girl peered up from her position on the floor, a curious expression on her face. "You came to me," she said through the water. Her voice was dainty and child-ish, matching her slender body eerily well.

Lina tried to answer again, but it was no use.

"No one comes to visit me anymore," the girl said. She drew circles on the ground with a finger as though the water didn't hold her back at all. "I haven't had a friend in years..."

Lina turned herself to face the strange girl better, and a lock of her hair floated lazily in front of her face.

"I'm glad you came to me," the girl added playfully. "I like having friends. Will you be my friend?"

All Lina could do was nod.

"Good!" the girl shrieked with delight as little girls are wont to do. Her voice echoed from the temple's walls despite the water filling the structure completely. "But one of my little pets made you sick," she went on.

Finally, Lina felt like she was making progress, but her vision had blurred to show only various shades of painful red and orange.

"I'll tell you how to fix it if you promise to keep a

secret," the girl said.

Lina felt her heart beating furiously in her chest—or perhaps it had stopped beating altogether. Perhaps she was dead. Regardless, she nodded as vigorously as she could, and the motion made her nauseous. She vomited into the temple, and she felt the bloody contents of her stomach mixing with her loose strands of hair.

"Just eat the Witherbite," the girl cackled as though it was the most obvious thing on the planet. "I don't like the taste, but it makes the sickness stop."

Lina could barely believe what she was hearing. She assumed the vine that was growing all over the temple was Witherbite, and she had seen hundreds of the creepers in the Guildhall of the Pestilent. She thought of Ayrik's corpse some distance above her on the surface, and she remembered the immense distance he had traveled when the answer had been in his own city all along.

"Just keep in mind," the girl went on in her strange, echoing voice. "If you tell anyone, I'll have to send my pets to kill you, and I hate killing my friends."

Lina nodded again, or at least she thought she nodded, still operating on the mere assumption that she was not dead.

Beneath her, the girl finished tracing whatever design she had been making on the temple floor, and then she elongated into her squid-like form to slither back through the pipes to what Lina guessed was her eternal home. The way the girl had spoken about her minions in the Guildhall of the Pestilent made her appear like some kind of god, an outcast member of the pantheon known to only a few living beings.

When the squid-girl-deity was fully out of sight, the water began to lower in the temple, and Lina swam desperately for the surface. She erupted through the water with a spray of blood and spittle, gasping in breaths as quickly as her body could take them in. She floated on the surface of the water as it slowly lowered her to the ground, her mind barely beginning to recover.

Lina was unconscious by the time she landed softly on the Witherbite vines covering the temple floor.

Chapter 17

Ilsander dropped from his horse with a thud, a sheen of sweat covering his forehead and face. He looked back toward Traxholm, and the village was completely hidden by the horizon. The half-orc rolled to his back in the center of the dirt road, offering a prayer of thanks to Kraxblade, his tribe's patron deity. The orcish god lived in the sky, far above the ground, and watched his clans from the stars as they carried out the sacred rite of war. Ilsander didn't know if the god saw him at the moment, but he knew it must have been more than luck that had kept him alive against a lich.

A handful of travelers came down the road from the east, and they gave Ilsander strange looks as they passed him, offering him a wide berth. Most of the people of Estria were not openly hostile to orcs or half-orcs, but they weren't exactly friendly to them either. Ilsander heard the group pass, but he did not open his eyes to watch them.

His shoulder and neck ached with pain. He worried that an infection would take hold on his burned flesh, and he had nothing with him that could prevent it. He wrapped a cloth bandage around the burns on his arm, grimacing with each pass of the tight cloth. The skin hurt to move, but Ilsander was thankful just to be alive.

Finally, when he had rested enough to calm his whirling mind and steady his racing heartbeat, he got back on King Arias' horse to continue eastward. The next major city was Azanthium, and as long as the lich from Traxholm did not intend to pursue him, Ilsander was still intent on finding his quarry. He would send a messenger to the king when he arrived in Azanthium. It would take the effort of the entire kingdom to bring down such a powerful being as a lich, assuming it was possible at all, and Arias needed all the time he could get to prepare.

Lina had no way of knowing how long she had remained on the floor of the underground temple. She awoke dizzy and hungry for blood, her thoughts incoherently dancing in a mire of pain. It took her several hours to pull herself up to a sitting position against the wall. She vomited again onto the floor, and her entire body shook with pain.

Finally, when her thoughts had settled into something close to coherent, Lina remembered the strange squid-creature's words. She eagerly grabbed a handful of Witherbite from the ground and shoved it into her mouth. The plant tasted sour and made her face scrunch together as she chewed. She had no idea how much Witherbite she needed to eat, or even if she trusted the girl's words, but she ate and ate until she could not stomach another bite.

Lina didn't feel any different. Her stomach was full of the strange plant, but the corruption on her arm had not changed at all. The infectious plague had swirled all the way from her hand to her upper chest, and according to Rhaas, it would be there forever. Lina collected a hefty amount of the Witherbite vine from the temple before fetching her sword and returning to the surface. It was dark outside, probably several hours before dawn, and the night air was cool against her skin. In the quiet grove of trees, her only company was a pair of corpses she had made.

When morning came, the staircase beneath the earth was gone. Lina's haphazard excavation was the only thing left to denote her journey. She felt a tinge of regret for Ayrik and the horse she had killed, so she dragged their bodies to the pit she had dug before and rolled them inside. Again using her sword as a shovel, she covered both of the corpses. By the time she was finished, her stolen weapon was so worn and pitted it was useless, so she stabbed it into the head of the grave as marker, though she doubted anyone would see it before it was completely lost to the elements.

Setting her sights back toward the west, Lina began the long walk toward Azanthium and, ultimately, Traxholm. Without the corruption withering her body, she could finally drink the lich's blood she had hidden in the dirt outside her master's home. Becoming a lich would elevate her to a level of power she could barely fathom, and the prospect quickened her steps.

It was the plan she had made with Rhaas, the plan she had pursued for most of the past few years, and the reason for her entire existence. She knew she was greedy, hungry for power and ruthless in the pursuit of it, but none of those emotions struck her as anything more than petty. Weak-minded men and women looked at the powerful among them with disdain. Lina viewed the conquerors of old, the liches, necromancers, and vampires of the past, as idols.

And she would become all three—the first in Estria to combine the strengths of every forbidden magic into one human shell.

Azanthium was at least two weeks away on foot, and Lina needed blood if she wanted to keep her strength over the long journey. When she found the original road she and Ayrik had traversed, Lina turned north, intent on returning to the same farm where she had procured rabbits in search of more nefarious sustenance.

Ilsander reined in his horse outside a small military garrison of Estrian soldiers. The city of Azanthium towered in the distance. All through the street, humans stopped what they were doing and stared. Ilsander figured none of them had ever seen either an orc or half-orc in the flesh before, and one of the mothers walking with her family even shielded her child's eyes from the sight of his green skin.

The vampire hunter didn't care. He was used to stares and hateful language cast behind his back wherever he went—and he knew he could kill every one of them if he felt the urge.

Producing his golden writ from one of his pockets, Ilsander showed it to the nearest guard. "I need to send an official message to the king," he said plainly.

The soldier, a young boy probably on his first assignment after enlisting, stammered with his eyes wide. "Th-this way," he finally spat out.

The boy led Ilsander into the garrison, and the half-orc had to duck to avoid hitting his head on the doorframe. Only a few soldiers occupied the inside room. All of their conversations stopped when Ilsander strode inside. With a smile, Ilsander showed them each his writ and stated his demand again.

"Certainly," an older veteran wearing the markings of an officer replied. He pulled a scroll of parchment from a nearby desk drawer and sat down, quill in hand. "What shall it say?"

"It would be best if only you know of its contents," Ilsander said, looking to the others in the room.

"Leave us," the officer commanded his underlings. The others exited the room in short order, though Ilsander guessed they did not trust him and were waiting nearby with their weapons ready.

"She was in Traxholm," the half-orc began. "The village is gone, destroyed by a lich. Wait to move against Traxholm until my return."

The officer stopped writing after Ilsander said the word 'lich.' His face was pale and his eyes were wide in disbelief. "Traxholm is gone?" he muttered.

Ilsander unceremoniously lifted the man's head up from his paper with a calloused hand. He waited to speak again until he was sure he had the man's full attention. "Traxholm is a wasteland. And the kingdom does not need every peasant taking up a pitchfork to go fight. This information cannot get out. Do you understand?" Ilsander's voice was like heavy stone, bearing all the weight and gravity of the world.

The man nodded. He continued writing on the parchment scroll, but his hand moved slower than it had before. "A lich?" he said quietly.

"Again," Ilsander stated, "do not let anyone other than yourself know. Until the king is ready to move, he needs to keep the knowledge as closely guarded as possible."

When the scroll was finished, the officer took a red candle from a nearby shelf and used it to drip wax onto the paper. He pressed his own ring into the hot liquid, stamping it with his personal seal. "I will take this myself," he said. "Under any other circumstance, I would send men to investigate such a bold claim before even writing it down. But you carry the king's writ. I believe you."

Ilsander turned to go back to his horse. "I appreciate your honesty," he said. "Deliver the message. Tell no one."

Back on the main road, Ilsander wasted no time heading for the larger city in the distance. He passed a handful of posters calling for Lina's capture with crude drawings of her likeness sketched onto them. When he reached the main entrance to Azanthium, Ilsander noticed a heightened military presence patrolling the streets.

"What happened?" he asked from the back of his horse.

An armed guard looked up at him, a bit of fear in his eyes. "Be gone, half-orc," he said. "There's a murderer running about." Ilsander understood the implication.

He had been in other cities when similar events had occurred. When the local investigators failed to turn up a real killer, the closest green-skinned farmer or merchant usually hanged for the crime.

"How many murders?" Ilsander asked, ignoring the man's subtle threat.

"Almost a dozen that we've found, probably more," the man replied. "You should get out while you can."

Ilsander patted the hilt of the sword on his left hip. "I'll be fine," he stated. "Point me in the direction of the murders."

The soldier nodded. "To the north. The whole area is swarming with investigators. There were also a couple down at the docks."

Ilsander rode on through the streets of Azanthium with his head held high. Almost every pedestrian that saw him turned to stare—even a handful of equally unusual halflings who happened to be haggling with a merchant over the price of metal ingots when Ilsander passed. When he reached the northern section of town, it didn't take him long to find the scene of the recent murders.

A guard hurried over to Ilsander with his hand raised. He flashed his royal coin before the man spoke. "I'd like to see where it happened," he said calmly.

The soldier stopped in his tracks, confused and relieved at the same time. "You're here to investigate?" he asked.

"Sent by King Arias himself," the half-orc answered, nodding to his writ as he tucked it back into his pocket. He slid from his saddle to the ground and handed the reins to a lower-ranking soldier nearby. "See to it that my horse gets fed and watered," he commanded. Ilsander found that he was beginning to enjoy carrying the king's royal seal. He wondered how much it would cost to get a seedy blacksmith to forge a copy before he was required to turn the coin back in when he returned to Estria.

A man who introduced himself as Patrok appeared to be in charge of the overall crime scene, and he led Ilsander with a few of their other soldiers up to the room that housed the carnage. The bodies were gone, but the blood staining the floor still remained.

Once Patrok explained the scene as it was when he had found it, he let Ilsander set to work on his own. The half-orc thought of attempting to locate Lina's footsteps with his magical powder, but the entire complex seemed to be full of magical implements and enchantments. "How were the men killed?" he asked. "And were the any witnesses?"

"My soldiers believed it was the missing woman from Estria, the princess," Patrok explained. "And she used a dagger."

Ilsander nodded. "There's isn't much I can learn from bloody floorboards," he said after a moment.

"We have the weapon," Patrok added.

That piqued Ilsander's interest greatly. "Show me," he said, following Patrok out of the augmentation building.

The soldier led him to a barracks near the center of Azanthium. Inside, the unburied corpses of the recently slaughtered were laid out on wooden tables. The putrid stench of their decay was prevalent the moment Ilsander crossed the threshold of the room. Another table held a dagger with a jeweled hilt, a small weapon designed for small hands.

Ilsander turned the dagger over in his hands. He held it next to some of the wounds on the corpses, and it seemed more or less to match.

"You pulled this from one of the bodies?" he asked.

"Down by the docks," Patrok said. "Witnesses said a woman used it. She ran with another, though no one got a good enough look at the second perpetrator to identify them. She left the dagger in a hurry, then escaped into the woods."

Ilsander handed it back to the man. "Have it cleaned and ready for me tomorrow. I'll stay here one night to rest, and then I'll take the dagger with me when I leave at dawn," he said.

"You can have a room in the armory," Patrok told him. "Anyone with a writ from the king is welcome to stay with us."

"Thank you," Ilsander said. He considered interviewing the witness who had seen Lina at the docks, but he knew it was her. There was no one else who would fit the circumstances.

Patrok led Ilsander to the central garrison in the heart of the city at a leisurely pace. People gawked at the sight of the tall half-orc who towered over the officer by more than a foot, and again he paid them no heed. His shoulder and neck both still suffered from the burns he had acquired, and every time he moved his head to look somewhere he was reminded of his brush with death.

"What is there to do at night in this town?" Ilsander asked once he had seen the bunk he was offered.

Patrok thought about his answer for a moment before speaking. "There are a few decent taverns down on the waterfront," he said. "You might like one of those."

"I don't drink," Ilsander replied.

"An orc that does not drink?" the man said. "I've never met an orc who doesn't enjoy a pint or seven of ale."

"And how many orcs have you met?" Ilsander laughed.

"Well," the man answered, "maybe five now, including you."

"Count it four," Ilsander laughed. "Only one of my parents was an orc. I'm a half-breed."

The man opened his mouth to speak again, but Ilsander didn't want to the dwell on the issue and pressed forward. "So what else does Azanthium have to offer besides liquor?" the half-orc asked. There were still several hours until nightfall, and though he was physically tired, he didn't feel like wasting an entire night just for a few extra hours of sleep.

"Our lord-magistrate is hosting a feast next week, and the festival events leading up to it were scheduled to begin today. There was supposed to be a joust, but Sir Gothrey, one of our most celebrated knights, failed to arrive," Patrok explained. "I believe a fireslinger is on the schedule tonight down at the parade grounds. I can take you there if you wish."

"Do you have a guild of mages here in the city?" Ilsander asked, wondering where they would have produced a fireslinger. Minor magical abilities, though uncommon, were somewhat easy to find among the general populace of the Estrian kingdom, but a wizard capable of producing enough fire to awe a crowd was a rarity. Ilsander had seen a shaman in his own tribe who had been capable of summoning great waves of flame from his fingertips with wonderful effect. He had also seen that shaman burn to death during a performance when something had gone wrong.

"Unfortunately, Azanthium has no sorcerers," Patrok answered. "The one on the schedule for tonight is a simple magician, nothing more, but she is impressive."

Ilsander shrugged. "Then take me there, if you would," he said. "Though a joust would have been more suiting to my tastes."

Azanthium's parade grounds were huge. Sprawling

fields surrounded two lists: one a smaller area designed for the vespers tournaments, and the other a much grander structure built for the main events in front. Most of the stands were full by the time Patrok and Ilsander arrived, and the show was already in full swing.

As an officer in the militia, Patrok was afforded a high seat in the wealthiest section of the stands which had an excellent view. There were only a few other soldiers in those seats, and each of them turned to see the tall half-orc take his seat. Patrok laughed when he thought about the commoners in the stands to their left and how they would likely shriek at the sight of such a hulking, green beast.

In the center of the list, the fireslinger twirled a long rope with a blazing orb on either end above her head, the crowd gasping in amazement every time the fire went around. In the royal suite to the left of the list, a group of musicians played a stirring tune in time with the fireslinger's fluid movements, accenting her jumps and landings with drums and strings.

At the end of one particularly rousing sequence, the fireslinger threw her rope to the ground where it landed in a perfect circle. She leapt into the center and cast her arms out wide, igniting the rest of the rope into a ring of blazing fire. The music began to build, getting louder and louder along with the cheers of the crowd, until it culminated in a high-pitched wail of strings over a furious pattern of drum beats. The fireslinger bent over at her waist and roared, issuing a stream of magical fire from her mouth that coalesced into the head of a dragon and traveled nearly twenty feet toward the crowd.

"Impressive," Ilsander remarked.

"Certainly," Patrok agreed. "She is a finely skilled magician."

The woman appeared far more talented that any of the tribal shaman Ilsander had known back in the north. "Maybe she is more than a simple charlatan peddling fancy tricks," he said after the woman spat a second dragon's head of flame from her mouth. "That display is beyond impressive. Where is she from?"

"I believe she is local here to Azanthium," Patrok replied. "If my memory serves correctly, she performed at last year's festival also."

The display concluded with a fiery arpeggio of explosions launched into the sky in an arc above the woman's head. She flung the fireballs one at a time from her open palms, and her red robe fluttered with every movement. When everything had subsided, the smell of smoke was heavy in the air. "She's human?" Ilsander asked. From the distance, he couldn't tell if her slender frame was naturally indicative of an elf or if she was simply lithe of build. He had never met an elf, but his tribe had told stories of the long-legged creatures as violent murderers and thieves.

"She's human," Patrok confirmed with a chuckle. "You would be admitted to the festivities tomorrow with your writ, should you choose to stay. I could arrange for you to meet her."

Ilsander shook his head. "My quest cannot wait," he said. "Perhaps I shall make an introduction upon my successful return. She seems like an interesting person to know."

"If you find our murderer, will you bring her back here to hang for her crimes?" the officer asked.

"She'll go to the king in Estria," Ilsander answered. "What he does with her is up to him. I was only hired to track her down."

"Perhaps the king would honor an official request for extradition," Patrok remarked.

Ilsander barely restrained his laughter at the thought. "I wouldn't count on it," he said.

When dawn came to Azanthium, Ilsander was already on the road. He took a considerable amount of supplies with him on his rested horse, and he had Lina's jeweled dagger in a sheath within his leather vest. The weapon was easily concealed and still in reach. His swords had been attended to by a proper blacksmith at the barracks, and most of the damage he had done to them in Traxholm had been repaired.

The tall half-orc enjoyed the solitude of the early

morning road. Azanthium was a sprawling city, but it was quiet. Several roads led out of from the center of the city in something of a pinwheel fashion, and Ilsander had chosen the one nearest the docks. When he was far enough out of the city to be on a relatively unused section of road, he knelt down on the ground with his pouch of magical powder in hand.

He sprinkled some of the powder onto the street and found Lina's trail almost at once. Few magically enhanced people walked the trail, and Lina's signature blazed so brightly in the orange dust it was impossible to miss.

Several miles outside Azanthium, Ilsander found a pair of corpses on the road. He drew his blades and approached slowly, opting to move on foot and leave his horse a few paces behind near the trees lining the side of the forest. He moved with measured footsteps, his eyes constantly scanning the forest for any signs of movement. Other than a few dark-feathered birds chasing each other through the underbrush, he saw nothing.

The two corpses were close together, both face down on the road in stinking splotches of their own dried blood. One of them looked like a knight. He had a single wound through the center of his chest, marring his expensive linen shirt with a copious amount of red. The other man looked poorer by far, perhaps the knight's squire, and his neck told all the story Ilsander needed to know.

Lina had killed him.

She had fed on the poor squire and left his body to rot in the sun. Ilsander dragged both of the corpses by their heels to the side of the road. Under normal circumstances he likely would have covered them with stones and foliage, but he couldn't afford to delay any longer. The bodies looked old, but the half-orc knew he wasn't far behind his elusive prey.

Once more in the saddle, Ilsander pushed King Arias' horse hard. The beast pounded the earth beneath its hooves with a furious cadence, taking its orcish rider far from Azanthium and closer to the wild edge of the Estrian empire.

Chapter 18

Lina watched the farmer and his wife from an abandoned water well quite far from their quaint homestead. The older couple had only one guest staying at their tavern, and that man had not exited the building all morning.

Luckily, the visitor had a horse. The creature was stabled outside the older couple's home across from the tavern, and Lina intended to steal it once she had consumed the blood of its owner. She waited until both the man and woman were inside their own home before she darted out from the ruined well to the tavern. She had no weapon other than her hands and her teeth, but against any unskilled opponent such tools would easily be more than she needed.

Inside, the tavern was lit only by sunlight entering through old, dusty windows. It was small and empty, eerily quiet for being almost noon. Lina went quickly for the stairs in the corner of the room, taking them two at a time. The upper level only contained three rooms. Two of the doors were open, so Lina crept up quietly to the third. She heard the sounds of someone breathing within, probably still asleep, and the door was locked. Rhass had attempted to teach Lina the subtle art of lock picking when the man had trained her as his protégé, but her fingers had never quite found the right touch for something so delicate.

Glancing once more down the stairs, Lina didn't see anyone in the tavern, so she took a running start and rammed her shoulder into the wooden door, splinter-ing the lock away from the doorframe in a single blow. The man inside the room yelled in panic, scrambling up from his straw mattress with only a few tattered bits of clothing covering his body. His eyes darted all around the room as he stumbled into the wall, yelling at the top of his lungs.

The man screamed and bellowed when Lina's fangs bit into his flesh. He was helpless against her strength, and his body scraped against the wooden wall behind him as he flailed. Lina tore and shredded with her teeth, raking chunk after chunk of meat into her bloody mouth.

Thrashing blindly against the pain, the man ham-mered down on Lina's back weakly with his fists. She grabbed his left arm just below the shoulder and fiercely pulled, disconnecting the bones and tendons from the

socket. She drank more, and the man started to go limp as he was drained. She let him fall from her arms down to the wooden floor in a heap of pain and ruin. He left a smear of blood on the wall behind him, and Lina licked at it, savoring the taste. The wooden notes under the acidic flavor of the blood gave it a complex quality similar to an aged spirit.

The man moaned on the ground at Lina's feet. His cries were soft and confused, every moment inching him closer to the finality of death. Lina looked through the room's meager accouterments for anything useful while the man struggled to hold onto his last hope of life. She found a few pieces of silver in a tight leather pouch hidden under the man's pillow on his straw mattress, then she pocketed the silver, turned to lick one last patch of blood from the wall, and calmly walked down the stairs to the tavern's main room.

Everything was quiet, and the two tavern owners were busy feeding their livestock across the street. Lina exited the tavern's front door as she wiped some of the blood from around her mouth with the back of her hand. She was sated, her bloodlust fully satisfied, and there was no possible way she could feel any stronger. She knew her brazen confidence wasn't the smartest plan, but she didn't care.

The woman tending to her chickens turned when she heard the tavern door open. She saw Lina and gawked, then dropped her sack of feed onto the ground in shock.

Lina looked the woman in the eyes with a devilish grin as she moved to the horse nearby. The woman's husband hadn't noticed the vampire yet, but he heard her when she spoke to the horse, taking the animal's reins in her bloody hand.

"You—" the man started, but his wife silenced him with a slap on the shoulder.

"Thank you for the horse," Lina said just loudly enough for the couple to hear. "Oh, and your room is vacant," she added with a laugh.

Lina rode the horse slowly through the center of the dirt street, casually cleaning some of the blood from beneath her fingernails. The husband and wife watched her every step of the way, but they didn't move. The chickens around their feet pecked noisily at the spilled feed, and the sound combined with the horse's steady hoof beats made a gentle song that brought a smile to Lina's face. The sun was high overhead and the breeze coming in from the north was just enough to keep her from getting too hot under her heavy cloak.

The vampire kept her pace somewhat slow, enjoying the calm weather and in no rush to return to Traxholm and reclaim her buried blood. She had monitored the progress of her corruption, and the black tendrils on her arm had stopped growing completely. The Witherbite had worked, and whether or not the girl Lina had seen in the temple had been real was something that didn't bother her any longer. She would bear her black marks for life, and that was a price the powerful woman was certainly willing to pay.

She rode until long past nightfall before stopping to rest for a few hours. She was still more than a day's ride from Azanthium, likely a week or more from Traxholm. Lying down with her back against a moss-covered tree, Lina drank in the sounds of the night all around her. Insects buzzed in the underbrush, a steady breeze rustled the leaves above her head, and an owl hooted every few moments from somewhere deeper in the forest. For the first time since she had left her father's city, Lina felt truly at peace. Everything she had planned, everything she had dreamed of since she had become a vampire, all of it was finally falling neatly into place.

Chapter 19

Ilsander was two days out from Azanthium when he spotted a lone figure dotting the horizon. The road behind him was empty, and his horse had begun to show signs of exhaustion the previous day. The animal was a strong beast capable of phenomenal endurance, but Ilsander had been relentless in the saddle. He walked alongside the horse, opting to give the creature a bit of respite in order to move his own legs and keep himself loose.

The figure in the distance stopped some ways away, and Ilsander immediately became suspicious. The silhouette was riding a horse, and as Ilsander kept drawing nearer, he realized he had found his mark. Swords still sheathed at his sides, he walked up roughly thirty feet from the mounted woman. "Well met!" he called to her, trying to sound as inconspicuous as possible.

Lina did not respond.

"Is there an inn nearby?" he asked casually.

The woman's eyes were focused on his swords, which the vampire hunter found to be extremely odd. Wherever he went, humans couldn't stop staring at the tusks on his green face—not the steel on his hips.

"I'm looking for a place to stay," he repeated, taking a few steps closer.

The woman rubbed her eyes and shook her head slightly, as though she was trying to clear some sort of fog from her mind. "Are you all right?" Ilsander asked.

"What do you want from me?" Lina demanded, her voice harsh.

Ilsander lifted his hands up to show they were empty. "What are you talking about?" he said. "I'm just looking for somewhere to stay. I'm tired."

"You're someone," Lina shot back sharply.

Ilsander's face twisted in confusion. "Aren't we all someone?" he asked.

"You've been looking for me," she shot back. She kept her seat on her horse, but her legs tightened and her forearms flexed.

"Wha—"

"Your swords," Lina yelled at him. "And the coin in your right pocket. And your necklace. Plus one of your pouches. You have magic about you."

Ilsander took a step back. His hands went to both hilts, ready to draw and fight. The woman unnerved him beyond anything he had expected. "You can read minds," he said dumbly under his breath.

Lina smiled. "Come to think of it," she began, "I left my weapon behind somewhere. I could use one of yours."

The half-orc drew his blades in a flash, the steel edges glinting in the sun. Lina was on the ground and upon him before he could set his feet, her hands moving back and forth in such a blur Ilsander could barely follow them. She pushed his wrists out wide to the side, and Ilsander staggered backward to shift his weight.

Lina's fist slammed into Ilsander's chest, but the half-orc was simply too large. A burst of pain blossomed across his ribcage as he grunted, and then he pushed back. He was far taller than the younger woman, so when he stomped forward she had no option but to retreat. Ilsander brought both of his swords in tight to his body and lunged. Lina dove backward to the ground and rolled, coming up beside her horse and out of reach.

"You've been looking for me," she said for a second time.

Ilsander scoffed. He swung his swords in wide arcs, stretching his shoulders and relishing the adrenaline of battle. "I know I cannot kill you," he said evenly. "Though have you ever felt the sting of moonsilver against your flesh?"

"So you're a vampire hunter," Lina surmised. "Who sent you? Rhaas?"

"Ah, your father mentioned that name when he hired me. Who is he, your lover? You're in league with that wretched monster in Traxholm?" Ilsander went on.

Lina visibly reacted to Ilsander's words, and the half-orc had hoped for exactly such a telling sign.

"So you two don't get along, is that it?" he mocked. "You're headed the wrong direction on this road if you pissed off that lich."

Lina had been about to move forward once more, but she stopped in her tracks and stumbled slightly, suddenly off balance, her mind reeling.

Ilsander charged, flashing his blades in from two different angles. His right hand went high for a horizontal slash while he stabbed forward with the left, keeping that blade low to his hip. Lina slapped his left-hand assault away with the back of her wrist as she dodged the elevated slash, but the moonsilver in the half-orc's sword only needed the briefest contact to begin its work. She screamed and her flesh began to bubble at the site of the touch. The moonsilver sword pulsed with magical light, and Ilsander was eager to let it have another taste of vampire flesh.

"Blood-sucking vermin," Ilsander growled between his tusks. He swung down again, angling both blades in parallel and cutting diagonally.

Lina tried to jump backward, but Ilsander's arms were far too long. The tips of both of the half-orc's swords cut two bloody slashes down the front of the woman's shirt and torso. She yelled in pain as the moon-silver charred her skin, audibly sizzling her chest.

Lina threw her cloak out wide behind her and ran. Having so recently feasted on human blood, she was inhumanly fast. Ilsander pulled himself up quickly onto Lina's horse and kicked the beast into pursuit. He kept one blade out in his right hand, leaning over the horse's flank to line up what would easily be a killing blow against any non-vampire opponent. The woman knew he was coming, and she cut sharply to her left into the wooded area on the side of the road.

Ilsander pulled up on the reins and turned, urging the horse into the forest as quickly as it could run. It didn't take long for the pain of the moonsilver to begin to slow Lina's fevered pace. She was twenty or more paces ahead of the half-orc, but she had to keep a hand to her chest to try and stymie the pain as she moved, and her breath began to come in ragged gasps as well. When he had closed the distance between them to only several feet, Ilsander leapt from his horse onto the vampire's back, crashing to the ground with his right sword still held out wide to the side.

He grabbed a handful of Lina's hair in his huge hands. He outweighed her by at least three times as much, and his gargantuan muscles bulged with power as he drove her head into the leaf-strewn forest floor over and over. She spat a glob of blood out in front of her, and Ilsander bashed her down again, using her delicate head to carve a hole into the ground. She gasped for air and screamed in pain all at the same time, a strange noise Ilsander had heard several times before from those he had captured or killed.

In an instant, Lina's head was wrenched backward by her hair and a moonsilver blade slid in along the side of her throat. Blood streamed from several cuts across her forehead, a ruptured vein in her nose, and multiple places in her mouth. The skin on her neck sizzled with unbearable, magical heat as the moonsilver ate away her flesh.

"Do not make this more painful than it needs to be," Ilsander growled into her ear. His breath was hot on her face, and some of her hair found its way into his mouth when he spoke.

Before Lina could formulate a response, she was yanked violently from the forest floor to a standing position in front of the half-orc with her back turned toward him. Ilsander pulled her cloak aside and lifted her shirt, resting the point of his sword in the small of her back, just above her belt. He applied the slightest hint of pressure, and the blade slipped into the skin, furiously burning a quarter of an inch beneath Lina's skin.

The two stood there in the woods for quite some time as Lina tried to regain her breath and composure enough to speak. Ilsander didn't mind waiting. Vampires were almost all the same when he captured them. First they would try to fight. Then they would suffer.

Once they had enough suffering, they all tried to bargain their way out. Finally, after Ilsander had rejected every offer they made, the vampires would submit to his control.

"I can give you gold," Lina said when her pain had subsided enough for her to think clearly once more. "You know who my father is."

Ilsander laughed her offer away and dug his sword another eighth of an inch deeper. "You will continue to heal—the moonsilver does not stop that—but you will continue to burn from the inside out," he explained. "No deals. No compromise. I'll deliver you to Estria and that is it. There are no other options."

Lina nodded slowly, and Ilsander withdrew his blade. She turned to face him, blood, dirt, and a collection of pine needles covering her face. A thin stick had entered the side of the woman's cheek, though she did not raise a hand to free it from her flesh.

"You belong to me," Ilsander told her in no uncertain terms. "I own you. I cannot kill you, but I can find you forever. If you run, I will hunt you down. Every time I find you will be worse than this. Remember the pain you felt when the moonsilver first touched your wrist. Keep that feeling alive in your mind. If you run from my custody, you will feel it again, and it will cover your entire body. Every inch of you will burn, and I will fall asleep to the sound of your screams."

Lina nodded. It was a small movement and there

was no enthusiasm behind it. Ilsander raked the flat of his sword across the woman's midriff, eliciting another round of painful screams that she tried in vain to stifle behind clenched teeth.

"I own you," Ilsander repeated. "You will not flee. You eat when I command you to eat. You breathe when I give you permission. You will sleep when I order you to sleep. Every movement you make belongs to me."

"I surrender," Lina said, her voice altered by the stick plunged through her mouth.

Ilsander reached down with a hand and ripped the twig from her face. He pulled his sword away from Lina's body and sheathed it, waving away the smell of burnt flesh. "Let's go," he said flatly.

He held out his arm to guide her back to the road, and the once proud vampire princess hung her head as she walked. The moonsilver burns would take time to fully heal, much longer than any traditional wound, and Ilsander counted on them serving as a constant reminder of her bondage.

Back on the road, Ilsander offered the woman a hand to help her back on her horse. Lina looked at him with confusion clear across her face. "Why are you doing this?" she asked.

"My name is Ilsander," the vampire hunter replied. "Your father hired me to bring you home. And I think there are a few people in Chancol who would like to see you as well, but your father is my employer, not anyone else. You will return to him at once, and I shall fulfill the terms of my contract."

Lina was quiet as Ilsander led her horse back to his. "You called Rhaas a lich," she said, remembering the strange words that had so thoroughly caught her off balance.

Ilsander nodded. "Does he have a huge sword?" he asked.

"The blade is probably taller than you," she answered.

"Then yes, Rhaas is a lich," he stated. "I looked for you first in Traxholm, but the lich slaughtered the whole village, and he was using their souls to fuel whatever evil it is he pursues."

Lina visibly deflated. "If what you say is true, we must return to Estria as soon as possible. My father must be warned. If Rhaas has the power of a lich, he is more dangerous than anything Estria has ever seen. He must be stopped."

Ilsander knew she was right. "Then let us not waste any more time. The sooner we return to your father, the sooner your friend can be slain," he said. "When will you need to feed next?" He kept his horse a step or two slower than Lina's, keeping a careful eye on Lina's back the entire time.

"You know a lot about vampires," the woman responded. "Is there anything else you do besides hunting my kind?"

"Not lately," Ilsander answered. "But I need to know when your bloodlust will peak once more."

"Why?" Lina dodged. "Will you help me feed?"

"Yes," he said at once, surprising Lina yet again. "I'd rather know that you're feeding responsibly and not slaughtering men and women in the streets to slake your wretched thirst."

Despite her dire situation and the pain throbbing all over her burned body, Lina managed a smile. "I won't need to eat for another few days," she said. "And don't worry, I've heard orcish blood tastes like shit."

"Good," Ilsander replied. "Now we need to get back to Estria, and you need to tell me everything you know about Rhaas."

Chapter 20

Lina did not try to escape. In fact, she began to some-what enjoy the strange half-orc's company as they traveled, though she never came close to trusting him. The two moved quickly along the roads between Azanthium and Estria, detouring once to avoid going too near to Chancol on the way. Their trip lasted six days, and they were both heavily fatigued by the time they reached the capital.

Estria's eastern buildings gleamed in the light of the seventh morning's dawn. Lina and Ilsander sat on the backs of their horses on a small rise a mile from town. "My father will not be pleased," Lina remarked.

"You will tell him what you've become?" Ilsander asked.

Lina let out a heavy sigh. "Yes," she said after a mo-ment. "If he hired you, he likely knew I was vampire already, right?"

Ilsander nodded. "He had his suspicions."

"Then let's not waste any more time," Lina said as she spurred her horse forward.

Commoners gawked when they saw the pair ridding through their streets. Women pulled their children back protectively against their legs as Lina passed. She had removed her silken sleeve and cast it aside, showing everyone her blackened arm as though it was a badge of honor. Ilsander wore a gruff expression, a grimace clinging to his mouth between his tusks. He had opened his leather armor to let the cool breeze find his muscled chest.

When they were close enough to the king's keep to be seen, a swarm of guards came out to meet them.

"Lina," Merren said, his voice shaking in disbelief. His body was tightly wrapped with linen bandages, and his visible flesh sported several dark bruises.

"Merren," Lina answered from horseback. She had met the man several times in her younger years, though he now looked so gaunt and battered he was nearly a different man.

Ilsander stretched his hands around his reins. "Has the king received my message?" he asked.

"Several days ago," Merren said. "The army has been summoned. Militias have been requested from every city in Estria. Come, the king will tell you more."

"Good," Ilsander replied. The soldiers made a circle

around the two as they entered the keep through the main gate.

"Lina..." Merren muttered from the woman's side. "Was... Was it you at Chancol?" he asked. "Is it true?"

Lina glared down at him from her mount.

The group went first to the royal stables where servants then led the two horses away. Once more with her feet planted on the ground, Lina stretched her back to ease the soreness of the saddle from her muscles. Her bones popped noisily in her torso. Merren kept his eyes on her, his expression one of disbelief.

Lina leaned close to the man's face as they walked up the steps to the audience chamber. "It *was* me at Chancol," she whispered, unnerving the guard further.

Merren swallowed. "And Maxus?" he said. "That was you as well?"

Lina smiled wickedly, letting Merren see the tips of her fangs. She enjoyed toying with the man's fragile emotions, and she winked as Merren looked away.

At the top of the grand staircase leading to her father's audience hall, Lina pushed her way to the front of the retinue. "Come, Ilsander," she said. "Let us do this together."

One of the soldiers flanking the heavy wooden door began to protest, but Lina silenced him with nothing more than a look.

"She's fine," Ilsander said. "She will not kill her father."

"How do you know?" Merren asked weakly. The bandage on the front of his chest was starting to turn red with small blotches of blood.

"Because I am here," Ilsander said with confidence. He turned back to the heavy door and pushed it open, the princess following directly behind him.

Inside the audience chamber, King Arias sat on his throne in front of twenty or more squabbling farmers in dirty clothes. The sides of the room were lined with members of the King's Shield, the best fighters the kingdom had to offer. Each of them stood in light armor with halberds and short swords, their backs straight and their faces blank as they watched over the king. The four guards nearest the door stepped forward in unison and lowered their halberds with fluid movements born from decades of training.

"You are free from your bondage," Ilsander whispered as the woman entered the grand hall.

"What is—" the king started to shout toward the back of the hall, but when he saw his daughter, he fell forward from his throne in an eruption of tears. The peasants bringing their claims before the king were quickly ushered out of a side door by a royally bedecked attendant.

"Lina!" the king yelled unceremoniously through his tears.

The vampire woman strode forward with her head held high. When she reached her father, she stooped down to lift him from the flagstones. "Father," she began, "I'm here. I'm safe."

The king nodded against her shoulder, his tears wetting her blackened skin. "Get my wife," he said to no one in particular. The only attendant left in the audience chamber hurried out of the door behind the throne.

Lina pulled away from her father's tearful embrace long before the man wanted the moment to end. "I'm not your little girl anymore," she told him.

King Arias nodded as he rose to his wobbling feet. The queen burst into the room behind him, rushing to her daughter for another painfully tight hug. Lina's mother was a small woman, and her bones could be felt under her clothing as though she had not eaten in weeks.

When both of her parents had regained their composure, Lina stepped away to show them what she had become. "Whatever you have heard, it is more than likely true," she stated without emotion. She tilted her head back and flicked her fangs forward from their resting place on the roof of her mouth. They made little clicking sounds as they latched into place.

The queen nearly fainted. She buried her head in her husband's chest, unwilling to accept the reality of what she had seen.

"I feared as much," the king said quietly. His words could barely escape past the lump in his throat. "The report from Chancol said you summoned a wraith. Necromancy?"

Lina nodded. "I'm not very good at it yet," she said honestly. "But I know a wraith that obeys my commands."

"You know our laws, Lina," the king whispered. "Necromancers are taken to the gallows and their bodies are burned by the river."

"And vampires do not get the gallows before the burning," Lina added. An execution by fire was not lethal to a vampire unless it was set by one who actually had the power to take such a life, but it was certainly an effective method. Lina knew her spirit, her mind, would live on in the ashes of her charred corpse, slowly regenerating, though it would be locked away in a vase and sent to the bottom of the sea. She would be trapped forever, though *forever* was not specifically true. Eventually, perhaps after thousands and thousands of years, she would regenerate enough to break from her watery prison. Then whatever was left of her would slowly float to the surface, requiring another few millennia to regrow into something that could stand on its own.

For a vampire, being burned and sunk was a fate worse than any death imaginable.

"You need me," Lina said. "Rhaas is a lich. Unless he has created another protégé, I am the only one who can kill him."

"So it was Rhaas who turned you?" King Arias quietly asked. "I should have drawn and quartered that wretched swine the moment he set foot in this keep."

"You never knew," Lina said, though her words were barely comforting.

"I saw the signs!" the king yelled back. "The missing servants! The blood found in his room! That bastard never ate when he was invited to our table! I was blind."

Lina shook her head. "You saw what you wanted to see, Father. There's no shame in that," she said.

"I hate to interrupt the tender moment," Ilsander said from several paces behind the reunited royal family, "but this business with Rhaas is dire. His power grows every day, and he must be dealt with swiftly."

The king brushed a line of tears from his face to look Lina in the eyes. "You believe him?" he asked his daughter.

"If he lies, I'll kill him," Lina answered, never taking her gaze from her father. "But it is likely true. I stole lich blood from Chancol. That's how I was poisoned." She held her right arm out for her parents to see more clearly. "It has been cured, but I left the blood in Rhaas' presence for a time. I was foolish, and I gave him the means to become what he is now. I should be the one to ram a stake through his heart and end his miserable existence."

"Perhaps the surgeon…" the queen began, but she could not finish her sentence before another bout of crying overtook her.

"It cannot be removed," Lina said. "But that is the least of our worries. We need an army to send against

Rhaas."

King Arias finally seemed to have regained most of his composure. "We are raising all the banners. We should be fully assembled within a month," he explained. "I sent out messengers the moment I had received Ilsander's message. Everything is moving as quickly as possible, but I fear the army will still be slow."

Ilsander cleared his throat. "I'll need additional payment if you want me to help," he added.

"*Can* you help?" the king asked somewhat incredulously. "Can you kill a lich?"

Ilsander smirked. "Allow me to return to my tribe. Only your daughter can actually kill the man, but I can certainly be of assistance. I will need to gather some things from the north first," he said.

"And your price?"

"I want a room in this keep."

"Why?" Lina asked, clearly taken aback.

"I have no home outside my tribe," Ilsander replied. "I would like to stay here when I am not working, and I would like to enjoy all the benefits of being a nobleman."

The king didn't waste much time considering the offer. "Fine," he stated. "Return to me in thirty days, and I will have an army. My generals shall work with you to end this threat."

"Give them heavy coats," Ilsander said with a bit of a laugh. "Traxholm will be a frozen wasteland of death by then."

Chapter 21

"I've never been to the north," Lina told Ilsander. The two had just finished a reception held in her honor in one of Estria's finest banquet halls. She had opted to wear a strapless dress, a fine silken garment worth more than most peasants' houses, and some of the nobles had gawked at her twisting, black corruption. She welcomed their stares, finding that her trials in the sunken temple had lent her an air of confidence she had not known before.

The half-orc wore a fine linen tunic with leather pants, and his bulging muscles constantly threatened to break free of his high-spun attire. "The north is a savage place," he said, flicking a chicken bone into a wooden bowl at the center of the table. "My tribe lives with several others following caribou herds for food. They build shelters and then abandon them when the herds move.

Their life is hard, but not without reward."

"And your shaman can help us kill Rhaas?" she asked.

"Yes," Ilsander replied. "Orcs do not suffer liches to live, either. Rhaas is a threat to the entire region, so the shaman will help us."

Lina nodded. She stood up from the table to return to her chambers on the southern side of the keep. "We will leave in the morning," she stated.

"Certainly," Ilsander replied. "Are you sure your human friend is fit enough to travel with us?"

"Merren is not my friend," Lina said. "He is one of my father's dogs sent to somehow ensure my safety."

Ilsander stifled a laugh as a pair of human nobles scurried through a door in front of him. The tall half-orc had to duck to leave the banquet hall, and his shoulders were so broad they nearly hit the sides of the doorframe. "I do not think the man understands exactly what you are," he said.

"Which man?" Lina asked. "Merren or my father?"

"Either," Ilsander answered.

"You're probably right."

Ilsander held the next door open so Lina could pass through ahead of him. "Meet me at the stables at dawn. The sooner we can get to the tribal lands, the better," he said.

"Agreed," Lina said. She headed left down a corridor and Ilsander went right, his fancy leather boots only making a muffled sound on the carpeted stone floor as he walked. The room he had been given was opulent, to say the least. It had previously been reserved for emissaries from other lands who came to visit the king, and it was richly appointed with all manner of tapestries and golden accents. A fire burned in the hearth across from the bed.

Ilsander took off his boots and let them fall to the floor at the end of his bed. A servant awaited his commands just outside the door, and he ordered the girl to bring him a bottle of red wine. She came back a short moment later holding two bottles, one sweet and one dry, and Ilsander had her place them both on the oaken writing desk against the far wall of his room. There was a large window there as well which led out to a short veranda, and Ilsander kept it open to encourage the breeze to cool some of the heat from the fire.

The vampire hunter was old by human standards, having seen more than seventy years, and he felt it that night. He had captured dozens of vampires over the last several decades, slaughtered twice that number of notorious bandits and murderers, and was solely responsible for preventing a military coup in the kingdom west of Estria.

Wine bottle in hand, Ilsander reclined against the headboard of his bed and drank. His feet extended over the bottom edge of his bed, but he had been told a new one was being built to accommodate his tall frame and would be ready in a week or two. He stared into the fire for a long time, wondering how he would possibly defeat such a powerful being, and he prayed to Kraxblade that he would have the strength and skill to overcome Rhaas.

A servant knocked on Ilsander's door just before dawn. When he did not answer, the girl pushed the door open slightly and saw the huge half-orc lying motionless on the floor in front of the open window. She walked up to him slowly, her heart beating wildly in her chest despite the obvious snoring indicating the half-orc was alive. She pushed an empty wine bottle from his grasp and knelt down to shake his shoulder.

"Mister Ilsander," she said several times as she jostled him.

Finally, Ilsander awoke with a splitting headache. He shielded his eyes, though there was not yet much light coming in from the world beyond his window. "You need to leave in an hour, Mister Ilsander," the young girl told him before retreating back to her post in the hallway.

It took Ilsander quite some time to clear all of the alcohol from his head. The bottle of sweet red wine was still on his desk, and he placed it in the bottom of his traveling bag before heading out the door.

The stables were already buzzing with activity when Ilsander reached them. He had lost his way twice in the complex hallways and passages of the expansive keep, but arrived on time nonetheless. The king and queen were there in full regalia with ten or so armored members of the King's Shield behind them. Merren already sat on his horse, clad in a tight-fitting metal breastplate that concealed his bandages and kept his back straight as he rode. His horse was laden with supplies, as were both of the others.

Lina stood near her horse in a simple outfit designed for speed, with a flowing shirt cinched about her waist under a leather belt and riding pants matching a pair of boots that came up to her knees. Ilsander considered his own sparse attire and wondered how much more expensive the princess' garb was compared to his. Even her horse's saddle was made of the finest leather, and the creature's mane had been braided with white ribbons. Though the half-orc had been in the castle several times, the sheer wealth the king and queen commanded still managed to give him pause.

"Here," Ilsander said. He offered Lina's jeweled dagger back to her on the palm of his open hand. "I took it in Azanthium. I figured you would want it back."

"Thank you," Lina said, slipping the weapon into her belt.

The king and queen each gave their daughter an awkwardly long hug before the trio of adventurers was allowed to leave the keep. Ilsander's swords rattled at his sides as the horse beneath him trotted along. "It will take us at least seven days to reach the tribal lands,"

Ilsander said after they had exited through the keep's main guardhouse.

"We don't have any maps," Merren interjected.

Ilsander laughed away the notion of a map. "The tribes are constantly on the move. When we reach their lands, we will have to find them."

"And if we can't?" Merren asked.

"We will," Ilsander said confidently. "It won't be hard to track the tribe. When I left fifty years ago, there were several thousand members, there are undoubtedly more now."

"And this Rhaas," Merren went on. "What sort of allies does he have?"

Ilsander shot the man a scathing glare he hoped would quiet his insistent questioning. "He can summon death elementals, though I am not sure how many he can control at once."

"He has other allies," Lina said. "He had a centaur friend a long time ago, someone from the west. Rhaas always relied on the centaurs to gather components for him."

"What kind of components?" Merren asked.

"For necromancy," Lina answered. "He never told me the extent of his designs, but I know he has something planned that goes beyond Estria."

Ilsander tightened his grip on his reins. "Then we shall head first for Traxholm. I'd like to know exactly what Rhaas has planned, who his allies are, and if he's moving. The whole army could reach the village just to find it empty while the lich is off somewhere else."

"Certainly," Lina replied with a smile. "Traxholm should not be far off from the route north."

"That is not in the plan!" Merren argued. His voice betrayed his fear just as clearly as his face.

Ilsander turned to regard the man's outburst for only a moment before ignoring it. "We can be in Traxholm within the week. We won't get very close, but we need to see what Rhaas is doing. Once we have our information, we leave for the tribal lands."

Merren continued to spout his objections, but neither Lina nor Ilsander paid him any attention.

North of the capital, the trio of unlikely companions stopped at the edge of King Arias' military influence to enjoy one final bit of civilization before entering the unsettled wilderness. The outpost, a small stone structure only a single story tall with towering trees on three sides, was two days from Estria. A small plot of farmland was near the door to the garrison, and a few stalks of corn looked ready for harvest. To the west, most of the landscape was barren and cracked. The land there housed minor clans of centaurs, trolls, and other beasts. The heavy woods to the north eventually gave way to tundra, and that was where the orcish tribes made their homes.

The garrison commander was lounging in a wicker chair under an oak tree when Ilsander, Lina, and Merren approached. She was older and unkempt, barely aware of the feeble road she was charged with protecting. Ilsander jumped off his horse with a heavy thud, and the woman finally looked up from her rest to acknowledge him, though she did not bother to say anything.

"We need supplies, and I have a writ from the king," Ilsander stated, producing the golden coin from his pocket.

That got the woman's attention. She stood up from her apparent nap and brushed a hand over her shaggy hair. "What can I do for you?" she asked. Her voice was hoarse, as though she had either been recently screaming or else had simply not spoken in several years.

"Supplies," Ilsander said again. "And a warm meal. We will not stay long."

The woman nodded, though she was still too busy fussing over her disheveled appearance to make eye contact with the large half-orc. "Rabbit or duck?" she asked before entering the garrison.

"Duck," Lina answered quickly, and the garrison leader disappeared into the building.

"Do you actually eat that?" Merren asked quietly.

Lina laughed. "The blood tastes fine, but the meat is like ash in my mouth," she said.

The skin of Merren's face went pale. "And you normally—"

"Let's be quick," Ilsander cut in, letting the thought of cannibalism mercifully drift from Merren's thoughts. "This is our last stop before the tribal lands. Rest your legs, but not for too long."

Lina led her horse to a hitching post in front of an old-looking bucket of water. "This woman should be relieved of her command," she said under her breath.

The inside of the garrison was only marginally better than the outside. Two racks of spears stood against a wall, though one of the shafts was so cracked it would be useless in battle. Opposite the spears, three large barrels of arrows and bolts appeared to be the only well-maintained objects within sight.

"Where is everyone else?" Merren asked. "Royal garrisons like this usually house twenty or thirty soldiers."

The woman scoffed as she set a meager-looking plate of overcooked duck in the center of the room's only table. "I was given six," she said, her voice as dry as the meat. "That was two years ago. I lost one to fever, one to a training accident with a crossbow, and the other four headed on patrol a week ago."

"You were left to watch over the outpost by yourself?" Merren went on.

"I stopped requesting reinforcements ten months ago as it never did me any good," the woman replied with a bit of venom in her voice. "As for my being here alone, a standard patrol is supposed to be eight. Seeing as I don't count for four whole soldiers and someone has to stay behind, that's what made sense."

"Uh huh," Merren said quietly. He stared down at the burnt duck meat he had on his plate, wondering if perhaps one of the woman's subordinates had actually died of malnutrition.

"I know it's the king's business, but where are you three headed?" the commander asked.

"You're right," Ilsander answered quickly. "It is the king's business."

"What do your patrols usually find?" Merren asked her, cutting the tension in the room.

"Centaurs have been coming closer and closer lately," she said absentmindedly. She turned back to the food preparation area and fetched a pitcher of syrupy red wine.

"This far east?" Merren asked. He tasted a morsel of his duck and returned it to his plate quickly, trying in vain to keep from showing his disgust. To his right, Ilsander had nearly finished his own portion.

"Like I said," the woman sighed, "they keep coming closer and closer."

"And has the king been told?" Lina demanded.

The commander only stared at the princess.

"When do you expect the patrol to return?" Ilsander asked.

"Probably in a couple of days," the woman answered.

"Perhaps we should move from here to Traxholm, then return to see what the patrol knows before heading north," Ilsander posited to his companions.

Lina thought for a moment before agreeing. "We should go now," she said, standing from the table.

Merren and Ilsander were quick to join her. "We'll be back in three or four days," the man said. "Keep your patrol here until our return."

The garrison commander offered a weak comment about the two plates still full of duck, but the trio left without looking back. "It has to be Rhaas," Lina said as she freed her horse from the hitching post.

"You're right," Ilsander added. "If Rhaas has centaur allies in the war he's brewing, your father will need more than just his army."

Merren just shook his head as he mounted his horse. "Why?" he muttered under his breath to no one in particular.

"Why what?" Lina asked.

Merren looked over to her. "Why would he start a war? That man knows the king. He knows Estria. Why would he bring so much destruction?"

Ilsander laughed. "For the same reason your human kings conquered this wilderness and built that outpost," he said. "The only thing orcs, humans, and liches all have in common is their burning desire to walk across a field of corpses to a newer, larger throne."

Chapter 22

The outskirts of Traxholm were easy to find. The group had ridden east for two days, moving as quickly as they could, and they felt the change in the air long before they ever saw what had become of the village. It was the middle of autumn, and Traxholm was always cold after summer since it was somewhat far north, but the cold that gripped the air even twenty miles from the village was unnatural. Frost clung to the branches, and frozen leaves crunched on the ground.

Still several miles from Traxholm, Lina could see the shining reflection of sunlight bouncing off ice. All the buildings in the town had been leveled, and a field of frozen death had taken their place. In the center of it all, Lina could see a thin line of smoke wafting up into the air, and it carried the scent of blood so vividly it felt like she was buried in a grave where she stood.

"What the…" Merren murmured.

"He's been busy," Ilsander remarked. "It was cold when I was here, but not like this."

The three of them stood at the edge of a frozen field, as close as they could get without risking detection due to lack of cover. "Rhaas was incredibly powerful, even by vampire standards," Lina said after a moment of staring slack-jawed at the marvelous creation of ice. "I was an idiot to leave the blood so close to him."

"How'd you even know about the blood in Chancol?" Ilsander asked.

"Rhaas told—"

"He played you," Ilsander responded immediately. "Don't blame yourself. He used you to get what he wanted. This was always his plan."

Lina's emotions whirled through a confusing pattern of shame, regret, and seething hatred. "Bastard," she scoffed quietly. "I'll gut him." Her grip on her reins was tight enough to start cracking the leather.

"It has to be you," Ilsander agreed.

"He will pay," she went on, her knuckles white and her face flushed with blood. "I'll drive my dagger through his heart."

Just then, something dark appeared in the distance toward the center of the icy fields. It grew rapidly in size, and Ilsander urged his horse a few steps backward. "Something is coming," he said, though the other two didn't need any warning. They moved back, struggling against their mounts to get the beasts to turn quickly. The stubborn horses moved, but not fast enough.

The black object came near enough to be identified, and Lina saw it for what it truly was. A skeleton armed with a spear was charging for them, and three skeletal dogs ran out ahead of the creature. Their feet beat the ice beneath them, filling the air with a steady cadence.

All three companions dropped from their mounts and drew their weapons. "All I have is a dagger," Lina said. She searched for any kind of heavy, fallen log to bash the skeletons apart, but there was nothing that wasn't completely trapped by ice.

"My swords aren't much better," Ilsander added through clenched teeth, setting his feet to take the skeletal charge.

The first skeleton dog lunged up at Ilsander, and the half-orc swatted at it with his right-hand sword. The weapon cleaved through most of the dog's ribcage, but the animated creature wasn't slowed. It came on, thrashing its claws and chomping down with its bony snout on Ilsander's wrist.

The second and third dogs went for Lina. They spread out to either side, running in at her ankles with their mouths open wide. Lina stabbed her dagger at the dog on her right, and her blade passed cleanly though the gaps in the creature's back. Her balance stolen by the ice beneath her feet, the dogs brought her down quickly, and her head slammed into the frozen ground with a loud crack that blurred her vision.

Merren yelled, though whether his shout came from the thrill of battle or the pain lingering in his wounded chest, it was impossible to tell. He rushed toward Lina and kicked out with his boot, catching one of the bone dogs on the side of the head, sending the creature flying into a tree. Several bones rattled loose from the dog's body, but not enough of them fell away to stop the vicious construction altogether.

The bone hound still on top of Lina had its jaws locked firmly on the meat of her shoulder. She stabbed at the beast over and over, but her dagger did basically nothing, only chipping away small flakes of white bone. Blood flowed from her skin as she struggled to get herself free.

Merren's hands reached around the chest of the bone dog, and the man pulled it up from Lina with a great heave. The creature fought wildly, but it had nothing immediately in front of it to kick or bite.

Scrambling to her feet, Lina quickly tucked her dagger back into her belt and squared her stance to the dog Merren was holding. The one he had kicked was back on its own feet as well, and Merren kicked at it again whenever it got near.

"Keep it still," Lina growled. She slammed her corrupted right hand through the undead dog's chest, reaching all the way to the thing's spine. She wrapped her fingers around the rough bone of the dog's vertebral column and yanked with all her strength. The string of bone came flying out in the woman's grasp, and the dog fell to pieces at Merren's feet.

Lina cast the bones away and turned her attention to the one remaining dog. Ilsander stood a few paces closer to Traxholm breathing heavily, a shattered bone dog at his feet. He was squared off against the hound master, using short strokes of his swords to keep the skeleton's sharp spear point from entering his gut.

Merren stepped backward, inviting the bone dog to lunge at him again. The undead creature took the bait. Merren caught the dog's leap, wrapping his hands around the thing's neck to pin it to his breastplate. Without a moment of hesitation, Lina slammed her balled fist into the creature to shatter its chest. She raked the bones away with both hands, quickly dispatching the beast.

The houndmaster lunged in at Ilsander with its spear in both hands, aiming directly for the half-orc's waist. Ilsander chopped down with his swords both moving in the same direction, deflecting the attack wide past his left hip. The skeleton struck hard, and parrying each attack didn't leave Ilsander any room to make an attack of his own.

Outnumbering their only foe three to one, Lina and Merren helped Ilsander fight off the houndmaster quickly. Merren swung his sword in at the humanoid's head while Lina, working on the other side, reached into the creature's ribs with her hands and started wrenching them apart. The houndmaster couldn't fight all three of the companions at the same time, and soon Ilsander was no longer parrying strikes but delivering them, tearing away bones with blow after blow until all that remained was a pile of inanimate white shards.

"We need different weapons," Merren said between breaths.

"And I need to feed," Lina added. She was doubled over with her hands on her knees, sweat falling from her forehead and freezing when it hit the ground.

Ilsander was by far the least exhausted and damaged of the three. He stood tall, his weapons still in his hands and his eyes looking toward Traxholm for signs of any other attackers. "Rhaas has been busy," he said slowly. "He will have an army before long."

Lina nodded. "My father's militia won't be enough, will it?" she asked hesitantly.

"I doubt it," the half-orc answered.

Merren finished wrangling the horses together and bringing them near. "We should return to the outpost," he stated. "If there are centaurs coming to join his cause, our only hope will be to stop them before they reach the village."

"What village?" Lina laughed. "He razed it all to the ground."

"Merren's right," Ilsander added. "If we can cut off the centaurs before they come here to reinforce Rhaas, it will help."

"And if it is an entire army of centaurs? Hundreds of them?"

Ilsander shook his head. "Then we're doomed," he said quietly.

The three only waited a few more minutes before leaving Traxholm and heading back to the west. Seeing the undead houndmaster had been more than enough to confirm their suspicions without ever seeing the lich himself. The ride back through Estria's northern wilderness was a somber one. Merren remained mostly quiet and passive while Ilsander mentally tried to concoct various plans for how they would possibly be able to dispatch a lich. All the while, Lina's hunger for human blood grew.

They could smell fire in the air by the time they were within a mile of the northern outpost. Ilsander kicked his horse into a gallop, and the others followed quickly behind him. Gruff, shouting voices filled the air. Ilsander, Lina, and Merren erupted from the trees at full speed, drawing the attention of roughly thirty centaurs all at once.

"Spread out," Ilsander called over his shoulder. He sat up tall in his saddle and drew both his swords, their metal edges ringing against his scabbards. Ilsander met the centaur nearest to him with a resounding crash. His horse thundered into the man-beast's chest. Surprised and unbalanced, the centaur staggered backward, and Ilsander sliced the creature's head from its shoulders.

Lina rode hard to the half-orc's left. She had her dagger held tightly in her blackened right hand, keeping the small blade low to her thigh. The centaurs at the outpost had already sacked the building, and many of their weapons were not within reach as they had been somewhat lazily reveling in their recent victory. Lina angled her horse toward one of the unarmed ones as the rest of the centaur war party furiously tried to organize themselves.

She lunged from her saddle at the last possible moment, flying through the air toward the shocked centaur, her gleaming blade ready. The beast thrashed on its hind legs with its heavy hooves, but Lina was too high. She crashed into the centaur's muscled, unclothed torso, and her dagger sank hilt-deep into the creature's arm. Lina wasted no time adding to the centaur's pain with her teeth. She drank from its neck, pulling the warm blood from the creature's body in thick spurts. It died a brief moment later beneath her body.

Lina bellowed into the afternoon sky as a flood of rejuvenating magic rushed through her muscles. She darted forward, ducked under a horizontal sword slash that could have easily torn her to pieces, and stabbed one of the centaurs in a hind flank. She pulled her dagger out fast, keenly aware of the possibility of losing it in the chaotic battle.

Merren didn't fare as well. He was a strong fighter in his own right and had won several tournaments in Estria, but he had not seen an abundance of actual combat. On top of his relative lack of experience, the man was still trying to recover from the grievous injuries he had sustained in the Estrian sewers. He turned side to side in his saddle, deflecting incoming attacks with his sword, but each movement brought a spasm of sharp pain to his chest that threatened to make him submit altogether.

He kicked his horse forward to get away from two of the centaurs to his right. The creatures pursued him hard, but Ilsander appeared on their other side and impaled one of them on his sword. The centaur tumbled forward into the dirt, taking the half-orc's left-hand sword with him. Merren blocked an incoming spear strike aimed for his head with the crosspiece of his own weapon, the force of the strike making his hand vibrate with pain. He raked his sword forward to push the spear clear of his body, then cut to his right with all the strength he could muster. Had the centaur been armored, Merren's attack would have done nothing. As it was, the man's blade drove through a foot of flesh, muscle, and bone before coming to a gruesome halt in the middle of the centaur's chest.

Merren roared with carnal rage and wrenched his

weapon free. Blood and gore spurted freely from the gaping laceration, and the centaur hit the ground in a heap of entangled hooves and arms. Still there were more than twenty of the beasts arrayed against them.

One centaur in particular appeared to be their leader. She was nearly a head taller than the others and wore shimmering bronze battle armor decorated with stag horns mounted to her shoulders. Her mane had been braided and set with small silver rings, and several designs had been shaved into the fur of her hide. She trotted forward in front of the rest of her surprised comrades and leveled a huge, bladed bow in Ilsander's direction. She drew an arrow from the quiver on her back and fired before Ilsander had time to fully react, and the missile cut through the bicep of his left arm.

Lina ran forward. She was significantly lower to the ground than the centaur leader, and she was fast enough to dodge the incoming arrows that screamed through the air at her. When she closed the gap, the centaur reared up on her hind legs, thrashing out with heavy, armored hooves. Lina ducked under one such attack and rolled across the ground, stabbing up over her head as she passed under the centaur's horse body. What would have been a death blow clinked off a heavy plate of steel barding.

Lina came up behind the centaur, but she was not fast enough. The leader kicked backward with her hooves and caught the vampire squarely in the chest, shattering

Lina's torso. She screamed in pain and writhed on the ground. Behind her, the rest of the centaur troop was huddled together defensively, waiting for their leader's command. Lina felt the bones of her ribcage stabbing inward against her lungs, eliciting a brutal wave of pain every time she took a ragged breath. The energy she had enjoyed just a moment before was gone in the blink of an eye, and her otherworldly strength vanished from her arms and legs as the magic was pulled into her chest to reknit her skeleton.

Merren urged his horse forward, his sword out to his side and a wild look in his eyes.

Ilsander cut him off before the man could throw his life away so recklessly against the superior opponent. Still on horseback, Ilsander gripped his one remaining weapon with both hands. Blood flowed freely from the cut just below his left shoulder, though it wasn't deep enough to render the arm useless. The half-orc charged forward and leaned to his left, keeping his sword between himself and centaur leader. The beast spun her weapon from side to side, the double-bladed razor whirling as it sliced the air.

Ilsander feinted left once, then up high, before finally striking from his right side. Against a lesser opponent, his movements would have been too fast to follow. The centaur leader was much more than her underlings, and she caught Ilsander's blade before it came within a foot of touching her gleaming armor. Her bladed bow crashed into the sword and locked with the blade. The centaur's expression turned from one of smug confidence to a mixture of surprise and interest when Ilsander matched her incredible strength.

He fought against the bladed bow, bearing down with all his might pushing into the hilt of his sword. The centaur gave ground, then yelped with pain, faltering. At the leader's rear legs, Lina's fangs were latched into the meat beneath a joint of her heavy barding. Ilsander pulled back and swung straight downward, connecting with the middle of the bladed bow where the centaur couldn't offer much resistance. The sword cracked through the weapon cleanly and didn't stop until it was nearly an inch deep inside the leader's skull.

The leader buckled backward. She was delirious and nearly out of the fight, but still had some semblance of life running through her thick veins. She thrashed out with a broken end of her bladed bow, and the razor edge found the skin over Ilsander's knuckles, quickly turning the back of the half-orc's hand into flayed ribbons of torn flesh.

Lina held on tight as the centaur bucked and twisted. She had her arms wrapped around the creature's haunches, her teeth locked into its veins. The centaur had plenty of blood to give. Lina's body strengthened once more, and the wounds she had suffered began to heal.

Ilsander shifted his sword back to his left hand. His

arm burned with pain, but the fingers of his right hand couldn't even move. He swung at the centaur leader with a large, sweeping arc, and the creature could only give a feeble attempt to block. Her bladed bow fragment came up and hit the blade, but it just slightly redirected the attack, angling it directly for her own jawline. The sword caught her below the chin, and Ilsander forced his last bit of strength into the blow. His weapon bit cleanly into the centaur's thick neck. She fell to the ground with a shudder, and she did not rise again.

At the leader's back, Lina continued to feast. She was fully engulfed in blood, her clothes and skin all stained a dark, even hue of crimson. She stood as her victim died, turning toward the rest of the warband with her blood-soaked hands held out to her sides, ready to tear the life from each and every one of them.

The remaining centaurs began to retreat. Leaderless and mostly unarmed, they looked to one another in confusion, then turned as a pack to run toward the west.

"How badly are you hurt?" Merren asked from his mount. His voice trembled with fear and his entire body ached.

"I'll live," Ilsander grunted. He clutched his right hand close to his chest. A few tattered strips of his skin hung loosely over his knuckles, and blood ran from them like a river.

Lina turned back on the fallen centaur leader for a final draught of warm blood. When she had consumed her fill and finally lifted her head to breathe, her body was fully healed. She twisted her back and her spine popped, sending a warm wave of relaxation through her tired muscles. "You need a surgeon," she said when she was close enough to see the wound on Ilsander's hand.

The half-orc grunted in response.

"I know how to stitch it," Merren offered. "But we didn't bring any needles or thread."

Lina looked at the partially burned garrison out-post. "I'll see what's left inside," she said.

"And what's left of the patrol," Ilsander added. "If these were the only centaurs heading to Traxholm to join Rhaas, they won't matter much. If there are more groups coming, we need to be out of their way when they get here."

Lina nodded and ducked into the ruined garrison. A small fire sputtered in one corner where a torch had been tossed onto a pile of broken chairs and other debris. Most of the smoke funneled out of a broken window, but what still remained in the room was thick and pungent. Lina covered her mouth and nose as she moved from the main room to the makeshift armory.

The unimpressive building didn't have much. Lina found two human corpses, one of which belonged to the woman they had met several days before, and the other she did not recognize. Both bodies were badly mangled. Lina rooted through the drawers along the back wall and made a small collection of the few things she thought might be useful. She emerged from the building a minute or two later with several knives, a few patches of tanned leather that looked unused, several strips of salted fish, and bag of metal bolt tips for a crossbow.

"No needle and thread," she stated, dropping what she had found onto a clear patch of ground. "There's some leather we can use to make a bandage. That's about it."

Ilsander slid from the back of his horse and went to the dead centaur leader. Beneath her polished bronze armor was a padded cotton gambeson, and the half-orc ripped a few chunks of it away to start making a field dressing. "If we weren't about to fight a war to save the entire kingdom, I'd take this armor back to Estria and have it melted down. That's over a hundred pounds of bronze right there," he remarked. The pain in his shredded hand made him wince as he wrapped two of the leather patches around his flesh with the cotton.

"I don't think any of these knives are sturdy enough to be useful," Lina said. She tested each one in her hand before casting them aside.

"Unless you plan on fletching some bolts on our journey, the bag of tips seems fairly useless too," Merren added. He tried one of the pieces of fish, and judging by his expression, it had been prepared in a much better fashion than the duck.

"Let's take the leather and be gone," Lina stated flatly. "Oh, and one of the patrolmen was in there too. Dead, of course."

Ilsander nodded. He tied off his makeshift bandage and dropped his arm to his side, cradling it on the inside of his leather vest. "Can you get my other sword?" he asked.

Lina slid Ilsander's sword from the center of a dead centaur. She flicked the blade to clear most of the blood from it, then removed the rest by wiping it on the dead creature's bare hide. "That was a good strike," she said as she carefully handed the weapon back to its owner, keeping the moonsilver edge as far from her skin as she could.

Ilsander returned the sword into the scabbard on his hip with a satisfying ring. "If we're fighting skeletons, I need a hammer. Against centaurs, I'll need my swords. Against the lich, I don't even know what might work," he said. "I feel like I'll have an armory on my back by the time I'm ready for this war."

"Just leave all your moonsilver at home," Lina laughed, her joviality untouched by the carnage surrounding them all.

"Ha, I never got close enough to test it out on Rhaas," the half-orc replied. "Maybe it will bring him to his knees as well."

Lina shook her head. "I wouldn't count on it," she said.

Chapter 23

When the forested northern border of Estria gave way to tundra several days after the three had left the outpost, the next path grew obvious. Several fires burned on the horizon, and a sea of tents and other temporary structures lined the edges of Lina's view. "I trust that is your tribe?" she asked.

Next to her, Ilsander was busy retying the bandages around his hand. The air was cool with a stiff breeze that swept across the ground for miles without anything to stop it. "I don't know. There are dozens of tribes that live out here. Mine is only one of many that follow the caribou herds," he answered.

"You're sure an orc tribe will just let us walk up and ask which ones they are?" Merren asked.

Ilsander shrugged. "Just don't do anything stupid," he said. "There isn't much love between the orc tribes and you humans, but there's not much hate at the moment either."

Lina rode on ahead of the other two, heading for the camp. "What, your reputation won't have us treated like royalty?" she playfully mocked over her shoulder.

"If you tell them you're the princess of Estria, you'll probably be held for ransom," he answered. "Is that the kind of royal treatment you want?"

"I'd have to live with foul orcs?" she scoffed. "Never!"

The three rode out across the open tundra at a slow pace. Ilsander took the lead, and Merren hung back slightly toward the rear.

When they got closer to the orc encampment, they passed a handful of standards stuck into the frozen ground. They were as tall as Ilsander on horseback and were made from sticks and sections of tanned hide still covered with fur. "Do those tell you which tribe it is?" Lina asked as they passed the second standard.

"Not exactly," Ilsander answered. "Every tribe marks their territory in a similar way. Sometimes they paint the fur, but the standards always look more or less like this."

"I see," Lina said. "When will you know if it is your tribe?"

A few orcs came out of the nearest tent to watch the approaching group across the tundra. Lina could see their general outlines, but she couldn't tell anything else specific about them.

"This tribe isn't mine," Ilsander said almost at once.

"How can you tell?"

"Look at me," Ilsander said with a smile. "When I left my tribe, I was considered average height. These orcs are small. I might only share half of their orcish heritage, but I certainly have the stature my kin enjoy. My fellow tribesman would tower over these orcs."

Lina couldn't imagine standing face-to-face with an orc taller than Ilsander. The huge, green vampire hunter was already more than a head taller than any human she had met. "Perhaps they will know where your tribe has gone," she said.

Merren came up alongside Lina. Despite the cold and the sharp wind, there was a noticeable sheen of sweat where his hair began on his forehead. "What if they're hostile?" he asked softly. "I don't think it is prudent for you to be so freely riding among them."

"What?" Lina said. "Perhaps you should stay back if you're afraid. I'm immortal, remember?"

The three neared closer to the edge of the tents and two orcs came out to greet them, or at least to greet Ilsander, as they largely ignored Lina and Merren. "You bring slaves," one of them declared. His tusks were larger than Ilsander's, and his voice was so throaty his words were nearly unrecognizable as a language.

Ilsander lifted his bandaged hand in greeting. "Not slaves. Companions," he corrected the two. "I'm looking for my tribe, the ones who worship Kraxblade in the sky."

"You must ask the chief," the orc replied.

"Of course," Ilsander said. He dropped lightly from his horse to continue on foot, and Lina and Merren both followed suit. Standing on the ground, the physical differences between the two new orcs and Ilsander were obvious. Ilsander's physical stature was larger by all measurements, and his head sat farther up on his neck—more like a human's head. The other orcs were permanently slouched forward, as though their shoulders led directly to their faces. Both of the presumed emissaries wore little in the way of clothing, just simple bits of leather covering their feet and groins.

"How fares the hunt, brothers?" Ilsander asked. Lina noticed the way his voice changed when he spoke to the orcs. His words slurred somewhat at the end, sounding more natural and relaxed.

"If we kill any more, we'll get too fat to ever move in the spring," the orc who had done all the talking answered.

"That is good to hear," Ilsander replied.

The inner areas of the camp were bustling with activity. There were hundreds of orcs, each hunched at the shoulders and the height of a tall human male, none coming close to Ilsander's towering frame. Not many of the orc tribe carried weapons, and Lina felt an odd sense of welcoming she had not expected.

Merren's reception of the scene was far different. He visibly shook in his breastplate. "They don't like us," he said so quietly only Lina's enhanced senses could hear it.

"Be quiet," she commanded him harshly.

The two orcs led them toward the center of the encampment where huge racks of tender, pink meat were roasting above a dozen or more different fires. Ropes were strung nearby to hold all manner of dried spices, most of which Lina had never even seen before. The smells came at her all at once, mingling together with the scent of the butcher's block behind it all to create an intoxicating aroma that made her mouth water, despite her inability to enjoy most non-cannibalistic cuisine.

"Wait here," one of the orcs told them. He ducked into a squat tent near a meat rack, leaving his companion to stay outside looking bored.

A few of the other members of the tribe came closer to investigate the newcomers, though they didn't say anything. Merren paced back and forth on a patch of frost, quickly turning the area into mud all by himself.

Only a short time later, the tribe's chieftain came out of the central tent. He wore a fur-covered hat Lina assumed was the orcish version of a crown, and he walked with the aid of a polished stick in his right hand. The chief, like almost all of the others, carried no weapon.

"Thank you for meeting me, mighty chieftain," Ilsander said. He held his hand out to his side at a right angle, and the chief nodded his approval.

"You seek the Kraxblade tribe?" the older orc asked. His voice was so crude and hard to understand that the first orc's tone might as well have been that of a skilled orator or poet.

"Do you know them?" Ilsander asked hopefully.

The chieftain nodded. "They have just concluded their Great Hunt," he said. "Their celebration should be easy to see from miles around."

"That is good, mighty chieftain," Ilsander replied.

"I trust you still know where the Great Hunt takes place?" the chieftain asked, turning a skeptical eye on the newcomers.

"Of course," Ilsander answered quickly. "We shall depart at once, mighty chieftain. Thank you for your kindness."

The chief held out a withered green hand, and Ilsander bowed to touch his forehead to the back of it. It was a strange, almost courtly gesture that seemed entirely unfitting for orcs to display. Not wanting to be rude, Lina stepped forward and offered the old orc the same motion of respect, which the chieftain did not turn away.

"We should move quickly," Ilsander said, climbing back atop his horse. "The Great Hunt is far away, so we shouldn't waste any time."

"Which direction?" Lina asked.

"North. Much farther north," the taller one answered.

"If they completed the Great Hunt, it will not be hard to find the tribe. Their revelry will carry throughout the tundra, and it will last for more than two seasons."

Following Ilsander's lead, Lina kicked her mount to a trot, heading north toward the horizon. "And what did they kill?" she asked, though some part of her wasn't sure she wanted to know the answer.

"Each tribe makes a Great Hunt every ten years," Ilsander explained. "I forgot that my clan was going to attempt one this year. It has been a long time since I have been back."

"But what do they hunt?" Lina asked again.

"Ice worms, great leviathans of the northern fields," Ilsander said with a bit of wonder apparent in his voice.

"How big are they?" Merren asked, his voice squeaky and unsure.

Ilsander smiled and leaned back in his saddle. "Probably the length of your king's castle from front to back," he reminisced. "They live on the ice, chewing it into huge chunks with thousands of teeth. When the caribou herds wander too far north, the ice worms burrow up from the ground to rip entire tribes apart in a single night. Killing one is the greatest honor an orc can achieve in his life."

"How many are there?" Lina wondered aloud.

"Hundreds," Ilsander answered. "There is a crater, a huge hole in the earth where they all nest and brood. It is from that place that they go out to feast."

"You'd know if one was near us, right?" Merren asked.

Lina turned to see if the man was being serious. "I'm fairly certain it would not matter," she told him when it was apparent Merren had not been making a poor attempt at a joke. "If there was a worm the size of a castle devouring the ice beneath our feet, we would be dead."

"You're right," Ilsander confirmed. "The Great Hunt requires hundreds of orcs—sometimes more than one tribe. But the meat you get from an ice worm is unlike anything you've ever tasted. Trust me, the loss of half a tribe's warriors every decade is an acceptable price to pay."

"Do the worms bleed?" Lina asked, letting a hint of her bloodlust creep into her mind.

"Indeed," Ilsander told her. "Each one has enough blood to sate every vampire in Estria for centuries."

Lina kicked her horse a little harder, urging it onward. "Then let's see this Great Hunt!" she shouted. They were just at the edge of the tribe's camp, and a few of the orcs nearby looked over to see her outburst.

It took the trio four more days to move far enough north to finally hear the sounds of celebration coming from the Great Hunt. A few orc standards were spread out along the landscape, but most of them were covered in a decent amount of snow. The wind was a constant force in the north, blowing frozen specks of frost in a horizontal line across the entire tundra without anything to ever stop it.

The days were short in the north as well. Nightfall came almost immediately after midday, though it was never perfectly dark at night. The stars above were brilliant and numerous, and the moon reflected so much light through the cloudless atmosphere that every detail of the bleak landscape was always visible.

"We're almost there," Ilsander said. There was an excitement in his voice Lina had only heard once before—when the half-orc had captured her. The tone was contagious, accelerating her own heartbeat, yet it was terrifying at the same time.

The three rode harder when they could finally see the tents and other structures set up on the horizon. They pushed their horses through the biting wind, everyone eager to see the aftermath of the Great Hunt.

When they finally arrived, the scene first struck Lina as nothing short of a battle. There were hundreds of orcs, maybe over a thousand in total, and every last one of them was celebrating in the most violent manner possible. A huge stage of sorts had been constructed from wood, rope, and bits of what Lina assumed was ice worm skeleton, and a group of thirty or more orcs played out a furious beat on huge drums from the elevated structure. Beyond all of the jubilation, still far-ther north, was the great carcass of the slain ice worm.

Ilsander's estimation of the ice worm's size was wrong. He had downplayed it, and by quite a bit. From her vantage point on her horse at a small rise less than a mile from the celebration, Lina guessed the ice worm's body could wrap entirely around her father's keep at least twice, if not more. The thing was beyond immense, and its mouth was so thick in diameter it was likely tall-er than most of the buildings in Estria.

"By the gods…" Merren whispered.

Ilsander laughed loudly. "I don't think your gods have ever been this far north," he said with a broad smile. "And they certainly have not witnessed a Great Hunt!"

Lina could barely comprehend what she was seeing. "You said your tribe worships Kraxblade?" she asked.

"Kraxblade lives in the stars," Ilsander explained. "He always watches the Great Hunt."

"All hail the mighty Kraxblade," the woman said slowly. She couldn't take her eyes from the gargantuan corpse on the other side of the tribal ground. Nothing she had seen in her life could rival the sheer awe the ice worm inspired, and Lina harbored no doubt that she would never grasp that same feeling again as long as she lived.

Ilsander trotted his horse down the gentle slope that would lead them to the revelry below. With the drums thundering in the air, everything else faded away. The gentle clopping of the horses' hooves was lost, the sounds of Lina's breath vanished, and all but her most rudimentary thoughts were blasted away by the incessant beat of celebration.

They descended the slope slowly, dodging thrown objects and the occasional orc corpse as they went. "Is this where it all happened?" Lina asked when they passed a partially eaten body. Lina had to lean close to Ilsander's ear for him to hear.

He laughed. "You think they killed the worm somewhere else and then dragged it all the way here?"

Lina offer a chuckle and leaned back in her saddle. To her right, a group of four huge orcs wrestled on the ground. She couldn't tell if they were actually trying to kill each other, or if they were merely nearing the end of a drunken brawl. Either way, it was all part of the grand celebration.

The majority of the festivities took place right in the center of the depression. Hundreds of orcish males and females in various states of drunkenness crowded on a mat of trampled furs the size of King Arias' audience chamber. Favoring discretion, Lina looked away to the other side where huge slabs of what she suspected was the ice worm's meat were being slowly roasted over several banks of blazing, open flames.

Behind the cooking racks of meat, the tribe's chieftain was unmistakable. The orc was gloriously large, as

STUART THAMAN

tall as Ilsander even when seated on his throne, and he wore the most opulent fur Lina had ever seen. In Estria, fox fur was in fashion every winter, and all the lords and ladies of her father's court would show off their latest cuts at every opportunity. Lina had always enjoyed the fancy clothing her father would buy for her, but everything seemed inconsequential in front of the orc chieftain's attire: a grand display of furs from animals Lina could not name that ranged from brilliant oranges and whites to deep russet shades similar in color to the ice worm meat nearby.

Ilsander dismounted and fell to one knee before the stone dais, still some fifty feet from the throne. It took a painfully long amount of time for the chieftain to notice Ilsander's supplication, and Lina felt awkward watching it all from horseback a few paces behind her companion. The chieftain raised his hand to his side, and if he said anything at all, it was lost under the drums.

Slowly, Ilsander got to his feet, and the chieftain beckoned him closer with a huge, green hand. When they were together and both standing, Lina gawked at the other orc's size. Ilsander was mountainous by the standards of men—and merely a dwarf next to the chieftain, who rose at least two feet taller than the vampire hunter. The two spoke for quite some time, their conversation accented by the chieftain patting the smaller half-orc on the back several times, a friendly gesture that nearly sent Ilsander sprawling into the ground. Finally, when everything was concluded on the dais, Ilsander returned with a smile.

"They have a place for our horses," he said, yelling above the constant beat of the drums.

Lina nodded.

"We can meet with the shaman tomorrow. For tonight, you're one of us. The chieftain specifically told me to warn you of the dangers of going near the center." Ilsander pointed toward the mass of orcs behind Lina. "He doesn't like his warriors associating too closely with humans," he said.

Lina looked horrified. "He thinks I am your slave as well?" she yelled back.

"No," Ilsander said with a shake of his head. "I think he just doesn't like humans very much."

Lina had no idea what to say.

"Let's get you some ice worm to eat!" Ilsander went on. He held out a hand to help Lina from her horse, then did the same for Merren. The three lead their agitated mounts a good distance away from the main celebration to a place where a handful of other horses were also being kept. The tribe's beasts of burden were shorter and hairier than Estrian horses, and layered with corded muscle. A single orc was in the makeshift stable to take the horses, and he was young, at least judging by his size.

When Lina finally got to see the tribe members up close, she understood how easily Ilsander could tell each tribe apart just by physical appearance. The orcs celebrating the Great Hunt all looked like they could be Ilsander's brothers and sisters, or perhaps his parents and grandparents. They shared the same curvature of their tusks, and they were all huge, the subtle features giving away Ilsander's half-orc identity hard to detect.

Ilsander led Lina and Merren back to the roasting meat racks near the chieftain. He carved off several pounds onto a wooden tray that had been resting on top of a barrel, then handed it to Merren. The portion was monstrous, but judging by the size of the carcass at the top of the hill there would be millions and millions more pounds of the meat. Ilsander handed Lina two empty waterskins and then opened the barrel where he had found the tray. Inside was a pool of thick blood emanating such a powerfully intoxicating smell that it made the vampire's head spin just looking at it.

"Fill them," the half-orc said when Lina didn't move.

She dipped the end of one skin beneath the blood's surface and watched it flow. Tiny flecks of something black dotted the liquid, and Lina wasn't sure the blood would be safe for her to consume, though the torrent of emotion welling up in her mind was begging her to ignore her intuition. Most wild beasts Lina had eaten had merely been enough to sustain her, and none of them had ever tasted as good as human, and the ice worm blood was something else altogether.

When both skins could not contain any more, Lina

followed Ilsander some ways away to a large tent with closed sides and a poorly constructed wooden door made from the bottoms of various barrels all strung together. The feast hall was quiet enough inside for Lina to rearrange her thoughts into a more coherent pattern, the idea of so much fresh blood so close still nagging at her mind. The drums continued to thunder away outside, but they were no longer loud enough to make her ears ring.

"Everyone else has already eaten their fill," Ilsander said, indicating the many rows of unoccupied benches and tables.

Lina and Merren sat down next to each other at the closest table, and Ilsander dropped down onto a bench across from them. "I think you'll like the blood," he said with a knowing grin.

"You've tasted it?" she asked. She removed the stopper from her skin and sniffed the blood once more. The smell was powerful and specific, inviting her to taste it.

"Everyone drinks the blood," Ilsander answered.

Lina brought the skin up to her lips and tipped it back, tasting the thick liquid hesitantly at first. Hesitantly became gluttonously after only the briefest exploration of the flavor, as Lina found it absolutely breathtaking. Before she realized it, she had drained the entire skin. Two lines of blood escaped down the sides of her mouth to her neck, and wherever it touched her skin she felt a slight tingle.

When Lina finished, Ilsander's eyes were nearly as wide as the platter of meat in front of him. "No... *No one* drinks that much," he said flatly, all the mirth stolen from his voice.

"Why?" Lina demanded, her enjoyment suddenly turning to worry. She jumped up from the table and immediately swooned, losing her balance and tumbling back down to her bench as the world began to turn within her vision.

"That's why," the half-orc said slowly. He watched her sway back and forth on the bench, impressed that she was still awake and at least partially conscious. "The shaman brews it with spirits."

Merren struggled to keep the woman from falling to the ground like a typical town drunk. The benches had no backs, so he had to wrap his arm around her to keep her somewhat upright. "What should we do?" he asked.

Ilsander ripped a huge chunk of ice worm meat off a slab with his teeth and chewed for a long while as he thought. Surprisingly, Lina kept herself awake, though not even close to cogent. She muttered a few unintelligible things as she swayed on the bench, and then her hand shot up to her mouth as though she would vomit.

Miraculously, Lina managed to keep the contents of her blood-filled stomach to herself.

"Perhaps her... unique gifts help her ward off the alcohol," Ilsander finally said. "In all honesty, any three orcs would be dead by now after drinking that much, yet she's still awake."

As if on cue, Lina's head slumped forward, and the last bit of her consciousness fled.

"Do you think she'll be safe?" Merren asked.

"Well you can't go back to Estria if the princess dies on your watch," Ilsander said with a grin. "You better hope she comes through in the morning."

The man's eyes were already as wide as they could go, yet somehow they grew even wider.

"Come on, little man, lighten up," Ilsander said with a bit of a laugh. Hearing his orcish voice use casual human slang unnerved Merren even more. "Lina will be fine. She'll wish she was dead in the morning when she wakes up with that headache, though."

Finally, Merren seemed to understand that his beloved princess would live. He looked at her one last time before turning to the plate of meat in the center of the table. The ice worm's flesh looked like a finely cooked beef steak, though it was far juicier and tougher than any beef Merren had tasted before.

Even though the meat was fresh from the roasting racks outside the tent, Merren found that some pieces of it were ice cold in his mouth, even cracking like ice when he bit through them. "Honestly, it's pretty good," he said when he was halfway through his portion.

Ilsander nodded in approval. "And there's more meat than these thousand orcs would ever be able to eat. I'm sure if one of them pointed you in the right direction, you'd be able to find the carcass from the Great Hunt ten years ago with most of the meat uneaten and still rotting away," he explained.

"Then why do you do it?" Merren asked. "Why bother with the Great Hunt?"

Ilsander leaned back on his bench, his eyes watching Lina snore. "The Great Hunt is the very reason why the tribes still exist," he said. "Without it, there would be nothing to look forward to, no reason to train. The tribes would eventually turn on each other, and then hunting orcs instead of ice worms would become the mainstay of tribal existence."

"So the Great Hunt is more of a distraction?" Merren went on.

"You could say it that way," Ilsander replied. "The reason each of your human cities don't turn to fight the others is because you have a king unifying every cause, right?"

Merren nodded.

"We have the Great Hunt," Ilsander said. "Each tribe strives to kill an ice worm once every eighty years. Each tribe then has seventy years to prepare as the cycle continues. While there is a great deal of competition surrounding the Great Hunt, there is also a sense of unity. If a tribe does not feel strong enough to complete the Great Hunt on their own, they will ask the others for assistance. In that way, we don't need a king ruling the tundra and telling orcs who to kill or not kill. Every tribe prepares for the Great Hunt. That is our government."

Merren finished his piece of ice worm steak with a smile. "I think I'd like that better than living under a king," he stated. "No taxes, no politics. It sounds like a dream."

"Perhaps the tribe will let you stay and gorge yourself on ice worm," Ilsander laughed. "You could always paint yourself green and walk around on wooden stilts like the carnival performers. I'm sure you'd blend right in."

"Seriously, if the ice worm blood tastes as good as it seems, I might try to stay," Merren said. Lina's second waterskin full of the strong drink was sitting next to her head, and the man picked it up carefully, as though he was holding a sacred object in a temple.

"Just go slowly," Ilsander told him. "It tastes good, but don't drink more than half a mouthful."

Merren nodded and let the blood touch his lips. It was surprisingly sweet, but thick and savory at the same time, and it had none of the burn he had expected from such a potent alcoholic brew. The small black flecks in the liquid added little bursts of a cooling, minty flavor to the blood that Merren could barely describe.

He knew he shouldn't drink much, but the flavor was so inviting Ilsander had to take the skin from him before he drank himself to death with a single drawn-out swig. Merren managed to keep his consciousness for a while, and even enjoyed himself, finally letting down his guard and relaxing.

Ilsander didn't partake in the blood himself, though he did eat three more helpings of the roasted meat as he regaled Merren with adventure-filled tales from his past life living with the tribe.

Lina woke up near her two companions in the corner of the large tent where she had passed out and noticed a few other orcs she did not recognize snoring loudly in other areas. The sun was high overhead, illuminating the cold tent with soft light through the thin fabric. Lina rubbed at her eyes, and a throbbing pain settled in behind her cheekbones.

The throbbing grew rapidly in strength, and it spread out over her entire skull like someone was hammering a new sword out of a chunk of iron while using her head as the anvil. One of the orcs kicked out in his sleep and knocked over a bench. The screeching noise the bench made as it hit the one behind it was amplified in Lina's head, echoing painfully between her ears for a long time after the object had stopped moving.

Merren was propped up against one of the tent supports, his bandaged chest exposed to the cold northern air. A bit of the ice worm blood clung to the stubble around his mouth, and Lina spotted her waterskin on the ground a few feet from the man's open hand.

Of all those remaining in the tent, Ilsander seemed to be the only one who had gone to sleep sober. Lina tried to stand, but the swirling vortex of pain behind her eyes and face sent her tumbling back to the ground. She groaned, and the noise only amplified her pain. With her eyes closed against the meager light, Lina summoned all of her strength and pushed up from the ground, then quickly vomited a glob of speckled blood at her feet. The act improved her overall state, and she pushed on her stomach to make herself vomit a second time.

When she could finally stand without clenching her eyes shut, Lina found the line dug into the ground which served as the camp's communal latrine. The tribe was alive with movement, and the incessant drums from the day before had gone thankfully silent. She watched a few of the orcs carrying huge chunks of bloody meat to the racks and marveled at the display of strength the tribe showed, each orc lifting what looked like more than its body weight in meat to be smoked.

Ilsander and Merren emerged from the tent a few moments later. Merren was buttoning his shirt over his bandages, and he had his metal breastplate hung over his left arm. He looked to have fared better than Lina on the blood, though he still shielded his eyes from the painful light of the sun.

"You lived," Ilsander said cheerfully. He slapped Lina on the shoulder. "Maybe next time you don't go so heavy on the blood."

Lina grimaced, but then nodded. "Can we see your shaman today?" she asked quietly. The sound of her own voice rattling in her head was enough to send another round of pain bouncing around between her ears.

"We will," Ilsander answered. He turned to take in the sights of the victorious tribe, and a smile spread between his tusks.

"Was it the shaman who you spoke to yesterday?" Lina asked him.

"That was the chieftain, the strongest orc of the tribe," Ilsander explained. "The shaman is the wisest."

Ilsander led Lina and Merren to the center of the depression, into the midst of the tribe's continuing celebration and revelry. All the excitement of the previous night still continued in full swing, and Lina noticed tall barrels of the ice worm's blood distributed everywhere amongst the tribe. She wondered how any of them could drink and carry on as they were without dying. The still form of an orc lying prostrate on a pile of furs made her wonder if some of them did die from the blood.

They found the shaman inside a large series of interconnected tents with smoke billowing from the top of one of them. The place was full of hot steam, and it smelled strongly of unrefined spirits. Ilsander lifted one of the tent flaps to usher them inside with an open hand.

Huge copper stills brewed the ice worm blood, and each of them had a wooden palette of black granules above heavy grinding machines mounted on the top. There was only one orc inside the brewery, but he didn't look anything like the stereotypical shaman Lina had envisioned. Her eyes were drawn to the black substance above the stills, her magical sense running wild. Whatever the black bits were, they were strongly enchanted.

The brewmaster wore a heavy leather apron over his chest with cloth pants that could have been from any human tailor in Estria. His head was bald, and he sported a scraggly beard on his chin that was as dark as the scorched metal implement he used to stir one of the vats. He looked a bit shorter than Ilsander, but his other features marked him clearly as one of the tribe's members.

"Ullr," Ilsander said, catching the orc's attention.

The brewmaster looked up from his work with a casual expression. "Ilsander, it is good to see you returned to the tribe," he said. His voice was distinct from all the other orcs Lina had heard, lacking some of the gruff tones and instead sounding more inquisitive than violent or oppressive.

"We have a bit of a problem down south," Ilsander began.

Ullr started to respond, but stopped when Lina's hand shot into the bubbling pool of blood where he was working. The woman scooped out a bit of liquid and drank it, then dipped both hands in for more.

It took Ilsander a moment to realize that Lina wasn't fully aware of what she was doing. He drew the longsword from his left hip and pressed the flat of it into the exposed skin on Lina's arm. She yelled out in pain, but she didn't stop going for the vat of blood.

"Help me hold her back!" Ilsander shouted to the other two.

Lina's fangs clicked into place, and her eyes rolled back in her head to show only the whites. She clawed violently after the copper still, reaching for it with her nails, scraping against the metal rim as Ilsander tried to wrestle his blade up against her throat.

"What abomination did you bring into my home?" Ullr asked. The shaman pushed Lina back, batting her hands with the wooden handle of his brewing tool.

Finally, Ilsander got his blade up to Lina's throat, using the pain as leverage to move the clawing woman away. Merren pinned her arms to her sides, and the two dragged Lina from the brewery like she was a belligerent drunk in a seedy brothel. Once she was outside, her muscles began to visibly calm.

"Pull yourself together," Ilsander growled. He dropped her unceremoniously to the frozen ground. Merren heaved from the effort, likely still hungover himself.

"I—"

"Control yourself," Ilsander commanded.

"I'm not sure I can," Lina muttered. She looked away, trying to hide her shame. "I'm not even hungry. Just the... the sight of so much blood. I've never seen so much in one place."

"Keep her outside," Ilsander told Merren. The man slumped down with a hand on Lina's shoulder.

"The shaman knows she's a vampire," he said.

Ilsander sighed. "He won't say anything. Vampirism isn't illegal in the tribes like it is in your cities."

"What would the rest of the tribe do if they found out?" Merren asked nervously.

"Probably try to hang her," Ilsander said.

"But she isn't illegal?"

The half-orc laughed. "That doesn't mean she wouldn't be hated," he said. He turned back to the shaman's brewery with a heavy sigh. "I'll get what we need as quickly as we can. Then we should leave."

"Good idea," Merren nodded.

Lina's fangs finally receded back into the roof of her mouth, once more becoming unnoticeable. "Thank you," she said to both of them. "I fought it as much as I could… Then everything went black. I don't know what happened."

Ilsander left her there on the ground and went back inside. "Ullr," he called, finding the bewildered-looking shaman behind one of his huge copper stills. "I'm sorry about that. She's a vampire and couldn't control her bloodlust."

Ullr nodded slowly. "You knew what she was when you came here?" he asked.

"Indeed," Ilsander said, patting the hilt of his left

sword. "I was hired to capture her, but now I need her help."

"And that's where I come in, too, right?" the shaman asked.

"You've always been the smartest orc I've ever known," Ilsander remarked. "There's a vampire in Trax-holm with the power of a lich. We intend to kill him."

Ullr's eyes went wide, but he otherwise hid his surprise well. "And Traxholm is far from the tundra, is it not?" he replied.

"Yes," Ilsander answered. "But the death of Estria would mean added hardships for the tribes as well."

"How?"

Ilsander cleared his throat as he tried to think of a response. "When Estria has been reduced to frozen ash, where will the lich turn next? I doubt he will cross the sea," he explained.

"This vampire-lich is perhaps afraid of boats?" Ullr joked. "I agree that such a being threatens the stability of our world, but that is no reason to help you." He let out a long sigh. "I will help you because liches are abominations of magic and an affront to all, humans and orcs alike, and as a shaman, I feel some need to help purge this world of certain atrocities."

"Thank you," Ilsander said. "I'll need a new weapon, if you're willing to help." He offered the shaman the sword from his left hip which Ullr himself had crafted several decades before. Moonsilver was a volatile mineral, something that routinely exploded when it was forged, and orc shaman were the only beings known to work it into weapons with any consistency.

Ullr pointed to the second sword he had made so long ago. "You do not desire two new weapons?" he asked.

"The lich is also a vampire," Ilsander added.

Ullr smiled, though it was an expression born of hopelessness rather than any enjoyment. "And that's why you need the girl," he concluded. "She's one of his creations, isn't she…"

"Perceptive again," Ilsander said.

"And if she turns on you?" Ullr went on. "If she joins her master to rule over a broken Estria at the lich's right hand?"

"Then this is the last you'll see of me, old friend," Ilsander responded.

"So you *must* succeed," Ullr said. "Perhaps you need to be asking Kraxblade for assistance, not a lowly shaman like me."

Ullr dropped his stirring rod down into the vat and turned a valve, releasing some of the black pellets into the mixture. He worked a bellows with his foot at the same time, drastically increasing the heat on the bottom of the still with a few easy movements.

"What will it take?" Ilsander asked.

Ullr shook his head. "I don't think you understand," he said evenly. "If it is a vampire who has become a lich that you intend to kill, you need far more than specialized weapons and that woman's touch. You need a miracle."

Ilsander knew the shaman was right, but he refused to leave empty handed. "Just give me something," he pleaded. "You must know how to contain a lich's power. I know you have something in your arsenal that would help."

The three companions, mounted once more upon their horses, left the camp an hour or so after nightfall. The revelry of the Great Hunt had begun again in full, and the constant drumming throbbed in Lina's head. Stronger than the noise, however, was the relentless urge to rip into the packs of blood in her saddlebags that tormented her with every passing second. She had several gallons of the brewed blood stuffed into every waterskin, and one of them, a particularly small leather pouch, contained the distilled essence of the ice worm's blood that Ullr had congealed into a thick, black sludge.

Ilsander carried his familiar longsword on his right hip, and his left held a squat axe. The weapon looked more like a kitchen implement than a tool of war, though the shaman had seemed confident it would have a profound effect if it ever cleaved into a lich.

Riding at the back of the group, Merren had been given the most by the shaman. The sword he had brought was still hanging from his side, and he had a huge morningstar slung in a baldric over his right shoulder. The weapon was heavy, though the handle had been expertly crafted from a length of slender, hollow iron wrapped with leather strips. Lina wasn't sure how many times the guard could swing such a large weapon before tiring, but she had to admit it was an impressive sight—and far better than any of their other weapons against a skeleton.

Lina's dagger was still tucked neatly into her belt, and the constant feel of it against her stomach was a welcomed comfort. The weapon was purely mundane, but she drew strength from the steel that she could not explain. From the jewels in the pommel to the sharpened point, she knew every inch of it as though it was a part of her own hand. She imagined sinking it into Rhaas' chest, her face just inches from his as he struggled for his final, ragged breath.

Lina kept that thought planted firmly in her mind as she traveled with the others back to the northern guardpost marking the border of Estria. Only a few miles from the outpost, they could see the evidence of a huge army having recently gone through the area. The grass was trampled, the smaller trees had all been uprooted and cast aside, and huge ruts of mud ran from west to east, each of them marked by thousands of hoof prints.

"Rhaas has his army," Ilsander said, bending down near one of the tracks. "They're too large to be normal horses. These are centaurs."

"How many could there be?" Merren asked. The tracks went on forever in both directions, and the mud was as wide as a river.

"Thousands," Ilsander said, giving voice to what all three of them were thinking. "He needed an army, and now he has it."

"Perhaps meeting him on the open field with Estria's soldiers would be foolish," Lina remarked.

"What would you suggest?" the half-orc asked.

Lina took her time formulating her plan. "Perhaps it should only be me," she said after a moment. "Or just the three of us. Infiltration and execution would be easier than organizing the entire army and plunging half the kingdom into war."

"And if the centaur army attacks us first?" Merren asked.

"Use our own force to push them back and hold the cities while we go to Traxholm," she answered.

"It might work," Ilsander added. "We need to return to Estria. We have what we need now—the only thing missing is a plan."

Lina nodded. "Right," she said. "Let's move."

Chapter 24

The kingdom was fully mobilized when Ilsander, Lina, and Merren returned. Their trip to the north had lasted twenty days, and the atmosphere in Estria was so different it felt like they were coming home to the wrong country as they passed through the northern gate. All of the businesses along the main streets had either been converted to military operations or were shuttered with heavy wooden boards. Forges burned hot in storefronts that once displayed baked breads and pastries. Dozens of men and women sat around barrels in a former farmer's market as they fletched arrows. Down one alleyway which used to provide access to the city's builders guilds, Lina saw a line of militiamen in crisp new uniforms firing crossbows at straw targets.

"They should be aiming at the outline of a horse, not a scarecrow," she remarked to herself as they passed.

To her right, a large complex which previously sold the finest silk and textile products had been converted to a staging area where new recruits were being processed by the dozen. Everywhere she looked, her father's city was getting ready for war.

The keep itself was the central hub of activity for all of Estria. The gates were wide open, and messengers came and went by the minute, transporting tightly rolled scrolls in every direction. Above the keep's inner guardhouse, only one man was left to control the flow of traffic into the castle. "My lady," he said with a respectful bow when he recognized Lina.

"Has there been any news?" she asked him. The clopping of her horse's hooves was lost under a hundred other sounds, and a messenger boy jostled into her side on his mount as he squeezed through the guardhouse amidst ten or more others attempting to do the exact same thing.

"You should ask your father," the soldier called back to her. "He'll be in the strategy room. One of the King's Shield should be able to take you there."

The strategy room was a place Lina had never seen. She had been past the door thousands of times before, but it was only unlocked when the kingdom officially called all the banners together for a campaign. All the lords of the various cities and provinces throughout Estria used it as a central gathering place during times of war, and it was likely the most defensible room in the entire land. According to Estrian legend, the kings and queens were never given a key to the strategy room as the access was limited by the captain of the King's Shield.

"Thank you," Lina called back to the soldier at the top of the guardhouse. "You may not be permitted within the strategy room," she said to Ilsander at her left. "I don't think anyone with green skin has ever been inside."

"I assumed as much," Ilsander replied.

A member of the King's Shield met the trio at the entrance to the keep. The man was tall and arrayed in shining armor, a glinting steel spear in his hand. Seeing the highly respected guards outside of their usual posts inside the castle was a strange thing to behold, and further proof of the heightened atmosphere of war throughout the whole city. Lina figured the regular guards were off helping to train the military somewhere, probably at the parade grounds southeast of the city proper.

Inside the first chamber of the keep—the audience hall—all of the guards were gone. The King's Shield member led them toward the center of the vast structure to a narrow staircase that curled upward for three stories. At the top landing, there were four doors, two on either side of a short hallway. To the left was a pair of storerooms where servants went in and out regularly. To the right, the first door revealed a narrow hallway which opened onto the castle's upper battlements. The final door held the entrance to the strategy room.

Voices drifted through the iron-banded door, muffled and distorted by the thick wood, each one overlapping the one before it. Lina could barely make out her father's deep tones among the vocal confusion. The guard stopped in front of the door and knocked twice, and the sounds from the other side went silent. A small panel in the top of the door swung open a few seconds later, and another member of the King's Shield presented his face to greet the newcomers.

The two guards exchanged a few words, and then the panel dropped back into place. Several minutes later, the full door swung open and the armored man on the inside pointed to Lina. "Just you," he said sternly. "The others can wait downstairs."

Lina nodded to her companions and stepped forward.

The inside of the strategy room looked far larger than Lina previously thought possible judging from the size of the exterior. The stone floor sloped downward at a gentle angle, ending with a flat platform several feet below the entrance. A huge table dominated the center of the room, and ten of Estria's most powerful politicians and military commanders sat around it. Lina's father was at the head of the table, wearing decorative leather armor as though he was about to venture out and kill Rhaas himself.

"Father," Lina began, walking toward the table of

Estria's best. The king looked up from a parchment map with fire in his eyes.

"You were successful?" he asked quickly. Some of the generals and nobles looked confused, but they didn't interject.

"I think so," Lina replied. "But there is an army headed for Traxholm."

The king nodded his head solemnly. "Centaurs, I know," he said. "You saw them?"

"We killed a couple of them, but there are hundreds, probably thousands," she answered. One of the generals, a man wearing a black silken doublet with gold epaulets on the shoulders, pulled a chair out for Lina to join them. She had seen him once or twice before and remembered his scruffy red beard, but she had no idea who he was or exactly how much influence he wielded.

"Were they all alive when you saw them?" the king asked.

Lina looked confused. "I'm not sure what you mean."

"One of the villages, which one was it?" King Arias asked the man seated to his left.

The nobleman ruffled through a sheaf of parchments before finding the correct one. "The village of Blueglenn," he said, sounding confident.

"Ah yes," the king went on, "the centaur army sacked this Blueglenn, more a collection of rundown farms than a proper settlement, but those horse warriors were all bones and magic. A few villagers managed to escape to Chancol, and the magistrate there sent a message via scrying pool yesterday morning."

"They were undead?" Lina exclaimed.

"So it was reported," King Arias replied.

Lina shook her head.

"Well, we need an answer, and we need one immediately," the king said, turning his gaze back to the rest of the men seated around the table.

One of the men, a grizzled old veteran bearing an impressive collection of scars on his face and exposed arms, stood with a list of figures in his hands. "We have three full corps of militia from the provinces, your highness. They're being trained now with pikes and crossbows, and they should be able to move when you need them. We also have a matching number of the regular army, most with decent arms and armor, though horses are lacking. We're also coming up short on food for the army, though there isn't any risk of starvation yet," the man reported.

"Three hundred thousand," King Arias said to himself with a smile. "It should be more than enough to crush this insolent lich."

"And you are set on meeting him in the open field?" Lina cut in.

"You would suggest something different?" the general giving the report asked incredulously.

"Yes," Lina stated as she stood from her chair. "I am the only one who can kill him. Ilsander and I can infiltrate his operation in Traxholm, and then I can get to him and cut out his heart."

The general stared open-mouthed at the princess. "And in the meantime, we sit idly by as our peasants are slaughtered in their homes by hordes of monstrous undead?" he demanded.

"Use the army to stop whatever hordes Rhaas sends against the people, but leave Traxholm alone," Lina explained.

"A plan of containment would be best," the general countered. "We should push the undead centaurs back into Traxholm, pin them down, and settle in for a siege. We can hold them in the village while you and that beast run in to get yourselves killed."

"A siege?" Lina scoffed. "What do you plan on doing? Starving out a bunch of undead who don't eat?"

The general clearly faltered, and a couple of the men on the other side of the table had to stifle laughs with their hands. "Well—"

"She has a point," the king said over his general.

"No matter the plan, we need to end the centaur threat before more villages fall," one of the other generals went on emphatically. "Once the centaurs have been eradicated, we can figure out exactly how to kill Rhaas."

A murmur of consensus came from everyone except the first general who had spoken, and the king seemed pleased as well. Arias stood from his position at the head of the table, and the room quickly fell silent. "We will move the army in five days," he stated. "We travel first to Chancol. From there, we can surround the centaurs and kill them." He turned toward his daughter with a loving smile. "Though I hate the idea of you facing the lich, I realize it is the only way. Take Ilsander and Merren. You can travel with the army, or on your own if you like, but head to Traxholm. See if you can end the lich before our soldiers get there."

Lina nodded. "Certainly, Father," she said. "We will leave at once."

Chapter 25

"With the amount of ice we saw in Traxholm, we're going to need some fire," Ilsander said once Lina had explained the plan to him. Merren looked nervous, though he felt more confident being back in Estria alongside thousands of soldiers in the city preparing for war.

"What do you suggest?" Lina asked.

"I saw a fireslinger in Azanthium," Ilsander replied. "I think she's worth hiring if Estria doesn't have its own fire mage at the guild."

Lina thought for a moment. "I don't remember if the mages guild has anyone proficient with fire or not," she said.

"It would be worth the effort to ask," Merren added. "I can take you there."

The three opted to stay on foot as they moved

through the city, none of them eager to fight through the bustling crowds on horseback. The mages guild used to be a towering spiral of marble reaching up to the clouds, but it had been reduced to rubble a little over ten years ago when an errant lightning strike had toppled the entire structure in a single night. The mages guild had then taken over an older building along the river that lacked all the prestige and opulence of their former establishment.

The guild was buzzing with activity when Lina, Merren, and Ilsander arrived at the front gates. Large wooden crates of supplies were being moved from several wagons by a complex system of pulleys and wooden platforms. One of the mages, a younger man with a telltale blue robe, paced back and forth as he issued orders to direct the boxes where they needed to be.

Lina tried to get the man's attention, but he didn't bother to acknowledge anyone except the others helping to move his supplies. The door to the building was open, so Lina led the other two inside. A few other mages were active inside, shuffling papers and organizing all manner of strange looking magical implements. "I guess they're all going to war too," she said.

One of the mages finally took notice of the group and came up to them. She was older, with bedraggled hair and an unkempt green robe, and her voice cracked as she spoke, as though she hadn't used it in weeks. "You have a message for us?" she asked.

"No," Lina said slowly. "We're looking for a fire mage."

The old woman tilted her head back and laughed like Lina had just said the funniest thing the mage had ever heard. When the mage finally calmed down, she had a crazed look in her eyes that spoke volumes. "You need to harness the sun!" she cackled, and a huge shimmer of light erupted from her fingertips in a radial pattern around each of her hands.

Lina shielded her eyes from the blinding light. "I think the mages here have come unhinged," she said to Ilsander. "We should go."

The old mage continued to laugh, throwing beams of harmless, bright light all through the room. Lina gave one final look to the other mages working in the building before she turned to leave.

"They've likely been hired to go with the military," Merren said when they were back outside.

"Hopefully they won't get the entire militia killed with their insanity," Ilsander remarked dryly. "Let's go back to Azanthium. We have a few days before the army moves out. If we leave now, we can make it to Azanthium before the army reaches Chancol."

"I agree," Lina stated with a nod.

The three headed back toward the keep to collect their horses and gather enough supplies for the trip. Behind them, the noise of the mages guild slowly faded away, lost to the bustle of the vibrant city.

Moving as quickly as they could safely push their horses, the three companions reached Azanthium in just under a week. They passed Chancol on the third day, and the city appeared completely mobilized for war. The walls had been hastily repaired, new ballistae were being constructed, and several units of soldiers were out in front of the city practicing organized maneuvers.

Azanthium was different. Without high walls surrounding the city, there wasn't much that could be done to prepare the place for a battle. There was a large contingent of soldiers stationed in the big port city, but most of them had traveled west back to Estria to join up with the regulars. What was left of Azanthium was basically a ghost town. All the nobles had left after the first reports of a battle had made it to the streets, and the merchants' quarter was overrun with vagabonds making the various stalls their new street-side homes.

No sails marked the horizon by the city docks. Every ship had left save for one; a small schooner with a destroyed mast and fire damage marring its starboard side. In the center of the city, all of the military garrisons had been boarded over and closed. Some soldiers were still left in the city, but they were few and far between.

"Where's this fireslinger of yours?" Lina asked. They stood alone in what used to be the central trading square, now eerily abandoned. The threat of open warfare clung to everything.

"I don't know," Ilsander said honestly. "Perhaps we should look for the mages guild here?"

"Not more lunatics," Merren muttered.

The three walked around the center part of the city for more than an hour, seeing only a handful of people, none of whom were useful. Near the southern edge of the city, a bit of commotion caught Lina's ear. She heard someone scream, a voice that sounded feminine, and then a chorus of male shouts came right after it.

Lina, Ilsander, and Merren turned their horses toward the noise without a moment of hesitation. The vampire didn't fancy herself as any kind of vigilante doling out extra-judicial punishment, but the potential for a fight intrigued her enough to get her moving.

In a tight alleyway between two abandoned waterfront warehouses, a group of burly men dressed as sailors made a semicircle in front of someone else. Behind them, one of the warehouses had caught fire, and thick burst of black smoke escaped the wooden walls as the structure began to collapse.

Lina watched for a moment as she tried to decipher what was happening. "You didn't pay!" one of the sailors yelled. His voice was hoarse, and Lina wondered if the men had been at their violence all morning. One of them kicked the prone figure in the center of the street. The woman shrieked, and then a sputtering of fire shot out from her body, leaping onto the nearby warehouse.

"You burned my boat!" one of the larger men yelled, delivering another kick to accentuate his point. As before, another burst of flame erupted from the woman. It spiraled directly up, then scattered in the wind to several nearby rooftops. The smell of fire quickly began to overwhelm the strong scent of the nearby ocean.

"I think that's our woman," Ilsander said, keeping his voice low.

Lina slid from her saddle. None of the men in the alley noticed her, and she crept up behind them with her dagger held close to her side. There were seven sailors, and Lina couldn't keep the smile from her face as she thought about draining each of them dry and leaving their exsanguinated corpses behind like back alley trash.

She grabbed the nearest man's belt and pulled him back several inches away from the others. He yelped, but only for the briefest of moments before Lina's dagger came out the front of his throat, its hilt pressed firmly against the man's neck. She let him drop to the ground.

Lina stood proud, flanked by fire on either side and a fresh corpse lying at her feet. "What's all this?" she asked, trying her best to sound like the dainty princess she once was. Her dagger dripped blood onto the cobblestones.

"What the—" one of the sailors began. He raised his fist, but Lina was faster than he could comprehend.

The vampire ducked below the sailor's poorly aimed strike, coming up quickly with her dagger planted deep in the man's abdomen. He keeled over on top of her blade, taking it down to the stones with him as he choked out his final, bloody breaths. Two of the remaining sailors charged at Lina, one from either side.

One of the men was a decent bit closer than the other, and Lina met him head on before the other reached her. She caught the man by his wrists, wrenching them backward violently and throwing him off balance. His neck protruded out with his arms behind him, and his mouth was so close to Lina that she could feel his hot breath on her skin. With a vicious jerk, she pushed the man's arms farther behind him, and the tendons in his shoulders pulled so tight they snapped.

Lina threw the sailor aside just in time to dodge a heavy punch aimed for her head. The sailor's second hand connected, but he was no match for the vampire. Lina roared with primal joy as she grabbed the man's forearm and threw him over her back. He landed with a sharp crack, and blood oozed from the back of his skull like spilled wine.

There were three sailors still standing, and none of them made a move toward Lina, instead cowering where they stood. The woman they had been roughing up was still lying on the ground several paces behind the last of her attackers. The fires on either side were growing to alarming heights, and the smoke in the alley was beginning to get in Lina's eyes.

"She—she didn't pay!" one of the sailors stammered. He held his hands up in front of him as though his feeble arms could offer any semblance of defense against the wickedly strong vampire. Even unarmed, Lina was so far beyond the prowess of the sailors that she hadn't even begun to sweat.

"She burned our ship!" another sailor pleaded.

Lina smiled, glad that she had finally found the woman she had been looking for. She stepped forward, bringing herself directly in front of the man who had spoken. "You'd kill her for not paying?" she asked.

The man swallowed hard. His eyes were wide, and his mouth kept moving despite no words coming out.

Lina grabbed a handful of hair on the side of the man's head. He screamed when she touched him, and he started to flail against her, but her grip was like iron. With a sinister laugh, Lina wrenched his head to the side and broke his neck. She tossed the body aside, eager to dispatch the two remaining assailants so she could finally speak to the fireslinger uninterrupted.

Both of them turned to run. They sprinted down the back of the alley toward the growing fires, covering their faces to keep the heavy smoke from their lungs. Lina sprinted after them, running up directly behind the man on the left. She grabbed him by the throat and ripped him from his feet, smashing his body into the final sailor in one clean motion.

The two men crumpled to the ground in a heap of arms and legs. The one Lina had thrown crashed through the side of the burning warehouse behind him, and a large section of the roof collapsed down on top of him, eliciting a pathetic scream as his flesh burned.

"No!" begged the only one left.

Lina towered over the battered man like a vengeful god come to collect the souls of the damned.

"It wasn't me!" the man kept on yelling. "I'm just a dockhand! I was trying to leave!"

Lina reached a hand down and picked the sailor up from his backside, setting him down on his own two feet as his comrade's screams finally died in the fire. She pulled him in close to her body, and her fangs clicked into place. The man's legs shook, all the strength gone from his body, and Lina had to keep him upright as she drank his life away.

When Lina had sated her bloodlust, she tossed the empty husk of a man into the burning warehouse to be cremated with his friend. The woman in the center of the alley had crawled away from the vampire, but Merren and Ilsander still blocked the only route of escape.

"Please..." she whispered, her ragged voice barely audible above the crackling flames.

Lina lifted up the woman roughly by her shoulders to a standing position. "Don't worry," she said, though her fangs were still prominently exposed. "You're the one we've been looking for."

The fireslinger fainted in Lina's arms.

Lina, Merren, and Ilsander sat atop a few crates and barrels on one of Azanthium's picturesque piers as they waited for the fireslinger to regain consciousness. They had the woman propped up against a wooden pylon with a few boards wedged behind her back to keep her from falling into the ocean. Their three horses were tied to a hitching post in front of the harbormaster's abandoned office not far away.

Finally, after nearly an hour of waiting and watching the waves lap at the pier, the fireslinger's eyes fluttered open. The woman tried to back away, but there was nowhere for her to go. Half a mile or so from the pier, the fire she had set raged through Azanthium, giving everything the strong smell of ash.

"Please don't kill me," the fireslinger said quietly. Her eyes darted from Merren to the half-orc, then settled on Lina who was casually tossing her jeweled dagger from one hand to another.

"So what was all that about?" Ilsander asked.

The woman gripped the edge of the dock, struggling to keep her fear in check. "They robbed me," she said, never taking her eyes from the vampire. "I paid them. I paid them twice over to take me from the city."

"They knew you had money," Ilsander concluded. "So they tried to take everything you were worth."

The woman finally let her gaze drift back to the wooden planks beneath her feet. "They took it all."

"You should be glad we found you," Merren cut in, his voice oddly cheerful.

"Should I?" she asked hesitantly.

Lina smiled at her. "Don't worry," she said. "I'm not hungry."

"And we need your help," Ilsander added quickly. He shot Lina a glare before going on. "You've heard about the lich?" he asked.

The fireslinger shook her head. "Just an army of un-dead centaurs running from village to village. Everyone fled. I tried to buy passage south on that boat, but those bastards knew I had more coin." She pointed to the burnt boat partially sunk several piers over.

"Well," Ilsander said, "there's a lich controlling them. He's already iced over half of the north, maybe more by now. We need your help to stop him."

The woman shook her head. She was smaller than Lina—short, with narrow shoulders and a narrower waist, and she had a tinge of red in her curly blonde hair that matched her fiery abilities.

"Will you help us?" Merren asked.

"Do I have much of a choice?" the fireslinger shot back.

Lina and Ilsander both laughed. "We will let you

go," the big half-orc said. "But what would you do here? Stay and watch the city burn? Wait for the centaurs?"

The fireslinger thought about the offer for a long time before answering. "They call me Cindana at all the festivals and magic shows," she said.

"And your real name?" Ilsander asked.

"I think I like the name Cindana better," she replied. "It fits, you know?"

Ilsander introduced himself and the other two, and then showed the fireslinger his writ from the king to further allay her fears.

"How did you learn the fire magic?" Lina asked. They still had a bit of ice worm meat with them, which everyone except the vampire shared on the pier.

"I've had a knack for it ever since I was young," Cindana said. She spoke casually enough to show she no longer feared the others, but she kept her eyes subtly following Lina's movements, ready to defend herself at a moment's notice.

"I saw you at the festival a couple weeks ago," Ilsander said. "You can clearly do more than parlor tricks. You had to have learned that somewhere."

Cindana pointed to the burning warehouses farther down the docks. "You're right," she said. "I picked up some things from a few others along the way, but a good performer never reveals all her secrets."

"Fair enough," Lina replied. "Though I suppose most of my secrets aren't very secret, are they?"

"Are you a vampire?" Cindana asked hesitantly, subconsciously backing into the pylon behind her.

"Don't worry," Lina replied, "I've never fed on another woman. Well, I might have, but at least I don't remember it."

"Comforting," the fireslinger said. She looked to the other two with a bit of nervousness showing across her face. "You have no problems traveling with one of her kind?"

"She's the only one who can kill the lich," Ilsander said.

"And she's the daughter of King Arias," Merren added.

Cindana eyes widened a bit. "So what's our plan? Just charge into this lich's fortress and run a knife across his throat?" she asked.

Ilsander nodded. "Yes," he said seriously. "I suppose that would work just fine."

"You haven't thought this out much, have you?" Cindana replied.

"The army from Estria will be pursuing the centaurs," Merren explained. "It is our job to get into Traxholm and kill the lich before he slaughters thousands of peasants parading around as an organized army."

Cindana looked longingly at the boat she had accidentally destroyed. "And there's no way out of the city," she said after a moment.

"Azanthium will be overrun before long," Lina told

her. "You'd have a month, maybe a little more before Rhaas' army sacks the city as he expands his empire."

Cindana let out a frustrated sigh. "Fine. And you need me to burn away the ice," she said.

Lina reached out a hand to lift the woman from the dock. "Welcome aboard," she said with a smile. "Now, let's get to Traxholm."

Chapter 26

Estria's army moved slowly. The soldiers were split into six divisions, each with their general and officers, and hundreds of civilian support followers trailing behind with their supplies and cookware. Count Astragon, a military veteran of forty years, led the most proficient of the divisions, and the only one with any cavalry.

His own horse was covered in steel barding with Estria's banner patterned across his saddle and streaming from his mount's mane. His division was in the lead. He had spread them out wide across the land as they moved from Estria to Chancol, gaining speed though losing a measure of their cohesion. He had his outriders scouting through the countryside to pick up the trail of the centaurs, and they hadn't been hard to find. The undead beasts left a rut of mud and destruction everywhere they went.

Astragon's scouts spotted the centaur trail a few miles north of Chancol, and it headed east in the direction of Azanthium. "We can catch them in a few days," the general said to his most trusted lieutenant.

"Yes, sir," the lieutenant replied. "The latest report says the enemy force is around twenty thousand strong."

"We outnumber them more than two to one," General Astragon observed. "We can pin them outside Azanthium, then when they stop to rest, we will surround the centaur scum. We cannot suffer a single one of the wretched undead to escape."

"Certainly, sir," the lieutenant replied. "We should be close enough to smell them in less than two days."

"Why are they moving so slowly?" Astragon asked.

The lieutenant shook his head. "I'm not sure," he answered. "Perhaps they are foraging. Or maybe they cannot travel very far without a break."

"They're dead," the general said. "I don't think they need to forage or rest."

"Then they lure us into a trap," the lieutenant concluded.

General Astragon's hands tightened around his reins. "You might be right," he agreed. "We must remain vigilant."

"Perhaps we should wait for the other five divisions to catch up."

"If we can trap the centaurs against Azanthium,

we'll take the chance," Astragon growled. "We're going to crush them. We have more than twice their numbers. The sooner we slaughter these centaur bastards, the sooner we can bring the glory of a lich's bloody head back to Estria."

The lieutenant snapped off a crisp salute before riding back to the other officers in the procession.

A dark, skeletal figure sat atop an equally undead steed. The creature beneath the warlord was large, a powerful, necromantic creature with thunderous hooves, but the warlord was far larger. The moon shone brightly overhead, casting its pale glow over the abomination and his army of thousands. The warlord was ready for carnage. He was ready to die again for his master—this time in glorious combat, not cowering in fear like the pathetic farmer he had once been. That life had been when he was weak, when he had had a name. Now... he had been perfected.

Behind him, there were only a few other skeletons riding the backs of the undead horde. He was one of a chosen few, the only reanimated skeletons deemed strong enough by their master to ride into battle as a leader. The warlord's only piece of armor was an old, rusted helmet that had belonged to his father, but that had been a different time, a different age. Despite only being transformed into his skeletal state a mere week ago, his past life felt like distant memories from centuries before that only flickered to life every now and then with hazy images and blunted emotions.

The beast beneath the warlord pawed its boney hoof at the ground, kicking a few errant leaves into the wind. The dirt was icy cold. If the beast had breath, it would have condensed into wisps of fog, but his mouth had not tasted the air in many days. Relishing the cold atmosphere, the warlord's only thought was conquest. Service to the master was the ultimate honor, and death was the ultimate sacrifice. The army behind him was anxious for their glorious ends as well. Their bones would become fuel for the cause, and the corpses of those they slew would power their master's cruel machinations.

A bitter, icy wind blew through the ranks. It was early fall in Estria and should have been warm, but the lich's might had frozen the land, blighting it with necrotic ice. There was a gentle bit of rain falling to the ground, and it froze into a wet slush in places where the ground had cooled considerably.

"They're close," the warlord hissed, his teeth clacking together as he spoke without lungs or vocal cords. The few undead centaurs near him pawed at the ground. They could sense the anticipation hanging in the air, the violence waiting to be consummated, and the battle only moments away.

The skeletal army was barely hidden behind the edge of a treeline several miles north of Chancol and a little ways to the east. The humans had gone past the gathered centaurs, blindly following a path that led them nowhere, chasing phantasms created by Rhaas for just such a purpose.

The moon was high overhead, full and shining with an eerie glow when the skeletal warlord finally gave the order for his troops to attack. They were almost directly behind the first human division, and the warlord smiled when his boney underlings crashed into the military baggage train with a chorus of otherworldly howls.

Undead centaurs trampled over the untrained humans, driving scores of terrified men and women into the cold dirt. Most of the centaurs were unarmed, using only their fists and hooves, though others held spears with sharp metal tips. The warlord carried a brutal, cylindrical mace covered with nails and spikes, and he swung it from side to side as his mount charged through a line of wagons carrying food and barrels of clean water. One of the caravan drivers shrieked and held up his hands to block, but it was a futile attempt, and the warlord's mace crashed through the man's head as though it was nothing more than silk.

The first centaur charge killed almost every member of the baggage train, and the rest threw down their meager weapons and ran before the horde, scattering into the icy wind. The warlord bellowed into the air and his underlings swooped toward the west, circling through the regulars of the army like a tornado of bone and death.

Astragon heard the screams coming up from the rear of his division right when he was about to call for the unit to halt for the night. They had made good progress during the day, and keeping the men moving several hours into the night had gotten them much closer to Azanthium than they had first expected. He knew they were hot on the trail of the fleeing centaur warband.

"See what that commotion is!" Astragon shouted to his officers behind him. Two of them turned their horses at once and galloped off toward the back.

"We don't have time for this," the count growled to himself. He felt his grand plans quickly unraveling, and his anger rose with every moment. He waited on the open road, his horse turning lazy circles in the moonlight, and he had to take his hands from his reins to keep his knuckles from going white.

Three or four minutes later, one of his officers returned. The man had panic written all over his face. "The battle has begun!" the man yelled. He waved his sword wildly above his head as he shouted. "The centaurs are here!"

Astragon reeled his horse toward the rear of his line, shouting commands to his officers until his voice was dry and cracked. At the end of the line, he saw the chaos enveloping his forces under the pale moonlight. There were centaurs everywhere. His troops had nothing resembling a formation or any organized tactic. His cavalry, several thousand mounted men carrying heavy armor in packs at their sides, had gathered on one side of the anarchy, but weren't fighting.

They were waiting for his command.

Astragon seized his chance to be a hero with a wild grin splayed across his face. He drew his sword, kicked his horse hard in the ribs, and flew through the center of the disorganized battle. A centaur came running in at his side and crashed into his horse's flank, but he chopped down fiercely at the same time, catching his blade on the skeletal beast's shoulder right when it hit him.

Free from the stray centaur, Astragon continued forward with all the speed he could muster. When he reached his pack of cavalry, he saw most of them were still unarmored, though they at least had their weapons in their hands. "Form ranks!" the general screamed. His voice struggled from the strain, but he was heard by many of them, and the command soon filtered its way through the ranks.

"Six deep!" he yelled. "Lances! Ready your damn lances!" He thundered his horse across the front of the group, shouting his commands above the din of slaughter and stirring his men into a frenzy. Unfortunately, most of the lances had been stored in the baggage train, so most of the men were reduced to wielding their swords.

When the cavalrymen were finally in formation, Astragon didn't bother to inspect them. Either they were ready and they would live, or they were not and they would die.

"Charge!" he shrieked, shredding what was left of his ragged voice. The cold air sent lines of sharp pain down his throat.

Still a long way from any kind of unison, the cavalry began to follow their general at a steady trot. Once the field was relatively clear of trees, they broke into a full gallop, an echoing chorus of hooves and warcries preceding them.

Luckily, most of the fully armored soldiers had positioned themselves at the front of each block, and the cavalry charge devastated the undead horde, sending bones flying up into the air in all directions. They rained down on the riders in the back lines, sometimes painfully, and sometimes carrying the telltale look of blood that meant they had been human. When the initial pass was completed, the field was significantly quieter than just a minute before. Most of the untrained militiamen were dead, trampled in utter agony beneath either the bone warriors or their own cavalry, but death was death and it didn't matter how they met it.

"A second pass!" Astragon tried to yell. He wasn't sure more than a handful of his troops heard him, but they were slowly remembering their training and were coming together into blocks for another round. In the field, the centaur army was far from shattered. They ran circles through the footmen, slashing the poor soldiers to ribbons, and bludgeoning hundreds of them to death under their hooves every minute.

Astragon waited until the majority of his cavalry was in position before waving them onward with his sword held high above his head. They pounded the dirt beneath their feet, getting a much better start than their first pass, and met the centaur army's flank with a tremendous impact.

The count took a backward-flying hoof to his chest that knocked him several feet behind his charging horse. The landing stole the wind from his lungs and blurred his vision, then his own soldiers attempted to give him room as they galloped past, their hooves slamming the ground just inches from the general's face.

At the last line, one of the beasts accidentally caught Astragon's right thigh beneath its hoof, and pain lanced through the man's body so intensely he couldn't force his jaw to move enough to vocalize it. He didn't have to look to know his femur was beyond shattered. He had been wearing hardened leather armor over his legs, but the horse and rider had weighed nearly two thousand pounds.

After what felt like eons, but in reality had been mere seconds, Astragon dared to look at his ruined leg. Several bits of jagged bone jutted up from his torn flesh. His armor had once been light brown, but it was now stained red. Even if he lived, the general knew he would never walk again, much less lead his division into battle. His troops completed their second pass as he looked on from the dirt and growing carnage. He couldn't see much from his position—hardly more than a handful of his riders battling the enemy—but what he did see brought him a shred of hope. Perhaps his death would not be in vain.

Doing what they had been trained to do, his men turned at the opposite side of the field to ready themselves for a third charge. Astragon heard nothing but his own heartbeat in his ears, and he knew they were coming. He could feel the thunder of their hooves shaking the ground beneath his crippled body. They came on faster than he thought possible, turning from small figures at the edge of his blurring vision to mountainous beasts of war in an instant.

Mercifully, Astragon did not survive the third charge.

The skeletal warlord felt the cold growing beneath his mount. He rode near the back of his underlings, preferring to watch their slaughter than to be directly consumed by it. With every corpse that fell to the dirt, the cold continued to grow in power. The reanimated farmer wore a small blue pendant around his bony neck, and it thrummed with the very essence of death. His master had made the pendant specifically for him, entrusting him to bring the relic to the weak humans so the lich could harness their power, and he reveled at the thought of returning to Traxholm having completed his task.

Soon, there would be enough death to put his master's plan into action. The warlord moved his mouth as though to smile, but of course he had no muscle or skin, so his teeth just clacked together in the same position they had held for days. His mount charging onward, the warlord watched with glee as another hapless, untrained footman was trampled into bloody gore beneath him.

Everywhere he looked, the sight of death met his hollow gaze. He used his hips to guide his undead horse to the right, chasing down a handful of fleeing soldiers who had thrown down their weapons and cast aside most of their armor in favor of retreat. The warlord rode past the slowest of the deserters, holding his mace out wide to catch the lead runner solidly in the back of the skull. The man's head exploded, and his running body managed two more awkward steps before crashing to the icy ground.

The warlord turned back again, slapping his bloody weapon against the bones of his palm, drinking in the fear all around him. Two of the humans attempted to shift course and run back the way they had come, but the warlord cut them off easily. He swung down from his higher position and raked his mace across the lightly armored back of one of the men, peeling a good chunk of skin away in the process. The second runner dropped to his knees, tears streaming down his face. The warlord brought his legs up beneath him on his horse's back and vaulted downward, angling his mace below his legs to land with it directly on the coward's spine. A series of wet snaps told him the man had broken.

There were two others before the warlord, both scrambling over each other's feet to get away. Laughing through his bony mouth, the skeleton stalked toward them and swung, destroying the first with a single, heavy blow. The second man grabbed a bit of broken banner from the ground and held it before himself like a spear. He got to his feet, wobbly as he was, and even managed to meekly stab twice before the warlord wrenched the debris from his hands.

Disarmed, the man once more took up his retreat. The warlord was about to strike him down, but a centaur came crashing through and killed the human beneath its hooves without noticing more than a sticky squish as it went by.

Finally, the warlord could feel his pendant calling to him. It was his master, and the time to unleash his power was at hand.

Yes, Rhaas whispered through the small pendant. *Bring them death!*

The warlord took Rhaas' magical necklace from his head and held it for a brief moment in his hand, then threw it to the ground and ducked backward, moving to cover his face from the ensuing explosion. What followed was not a violent conflagration of fire and shrapnel, but a blossoming of deep, purple ice that grew out from the gem like a system of vines.

Ice covered the battlefield. The humans, entirely unprepared for such magic, lost their balance and fell to the ground. Everywhere their skin connected with the frozen ground, it burned and cracked as all the moisture was stolen from it. The warlord knew the battle would be over in a matter of minutes. Without their footing, the superior human numbers meant nothing.

The warlord couldn't feel the ice gripping his own boney feet, and the cold meant nothing to his reanimated body. He walked toward the chaos of battle, dragging his huge mace behind him and relishing the screams of the humans as they fell, hundreds and hundreds of them dying beneath the undead horde. When he reached the center of the field, one of the centaurs came to a stop next to him, allowing the warlord to climb atop its back and resume his position of command.

There wasn't much left to command, however, as the entire battle had nearly come to an end. More than half of the centaur army remained undestroyed, and only a few hundred of the humans were still standing. Everyone else had either been killed or had abandoned the battle. The final group of enemies huddled together, knee-deep in the corpses of their comrades, their faces covered in blood and their legs shaking with fear.

The ice worked its way up their armor, slowly freezing them into place as they cowered. The warlord approached them on his centaur mount, figuring they numbered perhaps as many as two hundred, and not a single one of them had the strength to wrench their legs from the ice entombing them all.

"More fuel for the fire," the warlord taunted. He swung his heavy mace into the nearest human's face, shattering it in a shower of blood, sinew, and frozen shards of water mixed with flesh. The man's corpse didn't fall to the ground—it just stood there like some sort of headless scarecrow, a statue of grotesquery in a field of violent death.

These sacrifices will suffice, Rhaas' sinister voice echoed in the warlord's skull. The ex-farmer knew he had succeeded. He knew he had pleased his master.

A growing wail came from the center of the half-frozen humans. The ice traveled up their legs to their chests, seeping through their skin and reducing their bones to liquefied energy that Rhaas pulled through the ground back to Traxholm where he could feast upon it. Within the span of a few labored heartbeats, the entirety of the remaining human force succumbed to Rhaas' magic. Their empty husks remained upright, frozen in place until such a time as Rhaas wanted them to thaw, which was not likely to be soon.

Chapter 27

Lina, Ilsander, and Merren searched Azanthium for a horse that Cindana could ride, but all they were able to find was a single donkey that looked too old to be of any value. Cindana was small, and she threw a blanket over the donkey's back, though the creature was no faster than her own walking pace. Still, the fireslinger preferred riding to walking, especially if they were headed all the way to Traxholm.

The journey lasted several days, all of which were uneventful. They ate most of their remaining ice worm meat, and Lina drained all but two of her skins full of brewed blood to keep her energy high.

The battleground north of Traxholm was easy to find. There were bodies everywhere, some undead and most human, and the sight of their frozen carcasses told them that Rhaas had grown stronger. In the center of the icy field, two hundred or more corpses stood as a baleful reminder of the atrocities that had taken place several days before.

"It's going to get colder," Ilsander stated, looking out across the plain of ice. It reminded him of his tundra homeland, though the frozen north of Chancol was unnatural. Nothing about the ice appeared normal, as it held a deep purple hue reminiscent of dark wine spilled across black tiles.

Cindana summoned a bit of fire around each of her hands and held them outstretched to keep the edge of the frozen wind from reaching the group. They approached the upright corpses slowly, keeping their eyes on the horizon for any sign of the centaur army lingering behind. Everything was quiet. The men had expressions of pure terror frozen on their faces in white frost. When Cindana's magical flame got close to the corpses, their features started to thaw, and she held a sliver of hope that the soldiers would spring back to life, but they just fell to the ground, as lifeless as they were before.

"We should leave," Lina said grimly. "The more soldiers my father sends, the more powerful Rhaas will become in their slaughter."

"You're right," Ilsander replied. "We need to move."

"How much longer can you go without hunting?" Cindana asked Lina, a bit of nervousness playing in her voice.

"Still don't trust me?" the vampire asked with a

knowing grin.

Ilsander drew his moonsilver sword and held it up so the pale edge glinted in the sunlight. "If she gets a little too hungry, I'll stop her," he said.

Lina eyed the blade, but she didn't say anything.

"I still think you three are leading me to my death," Cindana said. There wasn't any mirth in her voice, and there was nothing the others could say to comfort her that wouldn't be a blatant lie. Instead, they all let the statement hang awkwardly in the air as they turned their mounts north for Traxholm.

With every mile they covered, the air got colder and colder. Lina remembered a winter she had spent in her father's keep that had gotten brutally cold. She had been eight, barely old enough to be permitted in the court-yard without supervision, and the snow had piled up around Estria in great drifts that reached up to her balcony on the second floor. That winter had been so cold her father had ordered the forges within the keep's walls to be run at all hours, and he had invited the poorest of the city to sleep next to them to keep the population from dying overnight in the street.

Lina had never experienced that level of cold again until she and her companions were within twenty miles of Traxholm.

"Your father mentioned something about summoning a wraith," Ilsander said to the princess as they began to make their camp at dusk just a single day's ride from their destination.

Lina smirked, but her teeth chattered together as she moved. She had her cloak pulled tightly around her shoulders, and she was thankful it was still intact through everything she had put it through. The heavy garment kept out the wind, but it didn't stop bits of ice from forming at her hairline and her eyebrows.

"The only wraith I can control is a *little* larger than your typical fiery denizen of the lower planes," Lina answered with a bit of sarcastic humor in her voice. "Without a purpose, it would kill us all just out of boredom."

Cindana was tired from constantly summoning her own magic to keep them all warm, but she let out a sigh and began her casting once again. The fireslinger laid a rope out in a circle on the ground and lit it with a snap of her fingers. It flared to life, giving off radiant waves of warmth in every direction, but the woman was exhausted to the point of collapse. Keeping her fire going for longer than a single performance was something she had rarely practiced, and heating four people for several days without rest left her looking little better than the frozen corpses they had found near Chancol.

"You—" Ilsander said through chattering teeth, "you should save your energy."

Cindana turned her head weakly, just enough to look at the half-orc through the corner of one eye. "If I save anything, we'll be dead by morning," she told him.

"I'll go search for more wood," Merren offered. He

had been foraging sticks each day before nightfall, but freely available fuel was becoming harder and harder to find. More often than not, any dead wood he came across was so frozen it could not be lifted from the ground without a chisel and several hours of painful work.

"I don't think our mounts will live much longer," Lina remarked as she curled her body next to her horse to conserve heat.

Ilsander looked at his own horse, one of the king's own, and shook his head. "I'm tempted to open the damn beast up and crawl inside," he said.

"If you slice that horse open, I'll drink all its blood before you get the chance to warm yourself in it," Lina laughed, though she was only partially kidding.

Cindana looked like she might vomit. "Please tell me you aren't serious," she whispered, edging closer to her magical fire.

"I'm saving my appetite for Rhaas," Lina responded.

"You can feed on another vampire?" Ilsander asked. "I've heard of it, but I've never seen it done."

Lina thought for a moment before answering. "I don't actually know," she said, "but I'm going to find out. I'll drink his blood soon, and then I'll tell you how it tastes."

"I'd rather not know," the half-orc replied.

Merren came back to the group empty handed after only a minute or so away. "There's nothing out there but ice," he said. He slumped down next to his horse in defeat. The creature made a bit of noise as Merren huddled next to it, but it didn't move. He wondered whether or not he would wake up next to a corpse, assuming he would awaken at all.

When morning broke, Cindana's donkey was the only animal still drawing breath.

"Looks like we're walking," Lina said quietly after confirming her own horse's demise.

"The animal casualties of war are often overlooked," Merren added. He was nearly on top of the smoldering rope Cindana had provided.

"If we move quickly, we can be in Traxholm by nightfall," Ilsander said.

All three of the others scoffed. "Twenty miles on foot?" Cindana said. "Not in this cold."

It took them two more days to walk the remaining distance to Traxholm. Cindana's donkey died not long after the horses, and they had eaten what they could of the creature after the meat was seared, though none of them had felt good about it.

A mile or two from the village, they saw Rhaas' new stronghold towering above the flat landscape like a beacon of ice and death shining brilliantly and calling forth wayward souls into the lich's fold. The structure was at least three stories high, and from what they could see of the outside it encompassed every single structure that was once a part of the farming community, leaving no trace of the prior inhabitants whatsoever.

"Do you see anything?" Ilsander asked Lina. Her magically enhanced eyes scanned the frozen fortress ahead, but she could barely discern anything of note with the intense glare of the sun reflecting off the white ice.

"Nothing," she said after a moment.

"And what are you expecting to see?" Cindana asked. Her voice was slow and choppy in the cold.

"The last time we were here, Rhaas sent a few of his minions out to welcome us to Traxholm," Ilsander replied. He gripped his weapons in his hands, uncontrollably shivering.

"How do you think we'll get inside?" Lina asked.

Everyone looked to Cindana for the answer. "I can burn a hole through the ice," she said, "assuming it isn't too thick."

"Should we wait until dark to approach?" Merren asked. He kept his fingers tucked under the edges of his breastplate to keep them warm against his torso.

"I'm not waiting," Cindana said defiantly. "I won't freeze to death out here waiting for the sun to go down."

Lina began walking toward the fortress, moving slowly to keep her balance on the ice and not giving a single thought to stealth.

"Here we go," Merren muttered under his frosted breath.

The four of them trudged forward seemingly unnoticed. No skeletal beasts came out to meet them, and the fortress showed no signs of life—or unlife. They saw no movement along the tops of the walls, and everything was silent, save for the crunch of snow as the four companions walked.

They reached the ice wall in a little over an hour. Lina took her pouch of potent ice worm blood from her back and dropped the rest of her supplies to the ground. Dagger in hand, she waited for Cindana to give them a way inside.

The fireslinger could barely control her movements in the freezing cold. Her hands shook, and her mind barely worked. She took her rope, held it against the wall a little above her head, and willed the fibers to life beneath her touch.

"The fire doesn't hurt you?" Ilsander asked as he watched the magical flames dance around the woman's fingers.

"It feels great," Cindana replied. "In fact, if I had a second set of clothes I would just light myself on fire."

"Good to know," Ilsander said. The ice wall began to melt, but the process was slow. As water came off the wall, it flowed down onto the bottom of the rope where it sizzled and popped, letting off a good amount of steam, and Cindana had to constantly reignite the rope to maintain her progress.

"Once we get inside, I don't think the hole will last very long before it freezes again," she said.

Lina smiled. "Once Rhaas is dead, the whole fortress should come down."

After half an hour of burning, there was finally enough of an opening in the wall for each of them to slip through, though Ilsander struggled mightily against the edges of the ice to get his broad shoulders to the other side.

The inside of the frozen fortress was somehow noticeably colder than the outside. The temperature didn't affect Ilsander much, as he was used to life in the northern tundra, but he knew he would not survive long inside the place without heavy clothing to contain his body heat. "We need to be quick about it," he said grimly.

"Where do you think he is?" Merren asked.

Lina held up her hand to silence them. There were a few ruined village buildings in front of them, and a soft, black glow emanated from behind a burned structure toward the center. "I heard something," the vampire woman whispered.

Three death elementals appeared in the sky above one of the nearest buildings, a frozen collection of stone and timber that was likely once a farmhouse, and they shrieked as they dove toward the group with their scythes held high above their heads.

"They're weak to fire!" Ilsander said, rolling to his side across the ice. He glanced back at Cindana, but the woman looked nearly dead. The effort she had expended to burn through the wall had drained her, and the fear she felt rooted her tired feet firmly in place. "Burn them!" Ilsander yelled.

Cindana didn't move. "I—I have nothing left," she stammered. She collapsed against the wall behind her, sweat glistening on her face and quickly turning into ice.

Lina met one of the elementals head-on. She turned away from its scythe as she stepped forward, accepting a hit from the weapon's shaft as she stabbed the creature in the chest with her dagger. Merren rushed up to her side with his sword drawn, his heavy mace still slung over his back, and chopped down hard on the elemental's collarbone. The creature shattered under the weight of the combined blows right as its other two allies arrived to join the fray.

The first elemental swiped horizontally, and its blade dug into the side of Merren's breastplate with a screech. The second hovered several feet in the air, focusing its attention on Ilsander.

Merren yelled in pain and fell backward, taking the elemental's scythe with him as he tumbled to the ice. Lina jumped at the creature's back. She landed between its wings with her dagger lodged in its spine, though if the beast could feel pain, it didn't show it. It launched upward from the ground with alarming speed, and Lina held onto the hilt of her weapon with both hands as she was propelled into the air.

Ilsander parried his opponent's scythe with the crosspiece of his sword, locking his bandaged arm against the death elemental's side. He chopped down at the same time with the short axe in his right hand, cleanly severing one of the creature's wings from its back with a single blow. Grunting from the effort of holding the elemental's scythe at bay, Ilsander reared back for a second chop with his axe. He angled the weapon closer to his own body and sank the entire blade into the creature's back. The death elemental shuddered once as it fell to the ground in a heap of bones.

Sixty feet above the fortress, Lina realized she had a problem. The death elemental she clung to wasn't slowing, and it wasn't returning to the ground either. It beat its wings furiously as it flew higher and higher, dragging her through the air on its back. Soon, the two were over a hundred feet above the ground, and Lina began to panic.

She kicked out with both legs at the elemental's wings, hoping to pin them down and force the creature to descend, but her plan didn't work. They continued higher, and Lina was out of ideas. She twisted her dagger in the creature's spine, then wrenched it free, a blank expression of fear on her face.

It took longer for Lina to reach the ground than she had expected. Her mind reeled as she plummeted, a thousand different ludicrous ideas swirling through her thoughts, each one more impractical than the last.

"Ils—" she yelled, and then everything went black.

Chapter 28

"By the gods," Merren mouthed. The dust and ice kicked up by Lina's collision with the ground was immense. The woman had landed several buildings away in a formerly one-room residence, destroying the home's roof and two of the walls.

The death elemental had fallen on the other side of the wall, and it didn't sound like it would be getting up anytime soon. Next to Merren, Cindana was barely clinging to consciousness as the cold air slowly stole away her life.

Ilsander was the only one who had fared well through the fight. He pulled the scythe from Merren's chest, and a little gout of blood followed it. "How deep did it go?" he asked.

Merren touched the wound with his hand. The pain made him suck in his breath, but it wasn't overwhelming.

"Just wrap it tight," he said. "I'll live." He unbuckled the side of his armor to expose the wound to the cold air, and Ilsander took a cloth bandage from his pack. He knelt next to Merren to wrap the wound, his heavy hands rough against the man's cold, pale flesh.

When the bleeding had slowed to an almost unnoticeable level, they both looked to Cindana. She was passed out against the wall, and her breathing was getting shallower by the second. Ilsander shook her by the shoulders, but she did not wake. "She has to get moving," he stated. "She'll freeze to death if we leave her."

Merren nodded. "Maybe we should turn back," he said.

Ilsander didn't respond. Using the back of his green hand, he struck Cindana violently on her jaw, whipping her head to the side. Luckily, the blow woke her up, though her consciousness was tenuous at best. "You have to stay awake," he commanded her. "Get it together." He pulled her up by her shoulders to a standing position, and a few pieces of her cloak ripped off, still frozen to the wall.

"We should run," Merren said fearfully.

"Lina isn't dead," the half-orc reminded him gruffly. He turned back to the fireslinger and slapped her again, this time not as hard. Finally, Cindana seemed to regain some of her composure and then stood without assistance.

"So… cold…" she stammered.

"Can you make any more fire?" Ilsander demanded.

With a weak nod, Cindana dropped a small orb of magical fire from the palm of her hand as though it had been there all along. The sphere fell onto her foot where it splattered apart, setting her pants aflame. "I can burn for a few minutes," she said weakly.

Ilsander wasn't sure if she meant she would die after a few minutes or only that her fire would run out of fuel, but he didn't intend to waste a single second. "Come on!" he shouted, taking off in the direction of Lina's crash landing.

Merren put his hand around Cindana's waist to keep her upright as they struggled to follow. It didn't take long for the fire growing up the woman's legs to become too hot for Merren to be near, so he settled on offering a few words of encouragement to her as she plodded along atop the ice.

Lina's body couldn't be seen through the wreckage of the house where she had landed. Most of the roof was gone, and the wall that had held the door had fallen forward onto the street. Ilsander pulled some of the debris aside to reveal a person-sized hole in the floor that led to the dark root cellar beneath the house.

The half-orc leapt down through the gap, angling himself to the side to avoid landing on the princess. He saw her foot sticking out from under a shattered wooden dresser, though it wasn't pointing in the correct direction. He worked furiously to unbury Lina, using the light from Cindana's fire to see.

A jagged wooden floorboard protruded from the center of Lina's chest, covered in blood and gore. The rest of her body hadn't fared much better. Lina's legs were twisted and shattered, and blood seeped from the sides of her mouth into a small pool beneath her head that also contained several of her teeth. Her ribs were perhaps the worst of her injuries. A few inches below her impalement, four of her ribs jutted upward, having broken through the skin like white fingers reaching up from the ground.

Ilsander wasn't sure exactly what a human liver looked like, but he was fairly certain Lina's was halfway out of her torso. He lifted her off the broken floorboard that held her in place, moving slowly to try and keep her as stable as possible. Lina still breathed, as the half-orc knew she would, but each breath she took spilled more of her blood onto the ground from her myriad wounds.

"By the gods," Merren gasped, looking over the edge into the cellar.

"Take her shoulders," Ilsander commanded. He handed Lina up toward the two humans, and Merren looped his hands under her arms to drag her upward.

Ilsander had to place a hand on Lina's stomach to keep the rest of her internal organs from spilling out as lifted her the rest of the way.

"She shouldn't be alive," Cindana gasped.

Merren stifled a nervous chuckle. "Neither should

you," he said. The fireslinger was nearly fully engulfed in magical flame, and most of her clothing had burned away to ash. Her skin was a pale, alabaster white, unmarred by the heat swirling all around it. For the first time since they had gotten close to Traxholm, Cindana looked like she was handling herself well, though her exhaustion was still plainly evident in her eyes.

When they got Lina to the ground level, Ilsander used the woman's heavy cloak like a stretcher, with Merren taking the opposite end. "We need to get her out of here," he said under his breath. "She'll recover…"

They ran toward the hole they had burned in the ice wall. Most of it was still there, though the opening was noticeably smaller than before. A new layer of fresh ice had grown around the edges, and it reflected brilliantly in the sunlight.

"She needs blood," Merren said. He set Lina's twisted legs down lightly on the ground so he could root through their belongings to find the last skins of ice worm blood they had. He found two and pulled the stopper from one, holding it to the vampire's bloody mouth and tipping it up to let it trickle into her throat.

The blood went down, but Lina did not stir.

"How long…" Merren's voice trailed off as he looked at the princess, the woman he had sworn to protect.

"I don't know," Ilsander answered, his heavy voice wavering.

Merren tipped more of the blood down Lina's throat

until the waterskin was completely dry. To his surprise, she did not cough it back out, and her breathing appeared to steady slightly, though it was still painfully slow.

"We need more," he said, pulling his sword from his belt. He scraped the edge of his blade down his forearm, wincing from the pain, and then held his hand out vertically over Lina's mouth. His blood ran down his arm in tiny rivulets to his fingers where they joined together to drop onto the vampire's tongue, making a steady, macabre rhythm.

Slowly, Lina's exposed ribs began to recede through her torn shirt. Her flesh was knitting itself together, and she even managed a pained groan. Merren ran his sword down the length of his arm again, increasing the bloodflow from his own veins significantly.

"Don't cut too deep," Ilsander told him, his eyes wide as he watched the man sacrifice so much for someone his own government would condemn to death.

"She needs more!" he pleaded. He looked from Ilsander to Cindana, preferring to offer Lina human blood over orcish, though he didn't quite know why, or if it mattered.

Cindana backed away, her fiery hands held defensively in front of her. "No," she stated flatly. "You cannot take my blood. I'll not be transformed into a monster."

Merren grabbed Lina's final waterskin from her gear, a small leather pouch filled with a highly potent mixture of the alcoholic ice worm blood. He had no idea what the shaman's refined concoction would do, but he didn't have a choice. Grimacing, he held the open end of the skin in the palm of his hand, letting the blood mix with his own as it traveled down his fingers into Lina's mouth.

Lina's body reacted almost at once. The slow healing that would have taken several weeks rapidly increased. Her legs straightened beneath Merren, and he heard her bones audibly snapping back into place. The regeneration brought a shudder of nausea to Merren's body, but he didn't stop feeding the woman from his own veins.

"We need more," Merren growled through the pain. He held out his sword to Ilsander, pointing it at the half-orc's wrist.

"I don't know," Ilsander said slowly, though he took the weapon. "Will it hurt her to mix three different types of blood?"

"We don't have a choice!" Merren barked back.

With a sigh, Ilsander ran his left forearm across the edge of Merren's sword to open his flesh. "Move aside," he said, pushing Merren out of the way. He held his hand over Lina's mouth and clenched his fist, forcing his blood down her throat. She choked for a moment and spat some of it out, then continued to drink with renewed vigor. Her consciousness started to flicker back, and her eyelids fluttered, showing only the whites underneath.

"More are coming," Cindana suddenly interrupted. Ilsander and Merren both looked to the sky, and they saw four more death elementals descending toward them from a high tower of ice situated in the very center of the village.

"We're doomed," Merren muttered. He slumped to the ground as the effects of losing so much blood finally caught up to him and his adrenaline wore off.

Ilsander raised his own hand above his head to slow his bleeding as he drew his axe. Surprising them all, Cindana wobbled forward, entirely consumed in flame, and reared back her head like a snake about to devour a mouse. She loosed a scream, and with it came a fiery dragon's head the size of a large wagon.

The flying elementals were consumed by the fire and reduced to smoldering heaps of bones, but the spell completely exhausted Cindana's energy. She fell back to the ground, her clothes burned away and the cold wind once more biting her flesh, only a few errant wisps of smoke twirling into the air serving as a reminder of the blaze she had conjured just seconds before.

Ilsander felt alone. He was the only one still standing, and he knew he could not kill Rhaas. He wasn't even sure he could get within arm's reach of the lich without being utterly obliterated, and, for all he knew, Rhaas could be hundreds of miles away, having left some lieutenant to defend his fortress. Or perhaps the fortress itself was just a grand decoy, a scheme to draw

Estria's armies into a fruitless war on the wrong front.

His frustration boiled over in an angry growl. "Stay here," he told his wounded companions. They didn't look like they were in any rush to follow.

Ilsander ran to keep up his core temperature, though it didn't help much. He went toward the tower in the center of the fortress, his axe in his right hand and his moonsilver sword in his left, his own blood making his grip slick.

The base of the tower was wide, and the structure tapered near the top, a few stories above the ground. Ilsander didn't see any obvious way inside. He thought about banging on the side of it to try and goad Rhaas into view, but he quickly dismissed the idea in favor of never meeting the lich in open combat again. In the moment, his desire for accurate information was beginning to wane in favor of his fierce determination to make it out of Traxholm alive.

Something caught his eye. He saw the village square mostly as it had been before, though the death pit he had seen had been carved out, and now a staircase made of ice presented itself. Ilsander hesitated a moment before stepping closer. The corpses filling the pit were gone, and the single flight of stairs led down to a shoddily built wooden door that looked like it might have been ripped from one of the houses nearby.

Ilsander paused to listen at the top of the stairs. They were muffled, but he could hear a steady pulse of screams coming up from the frozen ground beneath his feet. Whatever the lich was doing, it certainly wasn't pleasant. He inched closer and felt a subtle vibration working through the bottom of his boots.

The door at the bottom of the stairs moved ever so slightly, and Ilsander took off in the opposite direction. It might have just been a gust of wind that had rattled the battered wood, but it was the last bit of convincing he needed to abandon his ill-fated assault.

When Ilsander reached the wall where he had left his shivering comrades, the scene had changed drastically. Cindana still looked just moments from death, but Lina had almost fully regenerated. She crouched on her heels in a growing pool of blood, her hair shaking back and forth as she tore at a chunk of meat held in her hands.

The princess heard Ilsander's approach and turned, wild fury in her eyes.

"Kraxblade…" Ilsander gasped. "Save me."

Lina had Merren's severed arm clutched to her chest as though she feared it would be snatched from her without warning. She was covered in blood from head to toe.

Merren was barely breathing and sputtering on his back. He groaned in pain, and a spurt of blood escaped a fresh bite wound on the side of his neck.

"What did you do?" Ilsander exclaimed. He held his weapons in front of him as he backed away, feeling terror creeping into his mind from every direction.

Still holding Merren's arm, Lina darted past the half-orc with unnatural speed. She sniffed the air, picking out Rhaas' distinct scent among the panoply of other smells mingling in the air above the ice. Before Ilsander could move to stop her, she was out of sight.

Ilsander's feet felt heavy. He trudged to Merren's side, though he didn't want to look.

"Kill me," the man begged. His voice was barely audible.

Chapter 29

The volatile mix of brewed ice worm blood combined with the most exquisite pain she had ever experienced made for a potent fuel. The sensation propelled her forward down the ice-carved stairs of the corpse pit to the wooden door. Unable to fully stop on the ice, Lina simply accelerated through the barrier, shattering it without much resistance.

The interior of the underground complex was nearly lightless and made entirely of ice. A long hallway led farther north, and Lina could smell her prey at the end of it. She ran the length of the corridor and came to a sharp left turn that angled downward as well, opening into a huge square room full of alchemical implements spread out among several tables. Chains dangled from the ceiling, and naked bodies squirmed at the ends of several of them. They were humans, broken and bloodied—with large hooks protruding through the meat of their arms to keep them suspended.

In the center of it all, Rhaas stood at one of his tables. He was shirtless, perfectly at home in the brutal cold, and he peered into a small glass vial of blue liquid as though it was the most interesting thing in all the world. His massive sword leaned against a wall not far from his grasp.

"Welcome back, Lina," he said, never taking his gaze from his work. "I'm glad you have returned, and I must certainly thank you for the gift you left for me during your previous visit."

Lina growled.

"I do hope your friends out there survive, though it is not likely. My experiments go much better when the subject is alive. I'm sure you understand."

Lina leapt forward over the nearest table. She soared through the air, moving between two writhing farmers hooked to the ceiling, but she was not fast enough. Before she was halfway through her jump, Rhaas appeared in front of her with his huge sword held up before him, and he easily parried Lina's dagger.

"This place reeks of death," she spat in her master's face.

Rhaas dodged away from her, standing confidently with his sword held horizontally, not the faintest look of effort in his hands from hefting the massive weapon. "There are thousands of corpses here," he laughed.

"Your father's men died like pigs at the butcher, and I have harvested them all!"

A wicked smile crept across Lina's face. "I was counting on it," she cooed. She dove her mind through a swirl of magic down to the depths of the lower planes, down to her beloved wraith. The beast needed souls like a blacksmith's forge needed coal, and Lina had a fresh stockpile waiting to be delivered.

"Ah, my darling," Lina whispered into the lower plane where her pet existed. "I require you once more."

The wraith had regrown since Chancol, reaching its full, towering height. "Burn!" it bellowed with unchecked rage.

Lina saw the horde of trapped souls already imprisoned within the epic beast, remembering some of their faces as those of her army, mere pawns in her grand former scheme. She reached out with her mind to the wraith and beckoned it forward, tearing open a hole in the fabric of the world to bring the creature onto the material plane.

Unlike Cindana, Lina was not immune to magical fire. The wraith appeared in the room with a burst of heat, thundering into the icy chamber with all the decorum of an enraged bull thrashing through a crowded city market. Its body was so large it didn't quite fit, and the edges of its fire were somewhere in the ceiling beyond view where they hissed as they melted the ice at an alarming rate.

Lina sprinted back from where she had come, hoping the cold air outside would keep the fire that had sprouted on her cloak from charring her flesh. When she was once more in the village proper, she dove to the ground and rolled to smother the flames, laughing all the while.

The underground chamber began to collapse nearby. Huge holes grew in the ground around the staircase, and then they quickly turned from a patchwork of craters to a single, gaping chasm. The wraith roared in the center of it all, standing victorious among the destruction as all the structure began to melt.

Beneath the tumult, Rhaas crawled out on his hands and knees through the muck. He was badly burned, seared beyond anything a mortal could survive, but still he moved, dragging his massive sword behind him.

Lina watched as the wraith drank in the energy of the thousands of trapped souls Rhaas had imprisoned. The beast ripped them from their containers scattered about the ruins of the underground complex. They formed an azure torrent of gaseous energy, like a river flowing over the edge of the world into utter oblivion.

Rhaas used his sword to push himself up onto his feet. What was left of his skin looked horrid, but the determination in his eyes told a different story. He clenched his teeth, and then the current of souls rising up from the ground shifted course. More than half of the souls drifted away from the wraith, flowing instead into Rhaas' outstretched hand.

"Fight him!" Lina screamed at her pet. "Burn!"

"Burn!" the wraith echoed, its blinding fire erupting in potency for a brief second. The two adversaries fought for magical control of the flowing souls, and it appeared that Rhaas was somehow stronger.

Lina twirled her dagger around in her hand and ran, making a wide circle around her wraith so as to not be burned to ash by its fury. She ran past several frozen buildings beginning to thaw in the growing heat. When she had neared Rhaas' back, she charged straight for him, hoping his concentration on the souls was so strong he would not hear her.

Lina was wrong.

Rhaas whirled backward with his sword, and Lina leapt over the blade to avoid being severed in half. She couldn't turn herself enough in midair, so she landed to the lich's side and came up in a roll, quickly darting back to stab at Rhaas' legs.

The lich spun his sword again, knocking Lina's dagger from her hand. The weapon flew over the melting ice to land at the wraith's feet, the fire blazing so intensely the item likely melted before it ever stopped its skid.

Lina jumped a step backward to get herself out of the lich's range, and she saw that her plan was working. The stream of souls coming up from the ground had shifted back to the wraith, and only an errant soul every few seconds found its way to Rhaas. Still, it was too much. If Rhaas became much stronger, Lina wasn't sure she would be able to defeat him.

"Burn!" the princess commanded. Her wraith slammed its fists together above her head, unleashing a gout of fire in Rhaas' direction. The blast was overwhelming, and the lich nearly dropped his sword as he sprinted backward. The wraith attacked again and again, crushing its limbs violently in the air to summon massive bursts of flame strong enough to turn everything they touched into slag.

Lina followed her master with her finger. "Burn!" she yelled again, calling out the target for her wraith. "Burn! Burn!"

More fire cascaded down through the frozen village, but Rhaas was always one step ahead. With every ounce of fire the wraith poured into Traxholm, Lina could feel its tenuous position in the material plane beginning to fade. Rhaas was still funneling souls away from the wraith, and Lina would not be able to keep her pet in the world for long.

Rhaas came charging around a nearby building with his huge sword poised high above his head. Lina dodged to her left, trying to stay as close to her wraith as she could, and the lich crashed down onto the ground where she had been standing.

It took a moment for Lina to realize that she had not been her master's intended target. Rhaas' sword blew a huge chunk of the ground up in its wake, and the man released a torrent of pent-up souls at the same time. A spiral of ice shot out from the spot at once.

The moisture around Lina's mouth turned to frost, freezing her lips painfully shut. Her boots were frozen as well, pinning her to the ground. She struggled against the icy restraint, then knelt down to claw at her laces with nothing but her hands. She had her right foot free of the ice when she noticed that her wraith had been vanquished. It was still in the center of Traxholm, but was fully encased in magical ice that blocked every wisp of fire. Once more, the cold invading Lina's mind was on the brink of overwhelming. She quickly yanked the boot off her left foot and lunged, Rhaas only an arm's length behind.

Every step Lina took momentarily froze her skin to the ground, ripping the flesh from her body in bloody strips. Rhaas swung his sword in a horizontal arc, and Lina ducked to her right, cutting back toward her frozen minion. She felt the wind behind the mighty blade as it sailed over her head and took a few strands of her hair with it. Lina vaulted into the air and turned herself backward to face the lich, still keeping up a frantic retreat toward her wraith. She dodged another slash, then a third, and her back hit the tower of ice imprisoning her wraith.

"This is the end for you," Rhaas said evenly. He held the point of his sword to Lina's chest, the muscles in his forearm bulging.

"Perhaps," the princess agreed. She nudged herself

to her left, and Rhaas' sword followed.

Rhaas laughed. "Did you really think I would not smell the blood you had brought?" he mocked.

Lina didn't respond.

"I had known where you were the moment you came within ten miles of this village, and the lich's blood had been even easier to recognize," Rhaas went on. "I trained you better than that. You're a disappointment."

The ice surrounding the wraith cracked violently and exploded outward, knocking both vampires from their feet. Lina felt the point of Rhaas sword jab into her upper chest, and she gritted her teeth against the death she was sure would quickly follow.

Fire blew back over Ilsander's face and arms. He struggled to keep his footing, but the force of the blast was simply too much. He fell backward, somehow managing to keep both of his weapons in his hands, and hit the icy ground hard. He knew he had to act, and he wasted no time shaking the dizziness from his head and trying to spot Lina through the smoke and haze.

Finally, he saw her battered and bloody form crumpled under what appeared to have once been a merchant's stall. Rhaas was not far from her, his back against a fresh pillar of ice as though he had summoned it specifically to catch him.

In the space between Ilsander and the vampires, the wraith struggled to keep its body from receding back into the earth to the lower plane it called home. The creature was much smaller than it had been, perhaps only as large as a draft horse, and it clawed the ground with fiery hands, filling the air with a pungent smell. Ilsander ran near the creature, giving it just a wide enough berth to not get burned, and came up on Lina's side.

She didn't appear as injured as when the death elemental had dropped her through the house, but she didn't look much better either. Her stomach had been gashed open, and the wound poured blood out in sticky waves. Luckily, none of her organs were spilling out from the laceration.

"We have to run!" Ilsander yelled at her, grabbing the woman's fleeting attention for a fraction of a heartbeat.

Rhaas was slowly clambering back to his feet.

"Get up!" Ilsander bellowed. He threw one of Lina's arms over his shoulder and lifted, easily balancing the small vampire across his shoulders. Then he heard Rhaas, and he set his feet in motion.

"No," Lina softly whispered.

"Come—"

Lina bit into Ilsander's back and drank. The half-orc growled, but he pressed onward. Lina redoubled her efforts, shredding the flesh from Ilsander's bones as she feasted.

Ilsander dropped to his knees. The pain wasn't more than he could handle, but he had lost a considerable amount of blood throughout the day. He wasn't sure how much more he had to give. Still, Lina continued to drink.

Finally, Ilsander thrashed behind him with both elbows and threw the vampire off. He was gasping, and his vision kept turning and repeating over itself inside his head.

She was far from steady, but Lina stood on her own two feet. Rhaas' sword had broken into two pieces during the blast, and a long section of steel still attached to the hilt wasn't far from her feet. She picked it up, surprised by how much even a fragment of the weapon weighed, and stalked forward.

Rhaas was only slightly less disoriented, though he wasn't bleeding nearly as much. He held a sphere of ice in each hand, his arms out to his sides. He ordered the ice forward, and the spheres hastily responded. They shot out toward Lina, one from either side, and she only had time to block a single attack. One of them shattered against her stolen, broken blade. The other struck her in her right hip with enough force to spin her backward.

Lina used the blast for momentum and pushed off her back foot. She was only slightly misaligned, but with such a large chunk of steel in her hands, it didn't matter. The sword caught Rhaas solidly on the side of his shoulder. The man screamed and faltered, but he did not fall. He summoned another orb of ice to his palm, and Lina chopped it cleanly away before he had a chance to make use of it. Rhaas' left hand fell to the ground with a bloody thud.

Lina's last bit of strength found its way into her hand, just enough to maintain her grip on the broken blade, but not enough to actually swing it. She fell clumsily backward, and then her world went dark for the third time that day.

Chapter 30

Lina's eyes fluttered open. The sun was shining directly into her face, stinging her eyes from its position between two high, wispy clouds. There was a bird nearby, and its incessant chirping rattled within her brain, making her clench her teeth against the torrent of vivid sensations.

When she finally felt her mind calm enough to accept the world around her, she opened her eyes fully and propped herself up on her elbows. There wasn't any ice, and for that she was more than thankful. There also weren't any other human or orcish sounds. She was in the woods, and a small campfire ring was the only indication that anything other than woodland critters had been her company. The dry back of her throat told her she had been out for quite some time.

Propped against a nearby tree was the broken length

of Rhaas' sword she had used to cut the lich's hand from his arm. What was left of the blade had been cleaned, though not entirely. Little flecks of blood still stained the edge.

Lina waited for a long time. She waited and she listened, hoping to hear something of her companions, but there was nothing. She was alone.

When the sun started to slip beyond the horizon, Lina finally pushed herself up to her feet to move away and relieve herself. Her chest blazed with pain. It hadn't been bandaged, or if it had, it hadn't been done well. Blood crusted all across her skin in a nasty arc from one side of her ribcage to the other, and the back of her head throbbed with uncontrollable pain, far worse than any other part of her body.

"Blood," she whispered, half delirious. She sniffed the air, detecting the distinct scent of squirrels not far off, but she knew she would not be nimble enough to catch one.

She stumbled through the underbrush, weakly calling out Ilsander's name with a hoarse voice until long after nightfall. It took her several more hours to realize that no one was within earshot. She made her way slowly back to the campfire where Rhaas' broken sword remained and searched for her dagger, though deep down she knew it had been lost. The bottoms of her feet were cut and bruised, exposed to all the nuisances of the forest floor. They healed slowly, perhaps no faster than any mortal's wounds would heal.

Lina didn't sleep. When dawn came she was still alone, her knees cradled against her battered chest. She knew she would last for quite some time without blood, but what she would become when the bloodlust finally overcame her was something she feared, something unknown that shook her to her core.

Three days later, covered in sweat, dirt, and scabs, Lina found out exactly what that was.

Someone came to the castle today who struck my interest. He's an ambassador from a distant land, though I do not remember which. Perhaps he never told me. He's strapping, with a sharp jaw and even sharper wit.

I noticed him glancing my way during his reception. But he didn't eye me like the noblemen's sons often do, all full of lust and immorality. This man was different. He seemed to be inspecting me, judging me, and I think his smile meant I had passed his test.

I'm not sure what he had been hoping to find.

Still, I cannot deny that I am intrigued. He brought with him a customary gift, this very journal, one of the most beautiful possessions I now own. The pages are soft beneath the touch of my pen, and the ink flows into the grain in flawless strokes that look more like art than writing. What's more, the man had grasped my hand when he presented the gift. His touch was strong and lasting.

And his skin was ice cold to match the empty pallor of his complexion.

A loose piece of paper was wedged into the spine between the final page and the cover. An invitation of sorts, though not to the usual masque or banquet. When dignitaries come to Estria, they often ask for my attendance at some royal function or official reception. This mysterious ambassador's note was altogether different.

I think I'm going to accept. Something about the way he spoke, the way he carried himself, and the glint of ever-present knowing in his eyes told me I should.

I'll meet him tomorrow after midnight, after the man and my father return from a hunt.

Sneaking into the courtyard in the dead of night makes my heart race. I would never run off with such a man as the ambassador, and I get the feeling that isn't what he's after. He wants something more from me, and I have every intention of at least finding out what that something is. Perhaps he knows me from somewhere. Or maybe I'm a fool for accepting his gift and entertaining his invitation at all. The proper thing to do would be to run to Maxus, the captain of the King's Shield, and tell him everything.

But I grow weary of playing by everyone else's rules. I can handle myself.

And what was his name? I remember hearing it, seeing him smile ever so slightly when the herald introduced him in *the audience chamber.*

Rhaas.

That was it.

I'll meet him tomorrow night.

~ A torn fragment of the first entry in the journal of Princess Lina Arias, discovered in a previously unknown chamber beneath Estria twenty-two days after her disappearance.

About the Author

Stuart Thaman was born and grew up in Cincinnati, Ohio. He attended Hillsdale College and currently holds degrees in politics and German as well as a concentration in classical political philosophy. Now the author of four best-sellers, Stuart Thaman's latest release Shadowlith debuted at #2 in the United States and #1 in both Australia and Canada. He currently lives in Burlington, Kentucky, with his wife, his Boston terrier named Yoda, and three adorable cats: Ichabod Crane, Mr. Bagul, and Eleven.

You can catch up with all the latest news at www.stuartthamanbooks.com and be sure to join the mailing list for free books every month! Follow @stuartthaman on Twitter and be sure to add him on Goodreads too!

A DIVISION OF IRON WIND METALS

Chaos Wars is the fantasy setting for Ral Partha / Iron Wind Metals. The Chaos Wars Fantasy Battles game allows for two or more players to command large (or small) fantasy armies in battle against one another using tabletop miniatures.

Players choose from a wide variety of Fantasy Troop types, Dragons, Giants, Monsters, Artillery, Chariots, Air Ships, Heroes, Wizards, Clerics, and more to build an army. Designed with intentionally simple game mechanics, this game is ideal for introducing new hobbyists to miniatures gaming. The versatility and ability to customize forces ensures that veteran table top gamers will find new avenues to explore.

Iron Wind Metals produces over 2,000 different metal miniatures to be used in this game, or for other gaming, collecting, or painting purposes.

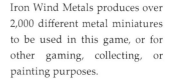

The Chaos Wars project is driven by our customers and the volunteers who desire to see it thrive. IWM offers opportunities for volunteers to join our demo team, paint miniatures for display, and generate artwork and writing to add to the official canon of the setting.

IRON WIND
METALS
10488 Chester Rd
Cincinnati, OH 45215

www.IronWindMetals.com

www.RalPartha.com | ChaosWars@RalPartha.com

This novel's primary character, Lina Arias was inspired by the Chaos Wars miniature SKU #51-469 "Vampire Queen"

Sculpted by Julie Guthrie

Made in the USA
Lexington, KY
02 October 2017